GENOME

Wanderer of Worlds

BOOK FOUR

ACKNOWLEDGEMENTS

Many thanks to the writers who attend the North Lakes Writers' Group, who listened as I read out various bits and pieces of the Wanderer novels and provided helpful comments about how to improve it, as well as pointing out what they liked. Without other writers to discuss our work, the adventure writing this project would be a much lonelier one. Also, many thanks to our constant helpers, the beta readers who read the stories in detail, following Daeson, Synjan and Hawke as they travel through multiple worlds. We appreciate that you pulled us up over every detail of our final draft—no matter how small the errors might be. We are pleased you found them, so that we could fix them. Warm-hearted thanks go to David Woodward, David Strange, Nicole Hary, Sue Strathdee, Kylie Crase, Fiona Moran and an extra special thank you to fellow author Jodie Lane whose keenness to read further motivated us all the more.

DEDICATION

For David, Darren, Jodi, Caleb and Aylish

For Jodie

TABLE OF CONTENTS

The Story So Far
1. The Round Of Pillars 1
2. The High Palace...............................20
3. White Cell 35
4. Guest Of Honour...............................44
5. Controlled Landing 67
6. The Three Navigators 84
7. Scene Not Unseen...............................94
8. High And Mighty 110
9. In The Belly Of The Beast 121
10. Out Of Control 135
11. An Unexpected Reality 149
12. Pretences And Propositions 157
13. Withholding Trust...............................176
14. Arrival In Na'ala 184
15. The London Portal 195
16. Uncontrolled Lust...............................204
17. Roman's Plea 213
18. Losses And Gains 220
19. Controlled Descent...............................229
20. Portal Bound 238
21. Controlling Destiny...............................249
22. Conscious Bias 256
23. Self-Defeating Prophecy 268

The Story So Far

DAESON ACCIDENTALLY LEFT his homeworld of Kharltae by Wandering into the cut-throat world of Trent. He was taken in by Omerri, who seduced and manipulated him for his truth-telling and Healing abilities. Omerri's companion in crime, Ellis, already had a Wanderer of his own—a Navigator named Synjan who he kept under his control, sending her on life-risking missions to advance himself.

Synjan and Daeson were kept apart for two years but finally met when Synjan was shot and brought to Daeson for a life-saving revival. Soon after, Daeson discovered that his relationship with Omerri was based on deception. He left the city and Omerri begged Synjan to bring him back.

Instead, Synjan took him to the Portal and bid him farewell. On a whim she grabbed his hand, and they entered the world of J'Bdyamn together. They stayed with the gentle Mukake peoples, who helped them survive in the tropical environment. While Daeson and Synjan learnt how to adapt, they also learnt about one another. During their stay, hostility was brewing with a neighbouring tribe, and when the Mukake went to war, Daeson and Synjan escaped for the Portal.

Unbeknownst to them, Ellis chose to pursue them, both personally and through his contacts—using an Authority Hunter, Hawke Donovan, to find them. Hawke had only just arrived home to his long-time girlfriend Brita but left her to fulfil the favour.

Hawke departed for Femme and ingratiated himself with the Authority Spies before being sent on a mission to penetrate the female-dominated civilisation. He was forced to remain with his contact, the Wanderer Clairvoyant Jinwa Woy, who made predictions about his success but ultimately abandoned him to the Femme Enforcers when they arrived to arrest them both.

With Ellis chasing after them through the Wanderer Portals and Hawke using all of the Authority resources available to him, Synjan and Daeson will have to be clever to stay ahead of their pursuers.

CHAPTER ONE

The Round of Pillars

BEFORE HIS EYELIDS fluttered open, before he was dazzled by a sun that warmed his skin, Daeson was reminded of his first two Wanders. He heard the chirping songbirds of Gredann's city garden and smelled the perfume of J'Bdyamn's jungle. Along with scent and sound came the peace of using the Portal.

He couldn't trust it. Wandering was dangerous, even discounting the threat of Authorities. The Portal was a seduction of worlds awaiting discovery, a promise of a better life. It could easily become an obsession; chasing a fantasy instead of living the reality.

Reality was the cool and gritty surface that his cheek rested upon.

Daeson opened his eyes and sat up, awkwardly extracting his arms from his backpack. Beside him, Synjan lay on her side, curled and peaceful.

They were in the middle of a circular concrete slab. Lines were etched into it, forming an intricate pattern he couldn't make out whilst sitting in it. The boldest lines travelled from the centre and ended at the columns that surrounded them. Daeson blinked at them.

The columns were tall—roughly twice his height. They were transparent, made from glass tinted different colours. There were twelve in all, positioned an exact distance apart. Inside each of them was a floating statue—a peculiar choice of artwork. Daeson wondered if the columns lit up to make a rainbow at night. During festivals in Gredann, he'd been impressed by the firebarrel flowers that lit up the night sky in pretty patterns—he'd watched them through a window, listening to the booms that followed each display.

Daeson shook off the last of the Portal's influence and stood, wiping his hands on the seat of his shorts as he looked around. The pattern etched into the ground was a many-pointed star. Beyond the paved disc, manicured grass stretched as far as he could see. Clusters of pink and orange trees lined a snaking path to a distant white building. It looked like several towers of giant toilet rolls stacked together.

Movement in the pillar closest to him captured his attention. Bubbles had disturbed the statue of the woman within, causing it to slowly spin around. He was curious about what painted face it had. Goosebumps prickled his skin when he saw the statue's open eyes. They were too realistic to be fake. He was looking at a corpse. What kind of world embalmed their dead in pillars of coloured liquid?

Synjan moved to his side, facing the woman in the turquoise pillar.

"Do you think this is a cemetery?" he asked. She couldn't see the patterns of those whose lives were extinguished, but she might know the reason behind the strange display.

"They're not dead. There's also another person below each of them, in the ground."

"How can she not be dead?" Daeson whispered, staring at the open-eyed woman now slowly turning her back. She didn't look like she was holding her breath.

"I don't know. Her pattern is the same as deep sleep. The ones below us are all male." Synjan briefly touched his arm, getting his full attention. "The men are beneath the women. We're obviously on Femme."

She sounded excited to know where they were but her choice of words confused him. Why was it obvious that they were on Femme because 'the men were beneath the women'? Synjan was saying something about many solid patterns, but he wasn't listening. On the previous world of J'Bdyamn, she'd described Femme as a slave world and said he wouldn't like it. He'd envisioned the mistreatment of people, of the rich controlling the poor, of allowing others to go hungry while food was plentiful and of an imbalanced society. He'd thought slavery was about being indebted. Had he misinterpreted? Something heavy formed in the pit of his stomach as he unfolded the meaning of 'men beneath the women'.

"Are all men slaves here?"

He startled her out of mapping—he felt her presence draw back sharply. She gave him a look that sat awkwardly upon her face—a cross between distaste and sheepishness.

"To the women. Yeah."

"What does that mean?"

"It means women are in charge. I guess I should pretend I own you?"

He felt a spike of anger surge through him, ambushed by her deception. Had Synjan purposefully kept that information to herself? Had she believed he might have chosen not to Wander if he knew what was in store for him?

"That detail would've been nice to know before we landed," Daeson growled.

"I'm sorry, I should've realised."

She sounded genuinely apologetic, and the truth of her statements quelled a portion of his anger. He couldn't let it all go. He was unprepared and it was her fault.

"At least we know where we are. What should we do now?" he asked through stiff lips.

Synjan frowned up at him, taking a breath and opening her mouth before she closed it and glanced over her shoulder. "Two women are coming."

He turned and watched their approach. They wore matching ankle-length dresses with wispy pink and purple ribbons that flowed behind them as they walked. They both also wore a band of blue-tinged glass wrapped around their eyes. Daeson was relieved to see nothing in their hands and, as they got closer, he noticed they were smiling.

Synjan stepped forward to put herself in front of him like she had in J'Bdyamn. No doubt she had the absurd notion she was protecting him. She was better qualified, but everything in him hated the idea. The feeling only intensified when he realised that it was his place now. He was supposed to belong to her.

Fighting a torrent of emotions down, Daeson resisted the urge to step up to Synjan's side. The women stopped a short distance away and held up their empty hands in a gesture that he accepted as peaceful. One of them was senior to the other—she had streaks of silver in her hair and carried herself importantly. She said something in a language Daeson didn't know and then translated.

"Welcome to Demkoi. Do you speak Authoritan?"

"Yes," Daeson said.

"Demkoi?" Synjan asked, alarmed.

"You might know our world as Femme. That is the Authority name for it," the woman answered. "My name is Chien and my colleague here is Lydette." Chien gestured at the younger woman, whose smile broadened.

There was a natural pause for them to respond and Daeson took grim satisfaction in introducing them. "I'm Daeson. This is Synjan."

"You will follow us, please," Chien said, not acknowledging the fact that he'd spoken.

"Why?" Daeson demanded, unwilling to blindly follow anybody. Synjan had insisted that he shouldn't ignore his talent for truth. Since he'd been blinded by assumptions, he would have to practise using his talent proactively and directly.

The younger woman—Lydette—looked at Daeson with wide eyes. Chien answered his question, addressing Synjan.

"We wish to take you to the waiting area and replenish your supplies."

Synjan glanced at him for verification. He nodded. It wasn't a lie.

"Okay," she agreed.

Daeson was disheartened to enter yet another world where Synjan would be accepted while he was merely tolerated.

Synjan picked up her pack and shouldered it as both women gave Daeson disapproving stares. Perhaps he was supposed to hold everything? Too bad. He was gratified by their displeasure and ignored the glares.

"We will place you in separate waiting rooms," Lydette told Synjan.

"No, we'll share a room. Thank you," she insisted.

The women bowed compliantly and ushered them down the path that led to the toilet-roll building. He wanted to thank Synjan, but with her walking ahead of him, he lost the impetus. Instead, he admired the strange hues of the trees and listened to an intriguing mechanical hum coming from beyond their destination. He didn't know what it was and figured he would have to see it to make sense of it. As the building loomed closer, Daeson could see it was built from tall white panels that slotted together to give a circular impression at a distance, but it wasn't actually round.

He wondered what kind of room the women would have put him in if Synjan hadn't said she would share. Would it have had bars? Were men kept in cages? Would he have to wear a collar and leash? He knew nothing about this world and there were no men around for him to observe.

"It's pretty here," Synjan said as his strides brought him close to her.

"Do you mean for a slave world?"

She blinked at him. "You're mad I didn't warn you."

He stifled a biting reply. He was upset, she knew he was upset and why, so there was no point taking it further.

They arrived at a white door. It was framed neatly in the building and would have gone unnoticed, except for the path that led directly to it. Daeson thought it would act like an ordinary door, requiring a push to open. Instead, it slid sideways into the wall. It reminded him of the fancy glass doors that belonged to the shops Omerri liked to frequent. She'd taken him along on her shopping trips until he'd eventually grown bored with complimenting her on each outfit she tried on.

They stepped inside a beige corridor salted with more white doors. These doors were framed differently and didn't slide open until Chien approached one and moved her hand in front of it. Apparently, these doors only opened for people who waved hello.

When they entered, Daeson wasn't impressed with the room even though its size was generous and its ceilings high. It was too stark, and without colour or character. Three doors lined the right-hand wall, and shallow pieces of furniture dotted the room. The most interesting item was a rotating abstract sculpture that water spouted from. He would've thought it a fountain and merely for decoration, but there were four drinking glasses set on a flat platform at the top.

"Is that for drinking from?" Daeson asked, pointing at the water feature.

Once again, Lydette boggled at him. Her surprise annoyed him. Even though this was a world with male slaves, she should understand that he wasn't one of them, and it was ridiculous for her to be shocked by his behaviour. It wasn't any better when Chien answered his question—once again to Synjan.

"The water fountain is for drinking. This is the main room. The door here," she gestured to the first door in the side wall, "leads to a kitchenette and eating area. All of the supplies you find within are yours to use or take. Here we have your bedroom."

Chien strode to the next door and waved hello. Through the open doorway, Daeson could see a large bed without sheets. "We expect your diplomat to arrive tomorrow."

"Our diplomat? What's that for?" Synjan asked.

Lydette interjected with imperfect Authoritan. "She come to ask, you stay or you go."

There was a deep frown on Chien's face before a tight smile took over. "I beg your pardon. The purpose of your diplomat is to ascertain your wishes. To see if we may fulfil them."

Daeson wasn't comfortable with Chien's explanation as there was a niggle of untruth within. Lydette's declaration had been sincere, but she was unable to communicate subtleties.

"Synjan," he said quietly, wanting to talk to her before she agreed to anything. It was strange to be offered things like food and supplies without requesting monetary payment in return. These women wanted something from them, and he found it unsettling.

His internal suspicion was reflected in Synjan's face. "We've just arrived. How do we know what our wishes are going to be?" she queried.

"You will be presented with the workings of our world and the role you would choose for yourself within it. The diplomat will have more information when she arrives."

"So I would choose to be a slave?" Daeson challenged. The answers sounded prepared and vague. He didn't like the direction of this conversation but felt like he didn't have permission to voice his concerns. Synjan was the only thing between him and imprisonment.

Spots of pink flared on Chien's cheeks as she

glared at him. In contrast, the other woman, Lydette, looked everywhere except at him.

Synjan laughed, drawing everyone's attention. The greeters looked dismayed by her reaction. Even though Daeson was confused, a spiteful part was pleased that Synjan had upset them somehow.

"As long we get to choose," Synjan said, giving him a pointed look. He was surprised by her statement. How could she believe they would be allowed to choose anything? He hadn't told her they'd lied but even without his talent, he'd expected her to be more suspicious. He was grateful for her desire to continue Wandering, for otherwise she might become enchanted by a world where women ruled over men. It would certainly be a safe place for her to live.

Chien pointed stiffly towards the third door at the far end of the room. "Behind that door is your bathroom, where you may shower and ready yourself for your distinguished visitor."

"Ready ourselves?" Synjan asked, her tone wary.

"There are clothes for each of you in the bedroom closets. Long dresses for the women, short for the men," Chien explained. "You will not be permitted to travel through our world in non-traditional wear. It would declare you to be... *Wanderers*."

Daeson had been about to question their intention to give him a short dress but the way she said the last word caught his attention. It had been strangely breathy. He got the impression that Wanderers were held in high regard, yet they'd disregarded him and his opinion at every opportunity. It made no sense.

A moment of group contemplation was broken when Lydette leant over to quietly say something to her superior. A furtive response came and they both stared at Daeson.

"Well, that's rude," Synjan declared.

"Apologies," Chien said, her tone unapologetic. "We were trying to decide what talent your partner has. We are having difficulty reading him. Is he a Shielder?"

"Reading him? You're Intuits, I gather?" Synjan demanded, her Dockside accent intensifying. Daeson had only heard her sound like that when her emotions were riled. He was curious that another Intuit would be able to lie—weren't they all forced to speak the truth?

"We are Intuits, yes. We know you're a Navigator," Chien murmured deferentially. "But we cannot read Daeson correctly. There are contradictory thoughts—is he a Shielder, an Intuit or a... *Healer*?"

Again, there was that strange reverential tone. His being a Healer must be a good thing. Perhaps they would stop mistreating him if he had an ability they liked. Lydette spoke to her peer in their language, prompting another indecipherable burst of discussion. After a few exchanges they had the grace to notice they were being watched and stopped.

"Tell us what you are," Chien prompted with an encouraging smile. He shook his head, denying them the information they sought. He considered they might punish him somehow and his heart beat faster at the thought. Instead, Chien tipped her head. "We hope you enjoy your stay."

The two women left the room and Daeson watched the door panel slide into place. Synjan approached the door and inspected it before waving her hands around like Chien. When nothing happened, she placed her hands flat on the door and tried to force it open.

"Did they lock us in?" Daeson asked.

"Uh huh."

"They don't want us exploring. They want to control what we see." He thought he was insightful about the kind of world they'd landed in, but Synjan didn't seem bothered.

"Yeah, but there's a shower so who cares?"

Daeson blinked. He watched as she dumped her bag against the wall and began stripping while heading for the bathroom. It was so absurd, so unmindful of their circumstances that it caused him to laugh. If they were locked in a room that held luxuries within, why not make the most of it? His laugh mirrored the one she'd voiced before—it wasn't buoyant in his chest but it made him feel a little better.

"I guess you're showering first," he said, relishing the idea of hot water stripping away the dirt and salt left on him from the previous world.

"You can join me if you like."

He watched as Synjan entered the bathroom, his expression neutral though inside he was reeling. The door remained open and he debated whether or not to take her up on her offer. He placed his backpack beside hers and perched on the couch. Several times he glanced at the door and imagined what it would be like to be with her. He'd certainly noticed her body. She had a familiar shape, if a little too muscular. Wrapping himself around her would be like being with someone from home—except she was his travelling partner. If they didn't work out as a couple, he risked losing more than just a potential girlfriend. When he finally decided the risk might be worth it, so much time had passed that it didn't seem right for him to join her.

Synjan exited the bathroom wrapped in a shimmery robe. Her skin glowing, her smile dazzling and her hair inexplicably dry, rolling over her shoulders and down her back in golden waves.

"You were noisy," Daeson said, filling in the silence. Her squeals had made him feel like his joining her was unnecessary. She smiled broadly at him.

"The buttons don't stick out like regular buttons, but you should press all of them. Especially the blue one." she said with glassy eyes before disappearing into the bedroom.

With trepidation, Daeson entered the bathroom and closed the door. The shower looked similar to the kind he'd used in Gredann city, but there was no handle to move left or right for hot and cold. How was he supposed to set the temperature?

Instead of a showerhead, small holes filled the roof and three walls. With some experimenting, he managed to get a warm spray trickling out of the shower roof. He found the blue button and once he pressed it, he was assaulted by pulsing jets of water streaming out of the walls. The spray hit his face and he cried out, squeezing his eyes shut and stabbing where he thought the blue button was. He was blasted by icy water and shrieked, flattening himself against the shower wall, out of the way. The next button he hit was 'off'.

The shower must have been pre-programmed to blow warm air once the water stopped. He liked the ease of it but the water evaporating off his skin made him feel itchy and uncomfortable, though it explained how Synjan's hair had been dry.

He used the second shimmery robe to leave the bathroom. Synjan wasn't in the lounge and he looked for her in the bedroom. She wasn't in there either so he figured she must have dressed and was investigating the kitchen.

By luck, he found his wardrobe first. He could tell because it held nothing but green or blue short dresses. They varied only in size—and some looked big enough to suit his frame. After putting a blue one on, he found the outfit comfortable in spite of his misgivings. When he came out of the bedroom, Synjan was at the drinking fountain. She'd selected a lovely lavender floor-length gown that deepened to a rich purple at the hem. Her tanned arms and shoulders contrasted the lightness of her hair, her curved body accentuated by the garment.

She was breathtaking, standing beside the water statue fountain and filling her cup from its spout. She was focussed on her task for a brief moment, one in which his breath was stolen. Looking at her dressed so nicely made him regretful that he'd lost a natural opportunity to have something more intimate with her. But deeper inside he knew his choice to keep their relationship as travel partners was best. They were too different. They wanted separate things. That didn't mean he desired her any less.

"You look... nice," he said, struggling for the right compliment. Inwardly he cringed at his own poor attempt, apologies and explanations dancing on his lips about not joining her in the shower. When Synjan looked at him fully, her expression changed from neutral to a pinched smile. It was a reaction to what he was wearing, no doubt. He felt inept and ridiculous while she was stunning. To her credit, she didn't tease him about his clothes.

"Thank you, so do you," she said. There was an expectant pause, made awkward by the knowledge of an unshared intimacy. To her, it was a rejection he hadn't meant to make. To him, it was the misgivings about the future of their relationship. On top of that, they were on a world where they couldn't be equals.

"I think this dress makes me look taller," Synjan announced, drawing herself up to her full, unimpressive height. She swished the skirt for dramatic effect and looked pointedly at Daeson, waiting for his agreement. He smiled, unable to comment in a way that would please her but grateful she'd lightened the mood again. She snorted and waved her hand dismissively. "You're no good for my ego."

He grinned. "You don't appear to be suffering."

She made a rude noise but her eyes danced. "I *am* starving, though," she continued and turned quickly so her dress flared once more. Daeson followed her into the kitchen. They made themselves sandwiches using ingredients they recognised before replenishing food supplies—mostly bottles of water and grain bars—into their packs.

When the entry door hummed open, they looked at one another and took their gear into the central area to see who had entered. Daeson had expected one of the two women who'd greeted them but it was someone different instead. A statuesque blonde woman carrying a small golden bag and wearing a multi-hued gown entered. As she moved, the fabric of her dress changed between yellow, pink and orange. Daeson was enchanted by the magic of it. Synjan began talking but was cut off.

"Are you our—"

"My name is Rinchuku Nama. You may address me as Diplomat Nama."

Daeson was surprised that when Nama spoke, she looked at him as well as Synjan. Nama glanced from the backpacks in their hands to each of their faces. Daeson thought her gaze lingered on him and he caught a tiny shift in her expression but he couldn't identify its intent.

"May I refer to you as Synjan and Daeson?" she asked.

Daeson figured that the Diplomat had spoken to the two women who'd greeted them to find out their names, but Synjan had a different idea.

"An Intuit," Synjan guessed, sounding unhappy.

"Yes, thank you," Nama replied, as though Synjan had spoken well of her. "You are a Navigator and what is Daeson?"

At first he was disappointed to once again be relegated to the status of 'too-unimportant-to-talk-to' but it was soon revealed why the Intuit was addressing Synjan.

"A Healer!" Nama looked pleased with the information she'd plucked out of Synjan's head. He remembered that the two greeters said he'd been hard to read and they'd misconstrued him as a Shielder—that would've been a handy talent to have. "You have an impressive natural block," Nama complimented him.

"Thank you," he replied, surprised to be spoken to. "We were told you would be coming tomorrow."

"Plans changed," Nama said with a tight smile. In the brief pause that followed, he took a breath to ask why the plans had changed when the diplomat got in first.

"I am here to demonstrate the use of the specs you will wear for the duration of your stay," Nama said to Synjan, then inclined her head at Daeson. "Men are not allowed to wear them. It would look out of place." She unlatched her bag and pulled out two pairs of wraparound glasses. One was tinged blue, the other was pink. She held the pink ones out to Synjan and then slid the blue pair upon her face.

Daeson dropped his bag and moved closer to Synjan, ducking so he could look through her glasses as she put them on. He saw a small picture display on the lens with the word 'Welcome' across it, then flashes of words moved across the lenses too quickly and tiny for him to read.

"I have put them on the slowest setting, so they do not distract you as we move through this world. If you look at something for long enough, you will be told what it is."

"I'm getting information about you," Synjan told Nama. Daeson thought she sounded impressed. He wasn't surprised—he felt the same way and he wasn't even wearing them. He didn't like being left out but at the same time he was relieved that he didn't have to wear them. He was a slow reader, only having learnt how to recently. He wasn't well-practised anymore.

"Are there any books here?"

"None that are accessible to men." Nama's tone sounded apologetic but Daeson noticed that she wasn't saying sorry.

"So men aren't educated here?" he asked.

"Of course they are, in order to be useful for their mistresses. Daeson, since you are a Healer Wanderer, you will enjoy great privileges living on this world. You have no need for concern."

He was surprised by her candour but her statement nagged at him. Something about it had felt wrong. Synjan picked up on it as well and identified it with a comment.

"If we choose to stay," she repeated flatly.

"Of course, should you choose to stay," Nama repeated. "Come. Bring your belongings and we will travel in my vehicle to your destination."

How does she even know what our destination is? Daeson thought. An amused glance from Nama had him believing that 'natural block' or not, she'd heard his thought.

Nama's car was a peculiar stretched oval shape, windowed and roofed with dark mirrored glass. When Daeson piled in after Synjan, he looked up at the sky and then around. It was like nothing was between him and the outside, except there were no fresh-air smells or sensation of wind. The hum of the engine was something he felt rather than heard and Nama drove holding two stick-handles that she operated independently.

Once they were out of the tree-lined avenue and onto the streets proper, Daeson stared at the strange beauty of it all. The pink and orange trees he'd first seen upon landing on this world were tame in comparison to the multi-hued plants they passed.

The few cars around them were sleekly designed; oval or wedge-shaped. They drove under thin columns that held narrow bridges for a different vehicle to drive on — sleek, long and white. He glanced at Synjan but her gaze was glued to the window on her side and he could see a line of text run along the specs she wore. He stared at her for long enough that she turned to look at him. All of the pictures and text that he knew was displaying on her specs went invisible. He wondered what the specs said about him.

"This world is so *clean*," she exclaimed, then turned back to see more of it. Daeson looked out of his own window and saw the boundary of a city. Where before there had been a few oddly shaped buildings, now were clusters of grand structures, both plain looking and fluidly designed. There were many cars—though none as sleek as the car he was in. There were many more pedestrians—not just women, but men too. All of them wore dresses, though the men seemed to only wear knee length while the women had a number of different lengths and designs.

"The men aren't in cages or on leashes," Daeson said.

"Why did you think they would be?" Nama asked through a smile.

"Because they're slaves," Daeson replied, feeling silly for his assumption.

"Is that what you did with slaves on your world?"

Daeson was offended. "No, I come from a world without slavery."

"Every world has slaves, whether legal or not," Nama said gently, like her words were in danger of hurting his feelings. He wanted to argue but her words were a truth that he wasn't too naive to deny. He was reminded of tales about people being traded and sold in the more dangerous parts of Kharltae... in cities he'd never had the chance to travel to. The bartender at the Queen—Misu—had described how he'd escaped a smuggler intending on trading him into slavery. Daeson considered the Techatachenti were likely to enslave some of the women and children from the Mukake.

It was too horrible to continue thinking about. "Why do so many of these men look happy?" he asked.

"Because they have a good, sheltered life as a slave. It is better than a hard, uncertain future as a free person."

Daeson disagreed but Nama believed what she was saying. He looked at Synjan and their eyes locked. By the press of Synjan's lips, he could tell she was holding back on a comment. While they were trapped in Nama's car and headed for a place they didn't know, on a world they had no understanding of, it was prudent not to argue.

Nama laughed, startling him.

"I know both of you dislike my words. It does not matter. You can choose whether you stay or leave. I do not care."

But the last statement she made was a lie. She did care, and Daeson had no idea why.

CHAPTER TWO

The High Palace

SYNJAN'S FIRST IMPRESSION of The High Palace was that of a graceful lady arranged upon a blanket of verdant finery. As their vehicle rolled up the circular driveway, she realised the building was constructed in two sections. The front was a wide and gently curved single storey that grew out of the grass on one side, rose up into a broad arch and then disappeared into the grass again on the other. The sun was high, riding its midpoint, and glinted off the textured panels of the silvery walls. The gardens surrounding the palace were poetry in foliage, complementing the entrance with a myriad of colours.

The second section rose to an inscrutable height. It was a tapering tower with many balconies, protrusions, and niches that appeared to be moving when she wasn't looking directly at it. Synjan guessed it had a dozen floors but the windows weren't positioned in a manner that helped her define storeys and her specs only offered the label 'High Palace, Ning'.

Their vehicle stopped at the loop of road closest to the palace entrance. Diplomat Nama turned and smiled at Synjan.

"Please, exit first," she invited, sparing Daeson a sympathetic look.

Synjan moved to obey, instinctively reaching for her backpack but their escort made a noise that gave her pause.

"Let Daeson carry your belongings," she advised.

Synjan sighed and got out without her gear. Seriously, would every world aim to separate her from her stuff? She smoothed her lavender gown and readjusted her specs, watching as Daeson shouldered both backpacks, looking dignified in the process. Synjan admired his broad shoulders almost as much as she respected his composure in the circumstances—she could tell he didn't enjoy acting the role of a slave. It left an itchy sensation beneath her skin also. She walked beside him as they followed their escort towards the breathtaking entryway.

"I'm sorry," Synjan apologised from the corner of her mouth.

Daeson smiled at her but it wasn't reflected in his eyes.

They passed two square-jawed, heavily-muscled males, each guarding a side of the wide doorway. The men didn't even glance their way. Synjan frowned at their lack of attention. Their uniforms of white dresses and golden sandals included gold weapons hanging from their belts but they looked unwieldy to her trained eyes. These men seemed decorative rather than purposeful and as they entered the carpeted foyer, Synjan's suspicion was confirmed.

Two women approached from their right, materialising from behind a huge, shimmering tapestry that was hanging nearby. They wore economical silver dresses and bore objects at their hips that looked distinctly like guns, though bulbous by design. They also moved with a precision that advertised their physical prowess. *These* were the Palace guards. Their appraisal of the visitors was sharp and though they exchanged words of greeting in their language with the diplomat, their gazes lingered on Synjan.

"Sister, be greeted," the ash-blonde said after her conversation with Nama concluded, stepping forward.

Synjan looked up—and up—into her unusually-coloured violet eyes. She was secretly pleased that she didn't take a step back, despite feeling like an insect about to be crushed. The woman was taller than Daeson! It was like being approached by the Mukake cliff face in human form.

"Be welcome," the giantess added, inclining her head to Synjan's murmured response of thanks before turning to frown at her colleague.

"The High Palace is a sanctuary," the other said, her brown eyes roaming quickly over Synjan before resting on her face. She had a warmer voice, though Synjan doubted she would be obliging just because she knew how to speak Authoritan fluently. "Our most gracious and magnificent benefactor, High Priestess Sorcha, blessed-be-her-name, resides here. To protect her and maintain the tranquillity of this oasis, all visitors are required to surrender their weapons."

Now Synjan did step back. "My weapons?" she frowned, looking between the two of them. With Daeson carrying her pack, she had nothing to hold and her fists clenched at her sides. The guards didn't miss the action. "How do you know I have any?"

"You were scanned. We will hold them only for the duration of your stay," Brown-eyes assured her. "They shall be returned to you as you leave."

Instinctively, Synjan looked at Daeson, marginally relieved by his brief nod that confirmed the guards were telling the truth. That didn't mean she had to like it.

"You'll keep them safe?" she demanded.

"They will be locked up, it will be fine," Nama concurred. "You will have to hand them over as men are not allowed to handle weapons," she added, glancing at Daeson before giving Synjan a pointed look that was unnecessary.

With a sigh, Synjan surrendered the gun from her bra first, then gestured for Daeson to put her backpack down. She knelt and pulled out the clothing atop her firearms, flinging a significant amount of sand onto the plush carpet in the process. The scent of the last world also wafted around her, tickling her nose and causing her to sneeze. The specs flew off her face and everybody watched them land a short distance away.

Nama scrambled to collect and inspect them. "No harm done," she assured as she returned them to Synjan, who took them humbly. She put them on the carpet beside her and pulled out more clothes and supplies.

The amount of sand surprised her as she'd been careful when packing everything away. By the time she got to her weapons at the bottom, there was a white ring of grains outlining her position on the floor. She should've been embarrassed that she'd brought half of J'Bdyamn's islands with her, despoiling the High Priestess' sanctuary... but she wasn't.

Silently, she ejected the magazines of her larger guns, assured herself the chambers were empty and the safeties were on, then held both of them towards the nearest guard. Woman-mountain took them without comment, brazenly leaning over to peer into the depths of Synjan's pack to be sure everything had been surrendered. She spoke to her colleague in their strange, blurred language and Brown-eyes responded.

"Your knife and ammunition also," she said.

Synjan scoffed. "What good are bullets without guns? It's not like I can fire them using my all-powerful mind or anything."

"Their chemical composition is potentially hazardous. All weapons are to be surrendered."

Synjan saw the futility of arguing and contented herself with sighing heavily and muttering about how she should probably surrender herself. She was silent by the time she stood and held out her precariously-balanced offering of sheathed hunting knife and three boxes of shells.

"Thank you for your cooperation," the giantess recited as she engulfed the proffered objects in her huge hands. She apparently had a few Authority phrases memorised.

Smoothing her expression so as not to sneer at their smiles, Synjan nodded and hastily repacked her clothes. She couldn't help mapping the guards as they walked away with all her material defences, feeling vulnerable in their wake. For a world bent on empowering women, these people certainly had a knack for rendering their visitors powerless, regardless of their gender. The sensation of being out of control worsened with every new encounter.

Daeson's hands appeared in Synjan's unfocussed line of sight and startled her. Again she froze as she realised she was not meant to be taking care of her own menial tasks. Guiltily, she looked at Diplomat Nama but their escort was distracted by a new group of Palace inhabitants approaching. Synjan took the opportunity to squeeze Daeson's arm gratefully as she stood, adjusting her clothing again. Her frequent grooming was less about presentation than it was about reassuring herself that her lightweight dress was still there.

The knot of newcomers were clearly not guards. They were draped in gold finery that implied their positions as palace officials. There were three women and one man. He remained a respectful distance behind his companions as they swarmed around Diplomat Nama, smiling and cooing in their language, gesturing at Synjan and Daeson without including them in the conversation. Watching the ebb and flow of it, Synjan deduced that these women outranked Nama and were planning to take over from her. This supposition was proven right when Nama bowed away from them and bade her farewell.

"Welcome, Sister Synjan and... Daeson."

The accented Authoritan drew her attention away from Nama and Synjan turned, trying to figure out which of the three women had spoken. They were all blonde and regal, staring with interest and polite smiles.

Synjan pressed her shoulder to Daeson's arm, feeling like they should present a united front. She couldn't recall a time where friendliness had unnerved her so much.

"Thank you. What happens now?"

Her blunt question was met with appreciative

titters from two of them.

"Now I shall escort you to your quarters," the woman who hadn't giggled answered.

"How long will we be here?" Synjan queried of her.

"It depends," a different sister spoke while a fleeting frown passed over the first one's brow. It seemed one of them was tiring of the others. The trio shuffled around and the serious one beckoned them to follow. Synjan chose not to press the issue.

Beyond the foyer, the High Palace was a study in tasteful opulence. The dominant colour scheme was gold but it was judiciously woven through the furnishings and decorations as a highlight rather than in an obnoxious display of wealth. The front section of the building was more significant than it looked from outside and was filled with sweeping hallways lined with doors or curtained alcoves and benches, settees or clusters of armchairs. Some were occupied by conversing women that paused to smile speculatively at them as they passed, before their native language resumed at a more excited pace at their backs.

After descending two sets of broad staircases and moving through a dizzying variety of corridors, their group came to a stop in front of two doors, side by side.

"These are your apartments," the serious woman said with an inclination of her head.

"We stay together," Synjan frowned, pleased when she saw an expression that might have been impatience sweep across the woman's face.

"I apologise, Sister Synjan, but you have separate apartments."

"They are very close together," one of the others interjected.

"You will have Phoak to assist you for the duration of your stay," the third said brightly and the man that had been silently following them stepped forward.

"Mistress," he greeted, lowering his head.

Synjan got the impression that his obsequiousness was a mask but his cloudy blue eyes were free of guile once he straightened up. She dismissed her paranoia as loss, of control and new-world disassociation. It had taken a while to settle in J'Bdyamn as well.

Phoak wasn't much taller than Synjan and was at least thirty years her senior but he took her backpack from Daeson effortlessly and waited between them while the serious woman spoke again.

"Daeson, please deposit your belongings in your suite and follow me," she requested.

"Where's he going?" Synjan cut in, alarmed by the notion that Daeson wouldn't be with her—and equally alarmed by the realisation that she felt incapable of being away from him for any length of time.

"He will be granted an audience with High Priestess Sorcha," the woman beamed.

"Blessed be her name," the other two echoed in unison.

"I'm sure I'll be alright," Daeson assured her and went through the doorway to his room. When he emerged moments later, Synjan engulfed him in a hug.

"I'll wait for you," she promised, feeling like the words sounded overly needy. She reluctantly let him go as the women urged his release. After he'd rounded the corner beyond her usual sight, Synjan sighed and led Phoak into her room.

'Apartment' was the better word to describe it. It

consisted of a luxuriously-appointed lounge and combined dining area, a huge bedroom and an extravagant bathroom.

"Shall I unpack your clothing, Mistress?" Phoak asked, standing at the entrance to the dressing area off the bedroom. The rack inside was crowded with a variety of Femme fashion, so the offer was unnecessary.

Synjan watched him speculatively, uncomfortable with having him serve her yet intrigued by the notion that she could demand information from him that none of the women would ever provide.

"I think everything in there either needs replacing or a damn good launder," she told him wryly.

"I will see to it," he nodded sagely.

She grinned at his solemnity, finding its presence when discussing sandy underwear highly amusing. "Thank you. Are you able to answer some of my questions?"

"Certainly," Phoak declared, his back straightening.

"Excellent. Perhaps we could talk while we drink something cool?" she hinted.

Phoak organised for refreshments to be delivered to the room and, while they waited for it to arrive, he helped Synjan sort her clothing. Another slave came to collect what needed washing. Synjan watched the way Phoak gave the boy instructions. Even though he spoke a language she didn't understand, she could see that Phoak held authority in the palace. She saw the same deference in the slaves that arrived with the drinks. They had also brought fruit and sweets.

"Please join me," Synjan invited, indicating the chair opposite hers as she sat. She took a little cake from the generous platter in the centre of the table and poured herself an orange drink she assumed was juice as Phoak complied. A quick check on Daeson revealed that he was sitting and conversing with a solid-patterned woman. Was he alright? What would they make of him? Would he discuss his truth-telling power? Would they be able to share some sort of insight about it? With a pang, she turned her attention back to her immediate companion. "So tell me, Phoak, how long have you lived in the High Palace?"

"My entire life, Mistress," he replied.

"How old are you?"

A wrinkle of concern flashed across his forehead but then it was gone. "I am sixty-eight, Mistress."

Synjan's eyebrows rose. "Does every Wanderer that visits this world come to the High Palace?"

"Oh no, Mistress. You are among a most lucky and elite group of Wanderers, to have been granted access to our world's most venerable building and its glorious inhabitants."

Synjan wasn't sure what to say to his gushing so she chose not to acknowledge it. "Why are we here?"

"Because your... partner... is a Healer."

She appreciated that he went to the effort of choosing his words so carefully. "And Healers are valued?"

"Everyone values good health, Mistress."

Synjan bit back a retort and ate instead. The meal she'd had earlier had been modest and, as the exotic tastes and textures of the new foods registered on her unrefined palate, she realised that she was still hungry. She didn't want to rush, though. She was intent on savouring every experience.

"Are we being kept here against our will?"

"If you wish to leave at any time, you may do so,

Mistress."

"*I* can, or *we* can?"

"It is not my place to answer such things," he demurred, lowering his gaze to the table.

"So what *can* you tell me?"

"I am a member of the highest ranked order of slaves on Demkoi, Mistress. My knowledge is vast and varied. I am able to answer most of your questions."

"But there are limits?" she pressed.

He had the grace to nod this time. "I am afraid my information is limited to that which is known to the Authorities."

"What?" Synjan blinked, disconcerted by any insinuated connection between her and the Authorities. "Why?"

"Because they are enemies to Wanderers and to Demkoi. They cannot be trusted."

"I would never speak to them."

"Voluntarily, perhaps," Phoak contradicted gently.

Synjan frowned at the implications. "Don't they have a base here?"

"Yes. They are kept closely contained."

"So you're worried that they'll force me to communicate what I know if I happen to go near their base?"

"You will not accidentally happen upon the Authorities."

"How do you know that?"

"If you do not become citizens of Demkoi, you will not linger in our world."

Synjan's eyes widened in disbelief. "You're kidding!"

Phoak appeared genuinely disturbed by her accusation of jest. "No, Mistress, I speak the truth."

"You're telling me I won't be allowed to explore your world, though? Unless I choose to live here permanently?"

"That is our policy, yes. Wanderers that plan to continue beyond our world are assisted through it as swiftly as possible, to protect them from Authority Hunters and our world from revealing anything untoward."

"So once Daeson and I leave here, we'll basically be escorted off the world?"

Phoak smiled reassuringly at her. "It is not as harsh as that, Mistress. The Diplomat that brought you here will accompany you to the Portal and though it will be a direct journey, it will not lack for excitement. You will constantly be exposed to the beauty of our world. I guarantee that the memory of it will remain with you as you spread your message through all the worlds you see."

"My message?" Synjan blinked, confused.

"That of the true Gods."

"The true Gods?"

"Naturally," he confirmed, behaving as if Synjan should know exactly what he was talking about. "The Authorities are ignorant, as we all know—belief in one God?" he scoffed. "A God that has no face or name, no purpose or betrothal to one of the higher callings as our Gods do. Wanderers are true followers, chosen of the Gods and blessed with powers that allow them to travel through the worlds performing their sacred duty, rejoicing in the glory of the Gods and spreading knowledge of their wonderment as they go."

"The wonderment of the Gods?" Synjan queried, wanting to be sure she was understanding the slave correctly. His zealotry was overwhelming yet utterly convincing. She didn't need Daeson to tell her that Phoak believed every word of what he was spouting.

"Of course," he said. "Perhaps you haven't been travelling for long but you would have seen the Round of Pillars when you arrived in our world. Surely that warmed your heart?"

"Uh, I was more curious about what it was for, to tell you the truth," Synjan laughed weakly.

"Each Round is a sacred place, like a temple. They are landing points for the Wanderers that visit our world. Each sister in stasis is an assistant to Panthea, the Goddess of Wanderers."

Synjan frowned. "Wait a minute. Dea is the Goddess of Wanderers on my world."

"That is another of her names," Phoak agreed, inclining his head. "She has many names and many true followers—all the Gods do. That is why the role of World Wanderer is so important. Too important to risk exposure to Authorities and tainting the purity of the message."

"There you go with that message business again," Synjan muttered.

"Wanderer women such as yourself are meant to rule the worlds. Demkoi is the only one so far that has understood this sacred purpose but I'm sure many more will receive the message as you travel on, speaking of the true Gods and rejoicing in their names. Should you be shown the mercy of our venerable Goddess and join a Fold, you will deserve a place in the World of Worlds."

There were numerous things he'd said that Synjan considered querying but the last struck a chord within her that hadn't twanged since she'd been a small child listening to stories upon her father's knee. She'd thought of them as tales of fancy, nothing more.

"The World of Worlds? I've heard of that! It's some sort of perfect world, isn't it?"

Phoak nodded. "A world created just for Wanderers, at the farthest edge of the Everyworld. Blessed by the Gods—and likely inhabited by them, too."

"My father used to speak of it," she breathed in wonderment.

Her companion nodded approvingly. "The Authorities malign it as fantasy and condemn our beliefs as radical and blasphemous but the faithful know the truth. On Demkoi, we are guided by our High Priestess and given the opportunity to welcome and protect all World Wanderers when they appear in our Rounds. It is as close to the calling as stationary devotees such as ourselves may get."

He seemed partially dismayed by the role he was forced to play and Synjan couldn't fathom the depth of the horror she felt on his behalf. Phoak had far more to mourn than the fact he could never Wander but he didn't appear to understand the scope of his bondage.

"Wanderers always land in your—what did you call it—your Round?" she queried.

"The Round of Pillars. That is correct."

"Isn't it dangerous that we always appear in the same place?"

"Why would it be?"

"The Authorities could stake them out."

"The Authorities have no jurisdiction here, their power is too limited for them to pose a threat."

"I was exposed to this notion on the last world I was in—Wanderers usually appeared at the same place there, too. It concerns me. It may be safe here but I doubt it is on other worlds."

"That is why the Goddess Panthea looks down upon you and blesses you with powers to help you Wander," he said with a deeply satisfied smile.

Synjan didn't have it in her to keep arguing because Phoak didn't have it in him to understand.

CHAPTER THREE

White Cell

WHITE.

At first Hawke couldn't make out any detail... then he saw imperfection in the whiteness; a seam. His gaze followed the seam to a corner and then downward, to a small table and chair. The furniture was also white. A tendril of anxiety threaded a path into his stomach.

He sat up, finding he was dressed in white pyjamas. Somebody either had an obsession or harboured resentment against colour. He rubbed his face with his hands as a memory surfaced.

Femme Enforcers had shot him with their bubble gun and watery goop had turned into a hard shell around his head, blocking his air. He'd passed out. Why wasn't he dead now? Maybe the goop could detect when someone lost consciousness. Bitches probably thought it was a humane way to pacify a prisoner instead of cuffing hands.

Hawke took stock of his surroundings. One bed, one table, one chair, no sink or toilet. Three white walls and an open space. Beyond it he could see a room like his own, with a narrow corridor in between. The opposite room was unoccupied, also missing its front wall. He didn't trust it—they wouldn't let him just walk out of here. Still, it would be prudent to check.

He got up, bare feet unprepared for the cold tiled floor. He picked up the chair and closed the distance to the open space. He'd learnt his lesson from the shock Woy's specs had given him when he'd attempted to drive her car. He didn't want to get blasted for touching some invisible wall. He tossed the chair, watching as the arc of its flight was interrupted by an invisible force. The chair clattered to the floor.

Even though he'd been expecting it, Hawke was disappointed. It was either the cleanest tough-glass in all of the worlds or he was being contained in a Shielded cell. Ironically, because of him, the Authorities had rooms like this at the DOME to prevent captured Wanderers from using their powers to escape. Hawke's Shield wasn't powerful enough to have a physical presence but it *was* enough to stop Controllers from taking over staff, Intuits to detect what people were thinking or Ghosts from walking through walls—theoretically. Nobody had managed to capture a Ghost to test it.

This Shield, the one that had the kind of physical force that could stop a projectile, would've been especially useful to him. Could it knock something down? Sure. Could it stop bullets? Absolutely. His blood was thin enough to taunt him with powers he could've had, with things he could've done, the Portals he could've seen, and just enough to isolate him from both sides. No, that wasn't true— Wanderers would have welcomed him just like the

Authorities had. He'd made the choice not to associate with scum.

Betrayers. The lot of them.

Even Synjan had betrayed Ellis by running away. That was all Wanderers ever did. Run away. Useless, fucking cowards. He could feel anger rising inside him, hot and unreasonable.

"Hey!" Hawke shouted, in case anybody could hear him through the Shield. "Hey! I need water!"

He heard footsteps, so the Shield didn't block sound.

The footsteps belonged to a tall, rigid woman who wore the silver uniform of an Enforcer upon her body and repulsion upon her face. He wasn't too impressed with her, either.

"I need water," he repeated, noticing that she wasn't holding anything. Her hands were flat at her sides, her shoulders stiff and slightly elevated. It was easy to see her tension, though she didn't look nervous. He thought it was peculiar that she wasn't holding a weapon—though the Shield wouldn't let anything through. If she was his keeper, then he was grateful the Shield separated them. She looked unstable.

"Do you speak Authoritan?" he asked, unable to remember the local word for water. When she said nothing, he mimicked eating and drinking.

"I'm going to need food and water, unless you plan on starving me to death."

"That is an acceptable outcome."

Oh, so the bitch *could* talk if she had something funny to say. He ground his teeth together, his jaw tight and aching as he held back a biting remark. To speak emotionally would be to his detriment. Maybe they were trying to psych him out. He was shitty with head games but he was smart enough to understand that silence was an easy out.

"Name and rank," she demanded of him, as though she knew he was from the Authorities.

"Fetch your superior." It was meant to come out as a request but even he heard it as an order. He doubted she would comply but he wasn't interested in speaking to guards in silver dresses. He might recognise the superiors by their silver robe, or golden crown, or some other fucked up formal wear.

She coughed a single burst of laughter and fury pounded in his temples. Funny-Bitch left without confirming if she was getting her superior or food and water. All he could do was wait. He returned the chair to the table and sat upon it, facing the blank space.

She took her time.

He'd counted every seam in the ceiling tiles, identified every loose thread in his bedclothes and tested the strength of the stitching in his mattress by the time footsteps returned. He put his case-less pillow on the bed and moved to stand beside the table. He looked towards the approaching sound, knowing it wasn't the woman because the gait was different. He was genuinely thirsty, even without his Shield to dehydrate him. He chose to conserve his energy, seeing no reason to employ his power whilst in a Shielded cell.

A man in a pastel blue dress appeared. He held a tray with several bowls and cups on it. Hawke tapped the tabletop thoughtfully, summoning a smile for his visitor. The man was young enough to be considered a boy. He probably had a special tool that allowed him to slip Hawke's lunch (breakfast? dinner?) through the Shield.

Instead, the boy looked up at the lintel at the front of Hawke's cell and then moved forward with purpose. Hawke watched him approach the table with professional focus, like he was a waiter at a fucking restaurant. The boy balanced the tray on one edge, arranging the bowls onto the surface. Hawke didn't pay attention to the food.

He sprang forward, his hip knocking the table and sending the tray to the floor with a clatter. The surprised youth reeled back but Hawke grabbed him and spun him around into a choke hold. The boy screamed something in his own language—calling for help, probably—as Hawke marched him to the Shield. He found that it was active when the pair of them thumped against it.

"Open it," Hawke growled.

The boy whimpered and spoke rapidly in his language.

"Open it! It's not hard to figure out what I want!" All he got in response were screams and blubbering entreaties.

Funny-Bitch appeared in the corridor and, true to her name, she smirked at them. Hawke suspected— no, he *knew*—that the loss of a serving boy would be of no consequence.

"I'll kill him," Hawke told her, bluffing regardless. The boy didn't react more extravagantly than he already was. He must not speak Authoritan.

"Go ahead. It will not endear you to 'my superior'," she taunted.

"Then open the Shield and I'll let him out," Hawke suggested.

"Let him go. Sit on your chair." Her gaze flicked to the corner of the cell. "Maybe pick up your meal from the floor and eat it."

It was a typical Funny-Bitch comment, she was always good for a laugh. Hawke let go of the serving youth—the slave—and backed away. The young man stumbled forward and leant on the Shield for support, clutching his neck.

Hawke hovered near the table, unwilling to follow her orders and sit, aware that he was unable to do anything to change the outcome of the situation. He could tell when the Shield went down because the boy fell through at the guard's feet. He wailed something as she gently helped him up and instructed him in their language. He staggered out of sight.

Hawke and Funny-Bitch stared at one another for a long moment, superiority glinting in her hard eyes and at the corner of her twitching mouth. He didn't look away and she left without a word but it didn't feel like a victory. He salvaged and ate what little he could from the spilt tray, sneaking a shard of ceramic up his sleeve. He lay down on the bed and positioned the shard beneath his body, ready to strike at the first person who entered his cell.

He thought sleep might not come but it did.

Hawke woke with an urgent need to pee.

"Hey!" He listened for footsteps but couldn't hear any. "I need to have a piss!" Still nothing. "You don't want me pissing on the floor of your fucking immaculate white room do you?"

He didn't want to piss anywhere other than in a toilet. If he was going to be kept here for an indefinite amount of time, he didn't want to stink up the place.

Funny-Bitch didn't make an appearance this time. Another woman in an Enforcer uniform—this one with platinum blonde hair—came to collect him. She held a bubble gun and peered up at the whatever-it-was that opened the Shield. Was it a retinal scan or a camera? Instead of stepping in, she gestured with the bubble gun for him to come out. He adjusted the ceramic shard in his sleeve.

As futuristic as this world was, they hadn't thought to put basic amenities into a holding cell. Advanced technology hadn't made them smart. With a veneer of scorn protecting the hollowness inside of him, he hurried out of the cell and down the corridor, glancing up whenever he passed similar rooms. There were four including his own, and he was their only prisoner. There was a small green strip above the open wall of each cell. Hawke supposed it was a retinal scanner of some kind. Ningalings loved the colour green, almost as much as they loved white.

Wait, was he even *in* Ning? He could've been moved anywhere. He cursed Jinwa Woy under his breath for taking him all the way out to the mountains. How did he know there wasn't another city on the other side? How did he know he was even in the same hemisphere? How was he supposed to find Synjan now?

"Here," Platinum directed. Hawke passed through a small doorway into a white tiled room. Communal showers, toilets and sinks greeted him. He didn't know if he was allowed to do more than use the toilet but he intended on showering and checking himself over to make sure these bitches hadn't implanted some weird nanochip into his body.

As he availed himself of the amenities, he

inspected the place for a better weapon, though it was an instinct that was already flagging. The guards kept themselves at firing distance at all times and the only people he was likely to come in contact with were inconsequential. Still, it was his first day (right?) so he couldn't give up hope that an opportunity would arise. Despite his revitalised determination, there was nothing—no visible pipes to untwist for a bat, not even a sink tap to dislodge. Water and soap poured out of holes in the walls to wash with, all operated by slimline buttons or handwaving. His only weapons remained his wit and a shard of broken plate.

The inspection of his skin yielded the same result. He was well-versed in searching for needle-pricks—a lifetime of DOME study and portal travel had trained him in that—but after poring over every likely injection site, he was positive that he hadn't been compromised. There were a few new scrapes on his arms and elbows but they looked more like the kind he would get from falling on tarmac rather than from a surgical implant. He'd most likely picked them up when he'd face-planted the ground at his 'arrest'.

He put his pyjamas back on and hid the shard up his sleeve again. When he stepped out, he was surprised to find Platinum standing upright beside the doorway rather than leaning against the wall. It would've been boring as shit standing there this whole time. He'd never had the patience for assembly when he'd been trained as an Authority.

He didn't bother trying anything on the way back to his cell. Platinum looked young but she was well-trained. He could tell by her posture and the way she didn't take her eyes off him. She didn't have to look around—he was on her home turf. She had every advantage. She appeared relaxed but she was weapon-ready. He didn't want to be smothered by the goop again or lose his one and only advantage.

Hawke noticed a large grate in the high ceiling. With no windows in sight, it was most likely an air conditioning vent and potentially a means to escape—except he'd need a ladder to reach it. He looked down the other end of the corridor where it ended at an anonymous T-intersection. The place was likely a rat's maze. Perhaps it was straight-forward but he was confident it would require multiple retinal scans to get out. There would be surveillance in the building, even if he couldn't see any cameras. Their technology was advanced beyond his understanding, after all.

No weapons, no map and everything was fucking white on white. Unless he formulated some kind of genius plan, he was here for the duration.

CHAPTER FOUR

Guest Of Honour

WHILE WALKING THROUGH the corridors, Daeson learnt that his companion's name was Yun Ti. He was fascinated by her violet eyes. She looked like a doll with white porcelain skin and a rosebud mouth.

"Where is your slave?" he asked, wondering if she kept him at her house or if she had a place for him here, like a nursery for grown men.

"I do not have one. I am a High Palace companion," she replied. Her voice was as soft and tiny as the rest of her. In stature she matched Synjan but in every other way she did not.

"I thought all women had slaves," he said.

"In the city of Ning, most women possess a slave. Only those with a position of special circumstances, like myself, do not."

He felt his stomach tighten and churn.

"That's not completely true," he said.

"There are also women who have lost the privilege because of inattention or mistreatment. Or perhaps as punishment for disrespecting a higher ranking

Sister. There are a few different reasons."

Daeson didn't want to pursue the criminal acts of women. "Are men happy here?"

"I cannot speak for the happiness of others," Yun said. She gestured down a corridor when they came to a T-intersection. "Do you like gardens? I can show you a magnificent one."

Daeson did like gardens and *would* like to be shown a grand one but the subject change took his attention.

"Am I not allowed to ask about the happiness of men?"

"Of course you may ask." Yun chose the left turn and Daeson followed her. "I answered."

"And the men who are not happy?"

"Happiness is a personal journey. There are men who are happy, those who are content, and others who do their tasks without satisfaction. As on every world."

They walked down a golden corridor. Large, colourful artworks adorned the walls while pot plants and sculptures perfectly filled each nook, likely designed for that purpose.

"But an unhappy man on other worlds can choose a different path," he pointed out.

"Are there not men who have limited options?"

He thought about his farm and the choice he could've made to leave it before it went to ruin. "I guess there are limitations but there's always some form of choice, even if the choice is a difficult one."

"What about the women? I have heard many tales of violence and inequality on various worlds. Do they choose that for themselves?"

"No, I..." The justification stuck in his throat. Of course women didn't choose to be less than equals. "I didn't—" *treat women differently to men*, he was going to say but couldn't. He *did* treat them differently but not because he thought they were lesser. "I wasn't raised in a place like that."

"Yet your answer reveals to me that you understand."

Daeson's time at the Queen of Hearts had shown him the lack of care men had towards women. They were despicable. Men like Nick, who would take advantage of an unconscious woman, or men who left bruises on the girls whose time they paid for. He'd voiced his protests and the answer he got back was always the same no matter who he asked: 'It's the way it is' or 'the strong always take advantage of the weak'. The truth of it had confused him. When he'd revealed his disgust, Omerri had called him naïve but Jade said it proved he was a better man than most.

"I understand," Daeson admitted. "But there must be a world that exists where the strong help the weak." Yun said nothing. Perhaps she thought he was foolish but he didn't care. He would like to find that world, or help create it.

The corridor became a marbled path. A giddy mixture of floral scents filled the air before they entered an open-air courtyard. Sunlight spilt down upon them, so brilliant that Daeson could not make out definite forms. In blinking to diffuse the glare, the riot of flowering plants blurred into a palette of intense colour around them. He closed his eyes and tilted his face to feel the warmth of the sun.

When he looked down again he was delighted to see an enormous circular fountain at the centre of the generous space, gushing water on and off in patterned bursts. From there, his gaze took in the rest; the meandering paths, the cosseted statues, the colours and shapes he'd never known in any other flower. No two plants looked alike. Every surface reflected the sunlight differently, all of them contributing to an overall dazzling effect.

"Wow," he breathed.

"It is spectacular, the Central Court Gardens. Not every citizen of Demkoi is invited to look upon this place. It is a shame and yet a blessing of Panthea that the garden remains special."

"Panthea?" Daeson asked, surprised to recognise a Goddess from his world. She was from the circle of the Old Gods, as with Portos.

"Yes, the Goddess of Wanderers," Yun confirmed.

On Kharltae—Daeson's world—Panthea ruled over travellers. It made sense that she would also be considered the Goddess of Wanderers.

"But why a blessing of Panthea? Why not Lile or Enigma for a garden?" He wondered if Yun would recognise the Goddess of Spring or the Mother Goddess.

"You know their names," Yun said, her large eyes widening. The wonder he saw in them made him laugh. It was nice having the answers for once.

"Yes, I know them," he said. On Trent where Jade had taught him how to read, she'd given him books about mythology. They'd been familiar stories with different names. He'd read them over and over, crediting his love for them as the main reason he'd finally made sense of letters and words.

"This garden is a tribute to Panthea because she is our creator," Yun explained.

They arrived at a bench sculpted to look like two long-necked birds bowing and intertwining. They sat together, staring at the wondrous garden crafted expertly around them. The peace allowed him to order his thoughts, to acknowledge the questions he wanted to ask.

"Why were Synjan and I brought to the High Palace?"

"Synjan was brought here because she is your travelling partner. You were brought here because you are a Healer."

"Don't you have other Healers here?" Daeson asked, looking around at the few women milling around in the garden, as if he could see inside them to their talent. None of them noticed him staring, they were too busy tending the plants. It was curious that women were doing the gardening—wasn't such a thing too menial for them? He didn't understand how this slave thing worked.

"We do, but the bloodline is rare."

He faced Yun, searching her face for clues but finding none. Her expression was carefully shuttered.

"Why separate me from Synjan to bring me here? What do you hope to achieve?"

"We wish for you to stay on our world. My task is to entice you."

The frankness of Yun's answer struck him and his mind reeled with arguments for and against staying:

It's a slave world. But it was a comfortable, advanced world.

It's a slave world. But it shared his beliefs about the Gods and Goddesses.

It's a slave world. But it was a world that wanted him.

And yet...

"I don't want to be a slave."

Yun shook her head. "You would not be a slave. Healers are never slaves."

Her statement was provocative but he wasn't

fooled by it. "I could argue that all your Healers are slaves."

"How so?" Yun asked, a smile playing around her mouth. She didn't believe him but was indulging him. That was fine.

"Because your Healers are required to use their powers. They don't get a choice how to live their life. It's just another kind of slavery."

For the women as well as the men, he thought. He wondered what Yun would say if he'd given voice to *that*.

Yun's smile was already gone. "If an ailing person was placed before you, would you not use your talent to save them?"

"Of course I would, but you would keep placing sick people at my feet."

"You have the power to save lives. You would resent doing it?" Yun asked.

He pressed his lips together and said nothing. He could see her point but her leading questions were making him feel selfish. Her expression betrayed her disappointment. Let her be disappointed then, why should he care? Except he did care—this strange woman from a strange world wanted him to save those who were dying and he was refusing her... because he didn't want to be a Healer.

As much as he wanted to help people, he wanted to choose his own path. He wanted to get married. He wanted to start a family. Even though he would never be a slave here, he could never be a husband, either. He was no woman's equal. He wouldn't be worthy of falling in love with. His talent, his ability, his *power*... wasn't a power at all. Others wanted to own it and use it according to their wishes. It didn't matter what *he* wanted.

"What's your talent?" he demanded of her. He felt grimy, dirtied by his refusal to help. Perhaps she would allow him a turn in conversation. He supposed he could have asked her nicely but his manners seemed to have disappeared along with his obligation to save every sick and ailing person on the world.

She hesitated. Her large eyes half-lidded as she looked away and to the side, as though she could no longer face him. Guilt stabbed him but he waited her out.

"I am a Speaker," she said softly.

"What's that do?" he asked, inwardly cringing at his boorishness.

"I will show you."

Yun made some odd sounds, clucking her tongue and hissing. A bee landed on the lap of her dress and instead of waving it away, she held out her finger for it to climb on. Its fuzzy brown and yellow body swayed as she lifted up her hand to show Daeson. Another bee buzzed around her thumb before landing. Soon she had thirty bees crawling on her dress and arms. As far as Daeson could tell, she wasn't stung by any.

She made a different sound and the bees flew away in unison, returning to their individual tasks of checking flowers for pollen.

"You're a Speaker of bees?" Daeson asked.

"Any type of animal or insect, whichever ones I wish to call. Birds, foxes, spiders, horses. The bees were handiest."

She looked out at the garden as she spoke and he looked as well, not having noticed the bees before. He spied some butterflies and wondered why she hadn't called them over—they would have made a more colourful display. He recognised that the bees carried the threat of pain with them and they hadn't shown hostility while being controlled.

"How do you know what noises you need?"

"The noises I make are not what calls them to me. I make sounds because it helps me to connect but some Speakers are silent. It is a connection within our minds that calls a particular creature to us and allows us to makes a request of them."

"You make a request? Don't you control them?"

"No, but I am rarely refused," she said, looking at her hands, held together in her lap.

"If a creature were to attack you, could you stop them?"

"Likely not. I would ask a different animal to fight for me." She looked out over the garden again and Daeson imagined a dark cloud of bees swarming to her defence. Such a thing would stop any animal.

"That's impressive," he said.

"Is it?" she asked, still staring ahead. He realised she hadn't looked at him once since he'd refused to talk to her about his Healer powers.

"I know it might sound heartless to you," he began, "but forcing a person to save a life loses the meaning behind the action."

"Not to the person whose life you saved," Yun countered, facing him.

"But you would be holding me hostage. You would have me exchange my life for theirs."

Yun's eyes widened and she scoffed. "Your life would not come to an end."

"In a way it would, for I would not be allowed to live it how I wished."

She lapsed into silence, uncertainty returning to her face. He was beginning to recognise that look in place of thoughtfulness now, for her doubt meant she was re-assessing her stance.

"Would you get no satisfaction in saving lives? You do not think changing your life would be a worthy sacrifice?" she prompted. Yun's intensity had dropped—he guessed she was in the middle of an internal debate.

"Leaving this world doesn't stop me from Healing people," he argued. "I would still Heal whoever needed it."

"But you can save more lives, here."

"Discriminately."

"I beg your pardon?" Yun asked, taken aback.

"You wouldn't put everyone who needed Healing before me. You would pick and choose."

"First you do not wish to save lives and now you wish to save them all?" she asked, but she was wary. They both understood that he would only Heal important people on this world; the women, never the slaves. This time the women didn't need his help. This time it was the men who were defenceless. This entire world was like the Queen of Hearts, and every woman was potentially another Omerri. He couldn't go back to that. His silence compelled Yun to talk again. "If you have watched someone die, you would understand."

Shock cooled his blood and numbed his fingers and toes. He sat up straighter without meaning to, the action causing Yun to look at him more closely. When he glanced her way, she lifted a hand to her lips, looking very much as though she wanted to put her words back into her mouth.

"You *have* watched someone die," she guessed, the words not needing to be said and brutal when spoken out loud. He blinked because his eyes were prickling. There were no tears, yet the threat of them remained. "Who was it?"

"My father," he said, and couldn't speak again for fear of a breaking voice. He didn't want to appear vulnerable in front of her, not after their disagreement. She would take advantage of it.

"And you were too young to save him," she said. She seemed respectful of his loss but didn't show the same kind of compassion Synjan had when he'd told her. Perhaps because he and Synjan shared the loss of parents.

"I didn't know I could," he corrected. "Otherwise I would have tried."

"How old were you when you lost him?" She reached out and took his hand and he gently squeezed it, grateful for the touch.

"Fourteen."

Yun murmured a noise of acknowledgement and then took his hand in both of her own, the action making Daeson feel awkward.

"Do not blame yourself. Most Healers do not get their powers until they become adults. High Priestess Sorcha was the youngest Healer to receive her powers, at sixteen. Most are eighteen or nineteen. You would not have been able to save your father at fourteen."

The truth of her words shortened his breath. He felt like he'd fallen a great distance but at the same time he felt *lighter*. His hairs stood on end and his skin prickled with the sensation of it. A surge of emotions launched from his chest up into his throat and stuck there. He struggled with them until a sob escaped.

He had permission to forgive himself, finally allowed to release the oppression of his guilt.

Burying it hadn't kept that ache away because as much as he'd pushed it down, it had lain deep within him.

"You are trembling," Yun told him. She stood and tugged on his hand. He stood and was enveloped by her light frame in an embrace. She was small and dainty, but he relished the feel of her hands around him, the beat of her heart and the smell of her perfume. Because of her, he could move forward without the weight of his father's death pressing upon his back. He felt his tears well and fall as his pain leaked out, escaping its prison of guilt and shame.

"Thank you," he said, over and over, the words turning into nonsense as he repeated them in her ear. He hid his face in her hair, burying the sensation of being watched and judged as he gave in to the release. When he had himself under control, she pulled away to gaze up at him. If she was uncomfortable with the strength of his emotions, she hid it well.

"Let me take you to a washroom so that you may freshen up, and then we will lunch together. We will be eating in the Grand Hall."

"Is Synjan joining us?" Daeson asked, rubbing his nose with the back of a hand.

"No. Only special guests are allowed to enter the living quarters of the High Priestess," Yun said with a proud smile. She gestured to the double doors that towered over the courtyard garden. "You will see Synjan later. For now, the glorious High Priestess Sorcha requires your audience."

Daeson sat beside Yun at a polished steel table long enough to seat twenty people. All of the chairs were empty except for theirs but a centrepiece display had been put on the table before them—an elaborately designed miniature fountain of the one in the courtyard gardens, but the water had been replaced with curved and rippling lights. The same rippling lights decorated the centre of each colossal wall panel that made up the Grand Hall, which altogether served to make him feel small and insignificant.

"Why make the ceiling so high?" Daeson asked.

"Low ceilings can make a person feel confined," Yun replied. "The Grand Hall allows a person to feel free."

"I don't feel free."

A messenger from the High Priestess approached them. He was dressed in a golden robe—the first man that Daeson saw in a dress past the knee. He was androgynous in appearance, a very pretty man. Daeson wondered if this was the reason he had an elevated position in the Palace.

"The High Priestess will be unable to join you until later in the evening. Enjoy your lunch and rest in the parlour. A tour of the High Palace is optional." The messenger made a strange gesture, then left.

Daeson looked at Yun Ti in surprise. "What's that signal?"

"It signifies the message came from the High Priestess herself."

The conversation lapsed as they were served by silent men bearing platter after platter of small yet elaborate dishes. Daeson ate his fill and, as he toyed with his second dessert—a scoop of something icy, he listened as Yun talked about High Priestess Sorcha. She complimented Sorcha's beauty, intelligence, talents and worthiness as a leader.

"Have you met her?" Daeson asked.

"Yes."

"Have you had a conversation with her?"

"I do not need a conversation to give High Priestess Sorcha my respect."

"Does she keep slaves?"

Yun blinked several times before she spoke. "There are multiple attendants who cater to the High Priestess' needs. All of them women," she added, placing her fork on the table and sitting back in her chair. With her hands in her lap, she looked relaxed, though Daeson sensed the posture was an act.

"Do the men respect her as well?"

"All citizens respect High Priestess Sorcha."

The statement was truth—or at least Yun's truth—and Daeson was astonished by her belief.

"One person cannot possibly be respected by every single person on the world," he argued.

Yun frowned. "Every *citizen*, I said. I am sure the Authorities do not respect our High Priestess as she deserves."

"But you couldn't know such a thing. You've admitted you don't know what people are really thinking. Just because someone shows respect doesn't mean that they feel it."

"There are many Intuits in this world. It is a dominant bloodline. The Intuits in the High Palace are always scanning for hostility or disrespect."

"But men are not allowed in here."

"Some are. You are, for instance."

He was, and he couldn't respect someone he didn't know. He thought she might be the reason that men were slaves in the first place. He couldn't respect a woman who'd implemented such a thing—or if she hadn't, she could at least dismantle it.

He wondered what would happen to him when he was discovered thinking negatively about Sorcha. He certainly wasn't looking forward to meeting her, though he was curious. "What happens if someone is discovered thinking an impolite thought? Do they get escorted out?"

"Yes."

His stomach clenched and a bitter taste sprang into his mouth. "You're lying," he said.

Her eyes widened and her cheeks flared pink. He thought it was because he'd caught her out but he was admonished instead.

"You are a *guest*," Yun hissed at him. "You should not make unfounded accusations."

"I might not be able to prove you're lying, but I know you did it."

"How do you know?" she said, lifting her head so she could look down her nose at him. With the difference in their height, she had trouble achieving the desired effect.

"I always know when people lie."

Yun stared at him without comprehension. Since she'd known about his Healer powers not coming forth until a certain age, he'd thought she might know something about his truth-detection ability. He hadn't told her directly and perhaps that was why she'd been surprised. He hadn't thought to explain his other talent to her. Now was a good opportunity.

"Ever since I was a child, I've been able to tell when people lie. It's a sensation I get in the pit of my stomach. Lies taste sour in my mouth, like I've eaten something bad. I also can't speak lies. Have you heard of others with this ability?"

Her staring continued, though her expression

changed from confusion to wariness. There were other, smaller changes in her features that he didn't recognise.

"Synjan said they're similar to Intuit powers. We discussed that it could be a power from my... that both of my parents gifted me their powers. As far as I can tell, I can Heal very well but I can't use the Intuit power to—"

"That is not an Intuit power."

"I don't understand."

"What you have described," Yun said, lowering her voice when a uniformed slave stepped forward to remove their plates. She waited until he'd moved away before continuing. "What you are describing is not an Intuit talent. Theirs is not a physical talent because their skills are performed mentally. They do not *feel* lies. They certainly are not prevented from speaking them," Yun said with a scoff, as though she'd had firsthand experience with a lying Intuit.

"Perhaps because it's been muddled up with my Healer power, it didn't come through properly," Daeson suggested. He and Synjan had discussed ideas about his secondary power in J'Bdyamn, before going to sleep together in the tent. She'd been surprisingly imaginative in her theories. "There was a baby on my world born with two heads, once. I wouldn't have believed it except people I knew had seen it with their own eyes and so when they told me about it—"

"Stop. There is no such thing as two talents in one Wanderer. It has never happened."

He was devastated that she didn't have answers for him.

"You can't know about every Wanderer on every world," he replied. "Maybe it has happened before, or maybe I'm the first. I don't know. I wouldn't have believed a baby could be born with two heads either, but it happened."

"That was two babies. Twins who didn't separate properly. Things like that happen often enough that there are medical procedures for separating them."

Now it was Daeson's turn to stare. "Are you saying I have a twin that was never born and who gave me his power?" he asked slowly.

"What? No. That's not—" The strike of a bell interrupted her. "Oh, the room is required for a function. We must leave. We will enter the parlour and continue this conversation there."

The parlour wasn't as intimate or comfortable as Daeson expected. They arrived in a six-walled room with a lot of curved chairs and low metal coffee tables that had designer holes in them. Slender drinking fountains were positioned at each of the six corners. There was a hexagonal rug in the centre of the room that most of the armchairs and settees were gathered around. He expected Yun to head for them but she moved to the far wall instead—the only one that didn't hold an artwork—and waved her hand to one side of it. The white wall became a window looking out over the gardens.

"That's amazing," he said, noticing the way daylight filled the room, reflecting off each white wall and brightening them all the way up to the tip of the high ceilings. He hadn't thought the room was dark before, but it was full of light now.

Yun selected an armchair close to the window. The chair was a bunch of cushions on metal rods and didn't look particularly comfortable. He headed for the chair opposite her but Yun urged him to join her on the one beside.

"But I prefer to look at your face when we talk," he

admitted.

"What a lovely thing to say. But you will be able to see more of my face if you sit beside me." Yun looked pleased. He found her attractive but the real reason he wanted to look at her was because he thought he could tell when she was keeping information from him. That was something his talent couldn't do.

Yun leant back in her chair. The cushions rotated on the bars so much that she'd ended up lying down. In the chair beside hers, Daeson pushed back and the chair glided into place beneath him. It was more comfortable this way and he mirrored her position. It struck him that it felt like lying in a bed with her. The idea both embarrassed and thrilled him and he found himself without words, waiting for her to carry the conversation forward.

"You know when people lie and you are unable to lie yourself," she summarised.

"Yes."

"That is not a Wanderer power."

"What is it, then?"

He watched her consider it, relieved that she was at least putting thought into her answer. She'd shown she could be dismissive. "Have you kept company with anyone who could experiment on you?"

Daeson was aghast. "I've had this power since I was a little boy."

"And your parents?"

"They—" *died*, he tried to say but couldn't. "I don't—" *know them*, but that wouldn't come out of his mouth either. He huffed his frustration and tried to explain himself a different way.

"Synjan thought it might be a merging of two powers. Even if it's not a true Intuit talent, is it possible that the... merging of my parents' powers could have, um..."

"Created a corrupted talent?" Yun finished for him. Daeson was relieved that she had filled in the words. Yun looked away, gazing out the window at the sky above the open courtyard. It was so vibrant a blue it didn't look real, but perhaps that was because he was looking through a special window. "Such an event has not been documented before. Perhaps if it is a merging of two talents, your Healer talent has given your Intuit ability a physical outlet. Have you used your Healer talent fully or do you have a weaker strain of that as well?"

Daeson thought of Synjan, of how he'd pulled her from the arms of death.

"My Healer talent is complete."

"You have saved someone who was dying?" she pressed.

"Yes."

She looked at him like she wanted to know more but didn't ask. They stared at one another until she spoke again.

"Do you find me beautiful?"

"What?" He thought now that she knew he couldn't lie, she was going to ask him increasingly embarrassing questions to prove it. He wasn't going to answer but she was looking at him expectantly and the question was harmless. It was a way to get her on his side, as well. "Yes, of course."

"Would you like us to be intimate?"

"I... why are you asking?" he prompted, feeling heat rise on his cheeks. She hadn't taken long to get to the embarrassing part.

"If you stay on Demkoi, I could be your companion," Yun said.

"What do you mean?"

"If you stayed, you would be able to summon me for intimacy."

Daeson blinked. "It's *my* decision?"

The conversation had taken an unexpected turn and as interesting as it was, he felt out of his depth. She was a great deal more sophisticated than he was and they barely knew each other. She was speaking frankly though, which meant she was using his ability to show him that this was all true. He could have her, if he wanted.

She looked different now. He suspected it was the new perspective she'd given him—one that included intimacy and familiarity. He'd challenged her words, her beliefs, and her response was to offer herself. Had she been evaluating him and found him worthy or was she merely a prize for him to enjoy if he stayed?

"Because I'm a Healer, you would become my slave?"

"Of course not," she said with a smile in her eyes. "I am a companion and I choose who I offer myself to."

"So if you found out later we're not compatible, you would leave?"

"No, once my choice is made, it is made. If another companion were to offer herself to you and you accept, you would have us both. If this is what you prefer, it is very likely. Healers tend to attract more than one companion."

He blinked slowly.

"I don't want multiple companions. I just want one woman."

After hearing his words, Yun shifted in her chair and it moved upright slightly. She beamed at him with excitement in her eyes.

"This suits me as well. You should accept me."

He desired her, he realised. There was a physical pang in his body when he imagined having her in his bed. He cleared his throat and forced himself to protest. It was easier to argue than to agree, since her offer worked solely in combination with this world.

"You don't know me and we haven't exactly been getting along. Why would you offer yourself to me?"

Yun chuckled. "The men on this world do not challenge me and I am not interested in women."

Daeson didn't understand what her interest in women had to do with her decision about him but he let it go.

"I could be a horrible person."

"That does not matter. I do not care about nice. I only wish to be with someone interesting and you wish to have a relationship as an equal. I am offering you a solution for both ideals. So stay."

He stared at her for a long moment. Her desire to partner with him was sudden and suspicious. Nothing she'd said was a lie but now that she knew he could detect them, she might be dancing around the truth.

"Is that the only reason?"

She paused, then: "Yes."

"You're lying."

"This talent of yours for the truth is impressive. I wish I had it."

"You might think you do," he grumbled. "It only causes me trouble."

"Better a warning than learning from a broken heart," she said.

"A warning doesn't stop a heart from breaking," he replied. He was looking out the window, up into the clouds and didn't want to look at her face. She made a soft noise of acknowledgement.

"Will you think about my offer?" Yun asked.

Daeson had already decided that he wasn't going to accept but he didn't want to tell her that. It would make things awkward and uncomfortable between them.

"How about we spend more time together, with a tour around the Palace?" Daeson suggested.

Yun agreed.

A messenger from the High Priestess found Daeson and Yun alone at the Grand Hall again, this time eating their dinner. The messenger was the same androgynous man in golden robes.

"The High Priestess will be seeing you early in the morning. Guest rooms have been prepared nearby."

Daeson turned to Yun. "I already have a room near Synjan."

"Those rooms are not conveniently placed for High Priestess Sorcha."

"Synjan will wonder—" *where I am*, wouldn't come out of his mouth. She was a Navigator and would know exactly where he was. "—what's happening to me."

"I can pass on the same message to Mistress Synjan as well," the androgynous man offered.

"I would like that, thank you." When the messenger left, he turned to Yun. "This is a change of plan, isn't it?"

"High Priestess Sorcha is constantly in demand."

"Is she Healing people?" Daeson got no answer so

tried again. "I mean, does she go around the world Healing people with her talent?"

"The High Priestess Sorcha does not 'go around' but some of her duties include Healing people, yes."

"What are her other duties?"

"Many ceremonies require her attendance. Also, whenever there are disturbances, her appearance calms the unrest," Yun boasted.

"What kind of disturbances?" Daeson asked. Yun blinked rapidly then smiled and shook her head.

"I spoke without thinking, forgive me."

Daeson sensed that even if he pressed his companion to clarify, she wouldn't. Logically he knew that the world wasn't perfect, that there had to be many citizens that were discontent with the idea of slavery—and surely not just the men. Some women had to be compassionate as well.

"What else can you tell me about Sor—High Priestess Sorcha?"

Yun's smile widened and she regaled the woman's merits. There were so many that Daeson was impressed in spite of himself.

Daeson's new room was more stark than the one he'd left beside Synjan, for the bed was the sole feature that took up most of the space. It was a sleek square of dark blue. Large, plush looking pillows lined the bed where it met the high golden wall.

Yun moved before him and reached for the belt of his dress. Undoing it would make the garment fall. Surprised, he captured her hands and held them.

"I won't be staying on your world," he told her. He didn't want to trick her into an intimacy that she wouldn't share with him otherwise. Not staying meant he wouldn't be accepting her as his companion, either. It was the gentlest way he could reject her.

"That is a shame," she replied, but she didn't look upset. He was concerned about her lack of emotion.

"Will I be allowed to leave?"

"Of course," she said. Her truth relieved him. "Once the High Priestess receives you, your Diplomat will take you and Synjan to the Portal. It will be a long trip, but nobody will use it before you get there. Word has been sent."

Daeson released Yun's hands and she untied the knot of his belt.

"What are you doing?" he asked, surprised yet excited that she would continue to undress him. Her offer of becoming his companion had led him to imagine intimacies with her, but he'd thought that opportunity had passed when he'd expressed his desire to leave.

"I am helping you prepare for bed. I am to stay by your side until you are received by High Priestess Sorcha," she said demurely, but the look on her face when she lifted her eyes didn't match her tone. When the garment fell to the floor, her hand strayed across his bare chest, the light touch of her fingers on his skin summoning shivers along his spine. "Would you like that?"

Daeson nodded. He would like that very much.

CHAPTER FIVE

Controlled Landing

ZEPHYRS CHASED AMONGST the leaves, rousting the shadows and throwing gleaming light upon the faces of the two Wanderers slumbering in the tropical clearing. As Ellis awoke, he squinted against the sunlight, turning his head to escape it.

It had been many years since he'd Wandered naturally and he was surprised. He felt sublimely rested and there was no chemical aftertaste befouling his tongue. After the numerous days he'd spent on a boat chasing down the Portal, it was of marginal consolation. He opened his eyes, blinking to settle his vision. Fyfe's face—less than a metre from his—stirred a momentarily-dormant ire and he was thankful that the brown-skinned upstart was quiet for once. He inhaled slowly and dedicated himself to enjoying the silence while it lasted.

As his senses whirred into full alertness, Ellis realised it wasn't perfectly quiet. Joyous sounds of splashing water and people squealing skittered towards him, carried on the soft breezes. He sat up and looked around, already finding the pulsing heat uncomfortable, the hovering jungle oppressive. Biting pinches along his arms drew his attention and he slapped at the detestable insects swarming over him. Water might make the situation bearable; the gush of large quantities falling accompanied the noise of people.

Fyfe sat up, a peaceful smile on his handsome face and his blue eyes sparkling. He stretched and yawned ostentatiously.

"Oh, *man*, that feels good!" the young man enthused.

"Keep your voice down," Ellis hissed, "you want to have the element of surprise."

Fyfe smirked at him and winked. "I always have the element of surprise," he told his companion loftily and closed his eyes. "Why, hello lovely wild naked people," he murmured as he used his Navigator talent.

Ellis gritted his teeth. "How many?"

"Six. All swimming at the moment. And your girl..."

Ellis' heart leapt as Fyfe Navigated farther afield. He didn't want to entertain disappointment but Synjan could be nearby and they'd walk right up to her in the next ten minutes. What would he say? What would *she* say?

"Nowhere," Fyfe finished decisively, opening his eyes to look at Ellis.

"Nowhere?" he repeated, his deep voice rolling around the word and coating it in dismay.

"Sorry, man. Pretty sure she's nowhere on the world—there aren't too many people on this world at all, really—and she's for sure not nearby. Maybe she's closer to the Portal. It's across a *lot* of water, almost on the opposite side of the world. She could be over there and I've not looked hard enough."

"You'll keep checking? To be sure?"

"'Course," Fyfe scoffed and Ellis's hands curled into fists as he fought the urge to strike his flippant mouth.

"I suppose we should go and meet our neighbours?"

"Yeah. These cats have the monopoly on land around here, that's for sure. If we wanna' get anywhere, we're gonna' hafta' be nice to them," Fyfe announced, springing lithely to his feet.

"How unpalatable," the elder sneered, annoyed by the notion they'd have to bend to the will of strangers. Fyfe held a hand towards him and he took it, suffering silently as he was pulled deliberately close.

"They've got the boats," Fyfe shrugged, smirking as Ellis' body pressed up against his. "Lots of water, remember?"

Ellis' lips became a thin line as he shook his hand out of Fyfe's lingering grip and stepped around him. There was a barely-noticeable path through the clearing. It disappeared amongst the trees blocking most of the sound. He headed for it.

They exited the parting in the foliage quite suddenly and were immediately noticed by the persons swimming in the pool at the base of the waterfall. They all struck for a different part of the lagoon's edge, where their weapons were laid beside their clothing.

"Ah shit! You should probably Control them to drop their spears," Fyfe urged in a rough whisper.

Ellis wasn't interested in enlightening him on the precise functions of his talent but the presumptuousness was irritating. "I'll see what happens," he demurred. "Striking first is not as important as striking truly."

"Whatever, man," Fyfe muttered, shaking his head. It was a passive aggressive habit that had permeated their travels from Bardon City to the Portal on Trent and Ellis was almost done with tolerating it.

The Wanderers watched as the locals scrambled to collect their weapons and clothing and then bustled towards them. There were enough of them that a few clustered in the background to speak excitedly to one another in an unknown language, gesturing at them in a manner that advertised they were the subject of the conversation. A man reached them first. He thrust his spear butt into the mud and puffed up his chest as he spoke at them.

"New Wandruhs! You come J'Bdyamn. Friends or enemies?"

Fyfe looked at Ellis but he deliberately blanked his expression, forcing the Navigator to communicate on his behalf.

"We're friends," Fyfe declared, his voice too loud, considering he was only competing with the waterfall. "We mean you no harm."

"No harm?" the spokesman queried, turning to bandy the term about with the rest of the group. None of them could decipher its meaning either, causing him to turn back with a wary expression.

"No harm, uh, we're friends," Fyfe repeated, silently appealing for Ellis' help to no avail. "Um, no fight. Friends!" he reiterated.

"No fight!" the spokesperson repeated and smiled as the words were repeated by his group. The offer appeared acceptable. "You come meet Bannan," he urged, gesturing for the two visitors to backtrack and precede the native dweller.

Before they left, the group of six took the time to dress. Although their clothing was simple, Ellis was surprised to see that it was made from woven fabric and dyed different colours. The men wore short pants or skirts without upper garments while the women had a strip of clothing to support their breasts and similar lower wear to their companions. He wasn't sure what he'd been expecting in such a remote environment but civilised apparel was certainly not it.

After a bit of manoeuvring, the large group worked their way to the clearing Ellis and Fyfe had awoken in. From there, the talkative male took the lead and their party headed in the opposite direction from the lagoon. Despite his best efforts to put one of the natives between them, Fyfe was behind Ellis in line. He seemed to feel it was his duty to lean forward and share every errant thought that sprang into his over-zealous head, leaving very little time for Ellis to think about where they were going.

When they emerged from the claustrophobic forest onto an open area above a vast ocean, Ellis closed his eyes and inhaled gratefully. His moment of silent reverence was interrupted moments later.

"Fuck. Me. Sideways," Fyfe breathed.

Ellis exhaled in frustration and opened his eyes. The sight of their welcoming committee traipsing over a spindly rope bridge suspended high above the murmuring ocean was impressive. When they were gestured towards it, Ellis stepped forward. He was delayed by Fyfe's hand on his arm.

"You think that's safe?" he asked worriedly.

Ellis regarded his companion coolly. "Did you see any of them die?" he bit out crisply.

"Nah, but that rope doesn't look very strong," Fyfe

mused.

"Wavering heart, empty hand," Ellis shrugged and pushed forward.

At the bridge's edge, he took a moment to adjust his bag—slung over his head and one shoulder so that it usually rested on his left hip—so that he'd have both hands free and then he walked out. He took a few awkward steps before he got the hang of riding the bridge's undulations but his feet were nimble and he very much enjoyed the view of the turbulent surf below as he crossed. The island ahead of them seemed larger than the one they were leaving behind and he assessed it curiously as he approached. It rolled gently downward from the pinnacle they were upon and there were gaps in the canopy off to the right that gave him some idea of the direction they would head.

They'd arrived in the later stages of the afternoon despite leaving Trent just before midnight. The sun, hovering level with them, cast a beautiful glow over the area, tingeing the grasses golden orange. While he waited for Fyfe to gather his courage and cross the bridge, Ellis meandered around, inspecting the foliage. He picked a berry off a small bush and crushed it between his thumb and forefinger, intrigued by its bitter, peppery fruit scent.

As soon as the last of their party was across the bridge, they continued down the slope into even thicker forest. It was obvious that a recent effort to widen the path had been made, as long grasses and small plants that had been wrenched from the ground lay dying beside where they walked, their roots wilted and their former greenness replaced by emaciated brown. Such casual destruction made Ellis wonder what had prompted the brutal landscaping.

His curiosity only grew when they got closer to their destination—advertised by many voices conversing in the distance—and he noticed scorch marks travelling in succession along trees that were lined up. They weren't large enough to have come from a fireball, their narrow precision suggested something more like a fiery arrow had travelled through the area and burned something quite large in a charred bowl in the dirt. There was more than one set of singe marks, like the flamethrower had had several attempts at setting his or her target alight. Without the technology of gasoline, only an Elementalist could have left these marks.

The outskirts of the village was discernable by the trees becoming sporadic, interspersed with stumps confettied by sawdust. They'd no doubt been culled to build the grass-roofed huts ahead. The tangy scent of bleeding sap nipped at Ellis' nose, telling him the settlement was relatively new.

They paused at a small cage built on the fringe of where the forest began to thin, separated from the civilisation visible some distance down the path. The cage was made of thin bamboo trunks lashed together with no roof on it. Two badly beaten men huddled inside, naked and ragged, cowering as far from their arriving party as they could get. It wasn't far enough to escape the spears that were thrust between the gaps to prod their skinny bodies or the laughter that erupted as their companions banged their weapons on the cage. Ellis recognised the petty act of reinforcing superiority for what it was; he'd been like these victors once. He knew better now but he said nothing.

After they'd had their fun, the native guides beckoned the Wanderers towards the village. As they followed, Fyfe shuffled to Ellis' side and whispered, "I don't wanna be in that cage, man. You won't let them put us in there, right?"

"No," he answered perfunctorily. Fyfe was too inexperienced to recognise the spoils of war and Ellis didn't feel the need to explain. Even if circumstances changed, he wouldn't allow the two of them to become this group's playthings. Fyfe must have read that in his eyes because he looked relieved.

The group attracted many curious stares as they passed with the two Wanderers. Ellis stared back, interested to see that most of them were filthy with forest-coloured paints, mud and even bits of plants stuck all over their bare bodies. They were well camouflaged even around their homes, where many seemed to emerge suddenly because they'd stopped blending into their environment. Their artfulness was appallingly clever and he suffered a delightful frisson of apprehension as he imagined them as adversaries.

As they went, a small procession of whispering children gathered in their wake, following them towards the highest point in the village area. Overlooking all the meagre huts was an enormous structure that spanned the breadth of the rise. Beside it was an even more elaborate stage—complete with a leafy backdrop and hanging light sconces. In front of this broad platform was a public lounging area where the village leader held court, able to watch the goings-on in every area of the village.

The warriors with them rearranged themselves to stand three abreast while they walked. When they reached the dirt at the edge of the huge grass mat that defined the lounging area, the one who'd first spoken to them announced their presence.

"We have new Wandruhs!" he bellowed and then the three men screening them from view moved aside.

Ellis barely had time to take in the scene before the man dominating it shifted. He was huge, his broad frame covered with fair, freckled skin and a wild red mane of hair and beard. He was reclining on what looked like a modern lounge chair except it was made from wood rather than cloth. It was covered with fur skin cushions and a colourful throw rug that wouldn't have looked out of place in some of the more unconventional Dockside residences.

Leaning on his elbow with his legs angled casually along his seat, he was clothed in a pleated kilt that reached his knees. His free hand fondled the bare breasts of the woman cowering on the mat before him. She was long-limbed and had the aspect of a warrior, yet she was doing her best to shy away from the big man's attentions. Wearing only a grass skirt and some sort of undergarment beneath it, she was mostly exposed. She seemed to be an outsider too, in spite of her dark skin.

At the announcement, her head lifted swiftly and she stared at Ellis with haunted, hopeful eyes that confirmed his suspicion. He was almost relieved when his view of her was blocked by the big redhead who leapt over her and invaded his and Fyfe's personal space.

"I am Bannan, King of the Techatachenti!" he roared, his face so close to theirs that Ellis felt the tickle of his beard and saw clearly the fading pinkness of sunburn upon his pores. The man had to be six feet five at least, he towered over both of them. Fyfe took a step back and Ellis did his best to keep his sigh of contempt to himself, lest Bannan think it was directed at him. "Where have you come from?" the king demanded, his booming voice carrying over their heads to the rest of the village—that were no doubt gathered behind them by now. His arms were the thickness of oak saplings and his legs like contoured stumps but the muscle in his flesh appeared loose rather than firm and opulence had bequeathed him a pot belly. Still, he was formidable and they would do best to tread carefully, not just because these people had the boats they sought.

"From Trent, Your Majesty," Ellis answered with composure, lowering his head to convey favour but not so low that he wouldn't see an attack coming or appear to be grovelling. Men like Bannan liked their dues but wouldn't respect cowardice. "The world before this one."

"Your journey has just begun!" the king guffawed, his golden eyes narrowing as they flicked between the two Wanderers. "What powers have you?"

"Fyfe is a Navigator," Ellis volunteered quickly. "I don't have the blood but have hired Fyfe to take me through the worlds."

Ellis' shoulders relaxed when Fyfe said nothing to contradict his statement and Bannan took it at face value. "What would drive a man to do such a thing?" the redhead growled shrewdly. "You're not a young man. Adventuring is a young man's thirst! What is your name?"

Anger flared but Ellis tamped it down, keeping his voice steady. "I am Ellis. My employee Wandered away from me and I seek her return. A blonde woman named Synjan, have you seen her?"

Bannan's look of glee was genuinely ignorant. "No, but if I had, she'd still be here, on my cock!" he roared, thrusting his hips obscenely to the delighted titters of his gathered village. "Instead, I have Paki. Come meet her," the redhead enthused and spun on his heel. Ellis noted how skilfully he moved for a man of his size. Bannan bounded back onto his lounge, his feet either side of the near-naked woman before it. He grabbed her face from behind and rubbed her cheeks, contorting her features for Ellis and Fyfe's benefit as they stepped cautiously closer. "I've only had her a few days so she doesn't speak much Authoritan yet, but I'm encouraging her to learn it," he grinned.

As he spoke, his hands roamed off her face; one went into her braided hair, the other to her breasts. She snarled and twisted in his hold, clearly angered when he pulled her hair. She tried to gnash his fingers between her snapping teeth. Bannan laughed, amused by her rebellion. It was only when she sang that his delight faded and he slapped her head hard enough to send her sideways, bellowing, "Authoritan!" at her.

Ellis raised his eyebrows at the woman. He'd heard a lot of languages in his time but one that was sung was novel. He wished to hear more of it but understood the danger. Paki hitched a sob and curled up, folding her arms across her abused skull.

Bannan watched her for a moment, then snorted with disgust and kicked her until she shuffled away from between his feet. She was careful not to touch the ground beyond the edge of the mat; Ellis supposed she had boundaries. Once she was out of the way, Bannan looked up at his visitors with renewed interest. "What are you still standing there for? Sit!" he ordered.

Fyfe headed to the seat farthest from the king but Ellis pushed him closer, seating the dark-skinned

Navigator between them for tactical purposes. Fyfe shot him a wounded look but sat where he was forced to, glancing at Bannan but mostly staring at Paki.

"You haven't had her long?" Ellis enquired.

Bannan chuckled. "Her people, the Mukake," he explained, taking a moment to spit on her as he said the word—she flinched as the viscous glob landed on her exposed back but made no move to wipe it off, "tried to keep this island from us. Believed it was for the Gods alone—the Gods being the Wanderers that arrived here," Bannan sniggered. He looked expectantly from Ellis to Fyfe, but the youth was too busy watching the spit slide over Paki's smooth brown skin to give a reaction. Bannan punched him in the shoulder to get his attention, then yelled in his face. "We are Gods to these gobdaws!"

"Gods?" Fyfe repeated, clenching his teeth as he grasped the place Bannan had hit him.

"I am, anyway," Bannan muttered dryly, then continued his story. "These fools thought the Gods owned this island, too," he indicated the Techatachenti villagers before he leant past Fyfe and spoke conspiratorially behind his hand to Ellis, "until I convinced them that my brother Gods told me this island was for them. It was the only thing that worked! We moved here. The Mukake didn't like it. There was a fight. We won. Killed most of them but we have two dogs left to feed from. Because I am a great and merciful God, I took three bitches into the village to breed with. The other two you can try but this one is mine," he said, nudging Paki in the buttocks with his toes. He looked directly at Fyfe as he said it. Intelligently, Fyfe nodded and the red giant eased back into his corner of the lounge. "Navigator, huh?" he asked.

"Um, yeah," Fyfe answered weakly, still massaging his arm. "What's your talent?" he asked.

Bannan smirked. "You'll see."

"But you Wandered here?"

"I did, many years ago. Probably ten, maybe more," Bannan said, tilting his head to look at Ellis behind Fyfe's back. Stories bloomed in his eyes, clamouring to be told, but he didn't share them. "How far behind your bitch are you?"

"Too far. She's been gone a few weeks."

"Where's the Portal?" Bannan asked Fyfe.

"Um… far across the world."

"How will you get there?" the king enquired. It was the opening Ellis had been waiting for.

"We really don't know," he said silkily, casting a hopeful look at Bannan. "I think we'll need to throw ourselves on your mercy and see if you can help us out."

Bannan grinned, his leonine eyes glinting gold in the late afternoon sun. "I could indeed. But you must stay for a while. I desire new faces to look at, new conversations with those fluent in my own language!"

Ellis didn't doubt that Bannan's desire was genuine but he thought it more likely that the man just wanted someone who could fully understand him while he bragged. If it got them a boat, Ellis was willing to play along. "Alright, but we won't stay too long. Our mission is urgent."

Bannan laughed gregariously. "As you wish, but it is your duty to take with you word of my generosity as you travel so that all the worlds will know my name."

Fyfe turned to look at Ellis then, his expression dominated by disbelief. "This dude," he exhaled quietly in Ellis' direction, widening his eyes for emphasis.

Unfortunately, Bannan heard him. Fortunately, he agreed. "Exactly!" he concurred, slapping Fyfe heartily on the back. Fyfe choked on some spit as he was smacked forward and Ellis smiled, feeling lighter than he had in days.

The scream was equal parts terror and rage. It rolled around the village far longer than any human should hold breath. Fyfe covered his ears and closed his eyes, trying unsuccessfully to block it out. The gleeful laughter and rhythmic sounds of flesh on flesh that came afterwards were worse.

"I hope you're not torturing yourself by watching," Ellis said quietly, his voice an intrusion in the darkness of their hut.

The owners had been evicted so that the visitors would be housed in the greatest of esteem, as Bannan's closest neighbours. So far, the position had only yielded them the loudest rendition of Paki's abuse.

Fyfe yanked his hands off his ears and glared across the grass mat floor between their beds. Moonlight accompanied the sounds of combat flowing through the open window holes but it was barely bright enough to make out Ellis' form.

"He's fucking sick," Fyfe hissed between clenched teeth.

Ellis was pleased that the youngling had the wherewithal to realise sound carried in both directions and keep his voice down. "I've known many men like him. Power is everything. He's enjoying her resistance so he won't hurt her too badly."

"Too badly?" Fyfe repeated in an indignant squeak. "How can you just let that happen?"

"Because it's not our place to interfere. It's *not* our *place*," he said, willing Fyfe to get the message.

"He's gonna' kill her and where will that leave you?" Fyfe huffed, punching at his rustic, scratchy bedding.

"Exactly where I am," Ellis snorted.

Fyfe went still and the tension in the air lessened. "You didn't notice?"

"Notice what?"

Fyfe leant up on one elbow and squinted at Ellis. "Oh, man, you didn't see how she reacted when you said Synjan's name and I did!" he crowed hoarsely.

The skin of Ellis' face crawled with apprehension, from his forehead to his chin. He turned his head and stared at the shadowy blob across the tiny room. "How did she react?"

"She flinched. Like she recognised the name. She's got info on Synjan and you're okay with that motherfucker killing her," Fyfe said, his voice betraying his disgust too much to let his smugness through.

Ellis was quiet for a great deal of time. "It will be dangerous," he warned.

"What will?"

"Keeping him occupied and oblivious while you do your best to get close to her. Keep it completely open and platonic, no matter what she does."

"Does? What's that supposed to mean?"

Ellis sighed impatiently. "It means she'll do

anything she can to get away. We're her only potential means of escape and you're clearly the softest place to land."

"Hey!" Fyfe objected. "If I'm such an easy mark, why don't you do it?"

"Because that would give you the job of keeping Bannan enraptured. Would you prefer that?"

Fyfe's ensuing silence spoke volumes, as did his petulant tone when he finally responded. "Fine."

"As soon as she figures out you want something from her, you're hers. Be aware of that. There are none so powerless as those who believe themselves in control."

"That's stupid."

"Why?"

"Because I have to be in control when I talk to her, you just said so!"

"The point is to be fully aware at all times and never relax your guard just because you *feel* everything is under control. It will only remain thus if you tread carefully and don't give away your desire for information."

"She already heard you ask Bannan about Synjan, she knows we're after her."

"She knows *I'm* after her, which is why she'll try to leverage anything you give her, to get to me. And also why I need to be the one close to Bannan."

"Your head must be one messed up place, man."

"Just stay focussed. Befriend her, stay out in the open with her, play down your interest in Synjan but get anything from her that you can—also anything about Daeson."

Fyfe muttered something beneath his breath that Ellis couldn't hear properly but the mocking tone came through. Ellis' hands curled into fists and he fought back the wave of irritation that threatened to drown him.

"We're not here to interfere with their lives," he reiterated when he was calm enough to speak. "We leave them as we found them. We're not looking to change the world, just find one woman."

"Awful lot of trouble for one while innocent women get fucked over right in front of you," Fyfe muttered sourly.

"Choice is an illusion, not a right. We're not getting involved in their petty squabbles. We'll be gone in a few days," Ellis argued and he was adamant in his belief.

CHAPTER SIX

The Three Navigators

MEALS CAME UNPREDICTABLY and the lights went off and on for inconsistent amounts of time. At first, Hawke was certain he could keep track of it. They were trying to fuck with his head by manipulating his benchmarks—food, toileting and sleep—but he was confident in his body clock. He would feel tired at night, awake during the day and hungry when it was a meal time. He'd been in his body thirty-eight years, it wouldn't let him down.

But these Femme bitches had a sophisticated understanding of what it took to reduce a man to complete ignorance.

First, they altered the amount of food they brought. Sometimes it was a filling meal, other times it was a snack with a protracted period of starvation afterwards. He was never able to savour it, despite knowing that eating quickly would leave his stomach growling later and his head aching. He learnt to eat everything on offer, even if it left him feeling bloated and ill.

Second, they left him thirsty. Water was never in abundance and sometimes they would disregard the necessity of a bathroom visit. He'd been denied for long, agonising stretches and one time, he'd been forced to piss in the empty jug. His urine had a strong, sour odour that made his stomach turn. His initial impulse to keep to his workout routine was quelled by the threat of dehydration. He wallowed in an unfamiliar, sedentary lifestyle, counting the breaths it took before someone responded to his cries for water.

Last—and most importantly—they fucked with time itself. He was bored so he slept. It was dark, so he slept. It was light but he didn't dare do too much, so he slept. When the lights were turned off, only the eerie green glow of the retinal scanner above the open wall was visible. That light wasn't strong enough to penetrate the extreme darkness of his cell. Turning them back on was akin to a spiritual experience as blinding white light shot straight through his closed eyelids directly into his brain. He got too much sleep but it wasn't restful.

Was he being drugged? He thought so, but it was subtle and cleverly disguised within his torture regimen. He was never this placid or unbalanced; they had to be drugging him. He couldn't taste it in the food and there were no needle marks, but he checked every day. He wasn't himself so he knew he was being juiced somehow.

Thoughts of Brita were guilt-ridden and mournful but he longed for the comfort of her presence. Thinking about her too much made him teary and he didn't want to cry. Cayden would've been horrified. Distractions were limited and fleeting. He couldn't hold onto any thoughts for too long. Woy's mocking voice often bullied him out of his dreams, where she'd push in between him and Brita, accusing her of being nothing more than a convenience.

Hawke had never been as aware of every minuscule function of his body. He ached all over, his eyes were always gritty and he had a love-hate relationship with every human that came near him, just because they were something to break up the monotony and give him food/water/attitude. His only relief was showering and he did that as often as they allowed, which wasn't often. It was glorious in its un-routine-ness (he thought a lot about words like that, certain he was creating essential additions to the Authoritan language). Once they'd let him stay in until his skin was wrinkled and the water had gone cold. Maybe it was because the drugs were being released in the steam and he was breathing them in.

Yesterday—or a few hours ago, he couldn't be sure—his ceramic shard had been discovered. He'd used it to cut open his forearm (he was smart about it, doing it curled in his bed facing the wall) to check that his blood was still red but a boy had walked in with a tray of food and water at that moment. Hawke had frozen and so the boy had walked out with the shard, handing it to Funny-Bitch. She'd made some kind of hilarious comment. He forgot what it was. Afterward, a new blonde woman visited him—he'd nicknamed her Empress because of how she'd carried herself, and she'd sewn him up like a rag doll with invisible stitches. He couldn't even find the wound anymore. Had that even happened?

Now he was waiting in the interrogation room and even though it was banal, he was energised by the change of scenery. Even on a different world and within a different culture, it looked the same as every interrogation room he'd ever been in. The walls were painted the same colour of bland. The metal table in the centre was unbreakable and nondescript. The chairs were the same degree of uncomfortable. It was intoxicating in its not-his-cellness.

Hawke had been lucky so far. He hadn't been questioned—though that looked set to change—and he'd been kept comfortable. Boredom was better than physical torture but being drugged was a deep concern. He hated not having a sharp mind. He inhaled to clear his senses, relishing the fragrance of air not dominated by his own scent. He estimated he'd endured between six and nine days in his cell so far and they hadn't changed his bedding yet. He was sick of smelling himself.

The door whooshed open and a short, matronly woman walked in. She wore the silver dress of the world's Enforcers but didn't carry herself like a soldier. She held a clear clipboard in one hand and a tall glass of water in the other. Hawke watched her set down her glass—his gaze lingered on it too long, giving away his desire. Out of his cell, he was Shielded. Water was required. Condensation dripped down the sides, leaving a delicious ring on the table. He swallowed.

She didn't immediately introduce herself. Instead, she scrolled through the tablet's runic symbols, reading whatever was on there. It took him a moment to realise she wasn't wearing specs and he made a soft noise of incredulity. Did they think he would forget what world he was on, or that eye contact would make a difference? Dormant anger stirred and he embraced it. Rage was useless to him alone in his cell but it was an effective defence here.

Her steady gaze met Hawke's tempestuous one.

She stared, he glared. Everything about her was stiff. Her posture, her tightly braided hair, the harsh lines on her face. Nothing moved. Hawke slid down in his chair, fingers linking together on the table between them.

"Name and rank?" she asked.

Hawke said nothing. There was no benefit to identifying himself. He was a Hunter of Wanderers in a world full of them. That would not go down well. He toyed with the idea of providing a false answer, using their rank instead... except he couldn't remember what they called themselves. *Yippees* or *Yoyos* or something.

"I am Yanjan Millana," she identified.

Yanjan, that was it.

"Do you think you are not expendable? That you will be bargained for?"

Hawke continued to say nothing.

"You must surely think it, to keep your silence. Are you so important that the Authorities would risk what they have established on our world? It has taken centuries of negotiations and tributes for them to set up bases in each of our major cities. Even so, they understand their hold is tentative. They will not dissolve the *Raoko Nakoi* for one man, even if he *is* important."

There was an expectant silence that Hawke didn't intend on filling, except he couldn't help himself.

"You're trying to confuse me with logic," he said. "It won't work."

"Then let me appeal to your emotions, Hunter Hawke Donovan."

His eyes widened at her knowledge of his rank and name. His stomach hollowed out and he sucked in more air, though breathing couldn't fill in the gap.

He hated that his reaction gave him away. She would know she'd surprised him and now she had the upper hand. He tried to console himself with the knowledge that, as his jailor, she would always have had the upper hand.

It didn't make him feel better.

"Did you think being a Shielder made you less vulnerable? We have knowledge of you. You are the only Shielder in the Authorities. You donate your blood so they can hold Wanderer prisoners and perform experiments on them." Her lip curled.

"I've heard you test out your new medicines on men. What's the difference?" He'd heard no such thing, it was a guess but an educated one. Slaves were treated like shit, no matter how pretty the world looked. It was the same on any world that used them; slaves of gender, slaves of race, slaves of economy. It didn't matter who or why people were slaves. They were always abused.

The Yanjan's eyes flickered. Had he hit his target? Who knew what was going on beneath her blonde-covered skull? She gave very little away. He was grudgingly impressed.

"You have been set up to fail," she told him. Her declaration was something he'd considered himself. "Do you believe Ambassador Woy would risk her life for you? She is in a perilous position even without your stunt."

Millana's words stung but they also gave him hope. No, he didn't think Woy would have risked her life for him, but she had told him from the start that her actions were constantly in question. Nobody trusted her—not her people and not the Authorities. A double agent could be a triple agent or could be working for herself. Her motivations were only clear to her own fractured mind. Perhaps not even then.

"You grow quiet and your eyes become soft," Millana said, her words hushed. "Could it be...?"

He let the sentence hang, wondering if she was talking about the level of drugs in his system. When he realised she was implying he was soft on Woy, he was shocked. The idea of his loving the freaky bitch that had led him down this crooked path was both laughable and frustrating. He'd trusted her in the end and that was why he was here. He wasn't going to admit anything.

"You'd think the Authorities would learn from their past mistakes," she said.

It got his attention. He stared at her while she twitched a smile, his curiosity apparent. He was a shitty spy, he really was. He'd always been terrible at hiding his true thoughts and intentions—and while Brita might have found it endearing, it was a fucking drawback during an interrogation.

Brita...

"Smug, much?" he spat, pulling his hands back and laying them on his lap.

"Hands forward."

"I don't have a gun in my pyjamas," he complained, but he sat up straighter and returned his hands to the table, palms flat. His gaze found the glass of water as she launched into her story.

"Some time ago, three Navigators from Demkoi fled to the Authorities seeking immunity. They opined that Wanderers who travelled from world to world were instruments of biological warfare and they disagreed with allowing them to travel through our world, unharmed. Their intentions were good, though misguided. There'd been a recent epidemic in Na'ala—a landmass south of here—that moved so quickly that Healers could not keep up. It claimed the lives of five thousand women before a cure was discovered and distributed."

"Five thousand *women*? Was it a disease that attacked just women? Or you didn't bother counting affected men and children?"

Millana continued as though Hawke hadn't interrupted. "The origin of the disease was never discovered but it was estimated that a travelling Wanderer had brought it. There was no proof but it was a scandal at the time. The Three Navigators promised to lead the Authorities to the Portals on every world, so that they could contain them."

She stopped talking and stared at Hawke, whose hands curled into fists on the table.

"Are you pausing for dramatic effect? Go on."

"They were taken to one of the Authority Base Worlds. They travelled with a group of soldiers to the Portal and declared its position. The Authorities had a half-blood Intuit with them for visual confirmation. They began construction on a wall to prevent the Portal from being touched. In retaliation, the Portal's energy beam grew until it released what was described as a pulse of light that killed the soldiers within the closest radius and blinded everyone else in sight of it. The Navigators were blinded and their powers stripped. The Intuit was far enough away that she retained her ability, though not her eyesight, and verbally documented the entire incident for the Authorities—and then she did the same for us."

Hawke was stumped for something to say. Yanjan Millana picked up the glass of water and held it near her lips, her eyes glistening. Hawke stared, unable to think of anything beyond his growing thirst. He wouldn't be able to stay Shielded for much longer without water to renew his ability.

She set the glass down without drinking from it, close enough to him that he would be able to reach it. He was almost certain it was drugged—she hadn't even taken a sip—but he was struggling to care either way. What was one more dose? It was water and he needed it. They knew he wanted it. He would not bow to their manipulation so he forced his gaze from it.

"Why tell me this?"

The story could be a lie, of course, but he already knew of the urban legend that some navigators had once worked with the Authorities and something bad had happened. Different accounts of the rumour depended on how drunk the storyteller was, but this particular, emotionless recount was something he could believe.

"You were intending on travelling through Demkoi until you reached the Portal, were you not?" she asked.

Hawke's breath abandoned him. Even if he'd wanted to speak, he couldn't. Their villainous machinations already had him dizzy and her words amplified the mind-fuckery to a whole new level—though he supposed it might have been shock. The Wanderer Portal could sense the presence of betrayers, and the Authorities knew it. After everything he'd done for them, after every experiment, every donation of blood and every bullet he'd put in a Wanderer's head in their name, their repayment was to trick him into a suicide mission. Failure meant being arrested. Success meant the Portal would have killed him.

"What do you owe them, when you are a Wanderer?" Yanjan Millana said.

Hawke's gaze sharpened and everything came back into focus. He swept his hand out, knocking over the glass of water, splashing some of it over his interrogator.

"I am not a fucking Wanderer," he seethed.

She must have believed him because he was sent back to his cell.

CHAPTER SEVEN

Scene Not Unseen

PEOPLE SWARMED AROUND them in numbers too great for Synjan's brain to process. It was all she could do to remain on her feet and keep Diplomat Nama in sight as they jostled their way across the footpath towards the transport terminal. She'd grown up in Gredann, which was always referred to as a 'city' but even then she'd known Bardon to be bigger. Both of them together wouldn't fill one pocket of the bustling metropolis that was Ning. Perfumed scents, blurred speech and multi-hued outfits assaulted her senses as she wove her way through the crowd. She'd already removed her specs because the information flying at her wherever she looked was another overload. It was difficult to catch her breath enough to check Daeson was okay with the bags, let alone air her concerns about him... about what he'd been through the night before.

Swallowing the lump in her throat, Synjan emerged beside the diplomat as they entered the station and the throng thinned out. Nama was waiting, watching Daeson manoeuvre his way through the pedestrians. Nobody gave way to a man so he was forced to stop repeatedly, acceding to the women striding about with their noses in the air and the will of the Gods upon their heads.

"Is there some sort of special event on today?" Synjan asked.

Diplomat Nama gave her a confused blink. "No, why do you ask?"

"There's just so many people," Synjan gestured feebly around them.

"This is usual. Ning has millions of residents and visitors are constantly drawn to where the region's heart beats. Good. This way," Nama instructed, turning as Daeson finally reached them. His expression matched his overburdened state. He carried Nama's luggage as well as the backpacks.

Synjan wished there was some way she could help him. At least his legs were long enough that he could keep up with them without too much effort.

"We're departing from gate five," the diplomat announced as she led her charges in the appropriate direction. As she walked, she leant towards them, her demeanour suggesting she was confiding something secret. "You're going to *love* the under-sea train."

Synjan came to a stop, unaware of all but the last word the diplomat had said. *Train*. She had the unnerving feeling that her head was a balloon attached to her shoulders by a string. Then Daeson was beside her, luggage set at his feet so he could hold her hand and look into her eyes. She held onto him, understanding with a sickening clarity what he went through on that bridge in the last world.

Diplomat Nama walked another few steps before she registered that her charges weren't with her. She returned with a perplexed expression, looking between them. "What is wrong?"

"You didn't tell us we were going on a train," Daeson explained. Synjan gave his hand a squeeze, grateful for his intervention.

"Do you know what a train is?" Nama asked, confused.

"We know," Daeson said. "Synjan's whole family was killed in a train crash. She was in it too. She was the only one who survived."

Nama's mouth opened and closed a few times as she tried to figure out what to say. She reached out and clasped Synjan's forearm, her expression sympathetic. "I'm so sorry," she apologised earnestly. "I had no idea."

It took a couple of tries but Synjan managed to swallow the panic fluttering in her throat and speak. "I'm sure your trains are far more sophisticated than Gredann's were. Plus, it was years ago."

Marginally encouraged, Nama nodded, her voice calm and inviting when she spoke. "Oh yes, it is the most technologically advanced train system in all the worlds. There has never been an accident. It travels through a tunnel beneath shallow, calm seas. Some of the tunnel is made of glass but it is heavily reinforced and not far enough beneath the surface to be under too much pressure. It is *extremely* safe," she repeated, looking at Synjan hopefully.

Taking a deep breath and exhaling slowly, Synjan nodded.

Nama expanded. "You shall have opportunities to look out at the living ocean and the gorgeous water because some of the carriages are designed for viewing—they have glass ceilings and walls. You feel like you are travelling *in* the ocean, it is spectacular," she enthused.

Synjan thought it very unlikely she'd enjoy such a sight but would reserve judgement for the time being. "How long will we be on the train for?" she asked, balling her free hand into a fist as the sensation of being out of control threatened to crush her. She wasn't sure how they'd even got to this point—she could only suppose Daeson had announced that they weren't staying in this world, since no-one had formally asked her this morning. She'd been gathered and shuffled out of the High Palace as swiftly as possible after waking. She hadn't even seen Daeson until he was deposited at her side on the driveway. She felt like a beige towel in a washing machine loaded with bright colours; out of place, dazzled and muted.

"Two hours."

Again she nodded and decided to try walking again. Part of her recognised that she shouldn't hold Daeson's hand and, with great effort, she let him go before she spoke. "And where are we going?" It was like a dance. Walk, breathe, speak, walk, breathe, listen. The rhythm asserted itself, making everything easier.

"South to the airship launch centre in Anjiang. Do you have a problem with flying?"

"I'm not great with heights but Synjan is fine with them," Daeson said.

"The airships are very gentle and also very safe," Nama assured.

"Sounds wonderful," Synjan said through her teeth. She met Nama's gaze and attempted a smile. "Fine. Sorry. It'll be fine. The train, I mean. I'm sure it will be fine." If she said the word 'fine' often enough, she'd believe it.

"You are in the safest hands possible," the diplomat insisted, eventually confident enough that she turned to look at where they were going. "Is that...? It *is!* It is my friend!" the diplomat exclaimed, distracted by someone she was seeing ahead of them. "Oh, I must speak with her. Stay close, please," she uttered breathlessly before putting on a burst of speed.

Synjan and Daeson exchanged a look and hurried after her.

"Satori!" Nama called, drawing the attention of an identically-dressed woman. She was also walking towards a doorway labelled with a few indecipherable marks and a large numeral five. She paused and looked back when her name was called, her face lighting up when she saw who it was.

"Rin!" she exclaimed, hastening over and throwing her arms about Nama.

Synjan and Daeson stood mutely by while the two good friends gabbled at each other in their language, obviously ecstatic to have met up. It wasn't long before Diplomat Nama gestured at them and Satori did the same to a man on her other side, drawing Synjan's attention.

Despite doing his best to look bored by the whole process, Synjan could tell by the hunch of his shoulders and the darting looks he was throwing around that he was no more comfortable in this situation than she was. He had to be a Wanderer going on the same world-exiting journey as she and Daeson were. His brown hair was shaggy and overhung his brown eyes but he met her gaze boldly, lips twitching dismissively as he looked from her to Daeson and then away, forced to conceal his restlessness beneath a guise of submission.

A decreasing chime trilled overhead, preceding an announcement in three different languages. One of them was Authoritan so they were able to understand that their train was now boarding. People funnelled themselves towards the nondescript gates and the two diplomats hustled their charges onto the train and into the correct cabin. Synjan was ushered in first, followed by Daeson and then the other man. Unsure where to sit, Synjan turned in time to see Diplomat Nama lean through the doorway and give them all a winning smile.

"Synjan, Daeson, this is Roman. Since we are all travelling in the same direction, you three might as well spend time together. I am sure you have much to share. I will stay with my friend. You will need to leave the cabin if you want to use the restrooms or go to a viewing car but Synjan can escort you. Synjan, your specs will provide you with any extra information you might need. Remember, it is all perfectly safe. I shall collect you when we reach Anjiang. Have fun!"

The door closed abruptly, leaving the three occupants blinking at each other. For a moment, awkward silence prevailed.

"Hi... Roman, was it?" Daeson asked, shuffling his and Synjan's backpacks like he intended to shake their new companion's hand.

"Yeah," the stranger confirmed before he shouldered past Daeson and sprawled along the seat to their right. It had three moulded backs with a bench base, all covered in a beautiful teal fabric. Roman didn't care how pretty it was; he shoved the armrests out of the way, pressed his knapsack into the far corner and sat against it, his legs sprawled along the seat. His back was to the window, the only entry in his line of sight.

Synjan admired his instincts but was annoyed by his cavalier attitude and blatant disregard for the furnishings. His sandals were filthy—how had he managed to get them caked in mud in such a pristine world?

Daeson ensured Synjan was seated with their bags nearby and sat beside her opposite Roman. She resented the fact that they'd been lobbed in with a stranger for the two-hour journey because they couldn't speak freely. She was loathe to discuss her train fears or the circumstances of Daeson's previous night with Roman staring at them and listening to every word. Something about his casual air prickled her skin and she was pretty sure she knew what it was. Recognition of a like-minded hustler.

To distract herself, Synjan fussed with her gear, taking the time to go through it and check that everything had been returned as promised. She supposed she wouldn't be permitted to wear her weapons but the desire to do so had her touching them all furtively until Daeson frowned at her constant rustling. She sighed and closed her backpack.

It was a little emptier now that she'd disposed of some useless clothing but she wondered if she'd be able to replace any of it. Femme's wardrobe choices were unusual and not suited to blending in to most worlds but where would she be able to find normal clothing? The next world? Twisting her feet, she looked at the slippers on them. Despite the fact that they were comfortable, they wouldn't last long during their travels outside of this world. In her bag were a pair of boots that the Mukake cliff face had ensured would need replacing, too. She released an impatient breath, wishing the train would just *go*. The longer she waited, the worse her nerves were getting and her—

The train started to move. She and Daeson were travelling backwards.

"Do you think that's a drink thing?" Daeson enquired, startling her.

She looked where he was pointing and noticed sleek-looking cabinet doors attached to the wall beneath the sealed window. There were six labelled nozzles at the top and a silver column on the side that held cups. "I'd say so," she agreed, putting on her specs so she could get some information. The nozzle labels were written in Authoritan but that didn't mean she could understand them. "Um... what do you suppose a phizon berry tastes like? Or a qandan star?"

"What?" Daeson asked and she laughed.

It lightened the weight on her chest. The two of them set about sampling the drinks—which were carbonated, flavoured water—until they found one that suited their tastes.

"I'm not sure how you can even drink that," she admonished Daeson, wrinkling her nose at his spectacularly orange-coloured drink. "It tastes like week-old groundwater."

"Better than your potion that tastes like wood. You're not supposed to drink wood," he countered, looking pleased when he drew another laugh from her.

Synjan glanced across at Roman, wishing he'd disappear. He'd watched them sideways the whole time they'd sampled drinks, and shook his head when Daeson offered him a cup.

Roman ignored her glares and closed his eyes. The strangest sensation came over her. Inexplicably, she felt drawn to him. She swayed forward, wanting to look at Daeson but unable to take her eyes off Roman. It didn't take her long to figure out what it must be and amazement replaced her discomfort.

"Is that what it feels like when I map?" she whispered.

Roman's eyes sprang open. The impulse to be close to him disappeared and Synjan broke her gaze to look at Daeson.

"Almost," he responded thoughtfully.

She looked back at Roman but his gaze was on Daeson. "What's your talent?" he demanded.

"Well, that's rude!" Synjan bristled.

"Healer," Daeson said at the same time.

Roman sat up, leaning forward earnestly, ignoring Synjan's outburst. "Did you say Healer?"

"Yeah."

Roman stared at Daeson and the look in his eye raised Synjan's irritation another notch. His stare moved to her and she thought he looked pleased by the annoyance he read on her face. She pressed her lips together, fighting the urge to snap at him as he looked analytically from her to Daeson and back again, then reclined on his seat. He was 'Roman Zhatoral—Visitor in Transit' according to her specs but she had plenty of far more creative names bouncing around in her head for him.

"Maybe you shouldn't just tell people that," she hissed at Daeson.

"Why not? It's not like I have any secrets on this world."

She sighed, knowing it was Roman that was upsetting her and not wanting to take it out on her travelling companion. He was her friend, he deserved better. She was concerned that Daeson was becoming too casual about announcing his talent, though. She imagined Authorities overhearing and arresting him, or his being shot immediately by said Authorities, or maybe being dragged away by strangers that wanted to monopolise his healing abilities. She was just being paranoid. She hoped.

"I need the toilet," Daeson announced, tossing his empty cup in the bin behind the cupboard.

Synjan smiled, relieved by the prospect of escaping the train cabin and eager to have some time alone with Daeson. "After three of those, I'm not surprised," she murmured. "Let's go."

The train was nothing like the rustic transport system she remembered from Gredann and that was her prominent thought as she followed Daeson out of their cabin. The carriages were very wide, with a central walkway running between berths in every carriage. They were extra long, too, so they wouldn't be back quickly. She looked in both directions down the corridor, pleased when her specs listed the features of walking either way and she could ascertain which direction was the shortest route to a restroom. With only a mild pang of guilt, she led Daeson the opposite way.

Checking they weren't followed out of their cabin, she walked beside him as best she could, waiting at his side when they encountered passengers going past. It was difficult to decide how to begin a conversation she felt was quite serious, so she began with something relatively neutral.

"So, that Roman guy is pretty intense. He makes me nervous."

"He's more quiet than intense, I thought," Daeson

said.

Slightly embarrassed—as well as disappointed and surprised—that Daeson didn't share her sentiments regarding their co-Wanderer, Synjan changed the topic.

"Hey, guess what? You know how, when we got here yesterday, I was noticing that this world is *filled* with solid patterns—like yours and Tagan's? It made me realise something. Solid patterns are *Wanderer* patterns." Her heart sped up as she anticipated his amazed reaction. The idea had come to her when she'd been waiting for him to return the night before.

His response was less than underwhelming. "Oh," he said with mild interest, leaning to the side as if it would help him see farther up the corridor of the carriage they'd just entered.

Synjan was disconcerted by his indifference and the rest of her realisations sat on her tongue like a bitter lozenge, too foul to swallow and too condensed to be released. After she'd made the connection about Wanderer talents having solid patterns, it hadn't taken long before a certain olive green pattern was called to mind. A cold sensation had washed from her head to her toes when she'd understood that Ellis had a Wanderer talent. *Ellis was a Wanderer.* She'd thought in circles about the facets of this revelation, why he'd never told her and what his talent could be, but she'd needed someone else to air her theories to.

Daeson would be that person for her but she saw that now was not the time or place to bring it up. Not only was his focus scattered, he'd been through something that was likely occupying most of his thoughts. It was selfish of her to think about things that were much less important than Daeson's wellbeing. She needed to let him know that she was there to support him.

"So, how was your night last night?"

Daeson looked at her, taking a moment before he responded. "I was given a new room."

She thought it was very telling that he'd chosen to begin with this statement. It was the truth but not anything close to the most important thing that had happened to him. She didn't respond right away either, debating how much she should push him to talk. What if he was an absolute catastrophe inside and barely keeping himself together? One wrong comment from her could dissolve him. She had to be gentle.

"Why?"

"I was told it was more convenient for the High Priestess."

Synjan sensed an opening. "What was she like?"

"We didn't talk much."

They had to move to let a rowdy group of young women pass and Daeson glanced sideways at her. He said nothing as they began walking again and Synjan allowed the silence, hoping he'd feel comfortable enough to elaborate if she didn't nag him. Much to her chagrin, he didn't speak until they'd reached the entrance to the male restroom. He pulled her aside rather than entering straight away and leant close. Keeping his voice low, he asked, "Were you watching?"

She sighed, loathe to admit the truth but also relieved to have it out. "Yeah, are you okay? I saw—"

"You shouldn't have seen anything! You shouldn't have been spying on me."

Synjan blinked, shocked by his vehemence. "I wasn't, I didn't mean to—"

"Are you saying you mapped me by accident?"

"No! I was just waiting for you to come back to your room so I was watching you all night. Off and on," she answered, her hands flicking limply between them as her emotions warred. She wanted to reassure him but guilt and concern about what she'd seen were undermining her message. Hopefully his truth talent would prove that she *hadn't* been spying on him, she'd just wanted to go to sleep beside him— J'Bdyamn had established a habit she didn't want to break— and they had lots to talk about.

"Are you sure that's all it was?"

"What do you mean?"

"You told me that you used to watch me with Omerri."

Synjan's mouth fell open at his implication. He thought she made a *habit* of spying on him having sex? What sort of twisted obsession did he think she had with him? "Not on purpose!"

Daeson stared at her.

The anger that flared was a welcome shift away from simpering uncertainty. "Look, I thought you were having a tour or something. I wasn't expecting you to be with... doing... "

"And did you stop watching when you saw?" he demanded.

Synjan felt the colour rise on her cheeks but she wasn't to be deterred from communicating her position. "There were four women in your room. It was *weird*."

"I didn't have sex with all of them," he defended.

More warmth covered her face. "Yeah, I figured that out," she mumbled.

As she lifted her gaze, Daeson spun and went into the restroom.

She sighed, uncertain about telling him exactly

what she'd seen and doubtful it would make a difference. She'd been in bed much earlier than he was, restless in his absence—of *course* she'd checked on him to see when he was coming back! When she'd seen him in bed with the first woman, it had jarred her enough that she'd watched longer than she should've, jealousy causing her pulse to spike.

A large part of her had felt betrayed. She'd remained celibate in J'Bdyamn against her will and he knew it. The last few days, there'd been a vibe between them that had got her wondering and thinking about Daeson differently. She'd always been aware of how attractive he was but it had felt like he'd finally started noticing her too. When she'd invited him to shower with her, she'd been genuinely hopeful that he would accept her offer and confirm her suspicions.

All that melted into an ugly mess of sour emotions when she saw him having sex with a stranger. Yes, she'd watched longer than she should've. Initially, it had been a matter of not believing his interaction was going to progress beyond a kiss and some fondling. When she'd figured out they weren't going to stop, Synjan had, pulling her mind's eye away. It hadn't been like the times when she'd seen his pattern with Omerri's. This time had stung. She hadn't *wanted* to see.

After waiting what she'd thought was a generous amount of time, she'd checked back on him only to find a surreal shift in circumstances had occurred. The pattern of the first woman lay beside him in bed, while another woman's pattern was riding him, with two more standing in the room watching. By the time she'd reassured herself that she hadn't fallen asleep and started dream-mapping, Daeson's pattern bled into the woman's abdomen. Soon after, she dismounted and left the room with the two watcher patterns in tow and Daeson was left in bed with his original lover. They'd argued and Daeson turned his back to her, curling up. Synjan had eventually fallen into a worried sleep.

She looked up as he walked out of the restroom, frowning as he caught sight of her standing there waiting for him. Had he thought she was going to leave him alone to get back to their berth by himself?

"It's the way it happened. It didn't seem consensual," she explained hurriedly.

His eyes narrowed. "By my observation, men want to have as many conquests as possible. Most of the Queen's customers had wives at home. Many of them paid for two women at once. What makes you think I didn't want that kind of experience for myself?"

"Because you're not—"

"Don't talk like you know what I want." Apparently he wasn't prepared to hear any more and he stalked off. She hurried after him, needing to trot to remain in step beside him.

"Did you say yes?" she pressed.

"I didn't say no," he bit out.

"That's not the same."

Daeson whirled on her. "Is it the same as forcing a conversation on someone who doesn't want it?"

His words were a slap and she stopped. "Daeson," she breathed, dismayed that he was likening her to the women that had accosted him.

To his credit, he stopped also. He turned to face her, his shoulders slumped with an air of resignation. He looked almost as hollow as she felt and it didn't reassure her at all.

"Just... no more. Please?" he pleaded.

Synjan nodded, realising she'd pushed him too far. It was too soon. He hadn't finished processing it himself and her pressing him was just making things worse. He was too good a person to be this mean, it was obviously her fault. As his friend, she needed to wait for him to come to her. She'd be ready when he was.

Nothing more was said for the rest of the walk and it didn't change when they re-entered their cabin. Synjan was determined to give Daeson mental space. She put their bags in the storage area so she could give him physical space as well, leaving the seat between them empty.

She disliked the way Roman's eyes sparkled while he watched this silent interplay and she despised the enjoyment he took in the obvious distress between her and Daeson. She refused to satisfy his curiosity by breaking the silence. It lasted the rest of the trip.

CHAPTER EIGHT

High And Mighty

THE ROOM SWAM out of focus as Hawke struggled to get out of his cot. With a great deal of effort he heaved himself into an upright position and then lay against the wall, out of breath. It felt like his arms and legs were made out of lead. He hadn't experienced this kind of doping before—nothing comparative had happened at the DOME. He was deeply concerned but didn't know what to do about it. He could still think but it felt muted—like he wasn't making connections as rapidly as he should. Half-formed ideas bloomed in his mind like impressionist paintings.

Detail. He was a man of detail and right now he had none. He heard a rhythmic clicking and didn't know what it was until a silver-dressed Enforcer appeared at the Shielded wall. The clicking must have been her booted heels. He should have identified that.

His chest felt like it was being compressed and a tendril of nausea wound tight in his gut—even his addled mind recognised it as fear. He'd felt it occasionally during his stay in this cell, but now it was present and undeniable. Something was going to happen. Something bad.

He didn't think he'd be able to walk, but supported by two Enforcers—*when had the other one shown up?*—he managed to force his feet into the rhythm of walking. Hawke refused to be dragged along like an unconscious drunk.

This interrogation room had a sky blue couch in it. Hawke stared at it, thinking it wasn't real, until he was dropped onto its soft cushions. Had he completely lost his mind? There was no such thing as an interrogation room with a couch in it. He caught himself at a lean and went through a great deal of effort to pull himself upright again. The back of the couch was comfier than the wall of his cell so, if this was a hallucination, it was a good one.

The two Enforcers had left by the time he was upright but then a different one entered the room. He recognised her—the short, plump one with eyes of steel. The first time they'd met, she'd told him a story about blind Navigators. The other times he'd faced her, she hadn't been so friendly. She had a maternal appeal but there was nothing soft about her beyond the roundness of her body.

"We are going to have a nice, long chat," she said.

"No," Hawke replied, surprised that his word wasn't slurred. What kind of freaky drug could wipe out motor function, mute his mental capacity but leave his communication intact? It was only a single word, perhaps he should try more. "I don't want to talk." Every word was clear—at least, to his own ears.

"You don't have to talk," Yanjan Millana said with a glee he mistrusted. "You just have to *think*."

Of course, they'd gone after his Shield. He had to get his Shield up—but his focus was off. He could feel his skin pulsing, like every muscle had a tic. On, then off. On, then off. Like a torch losing battery and flickering in the darkness. He struggled to keep that light on. Staring at Yanjan Millana, he saw her smile widen.

And then he was left in the dark.

"What is your mission?"

So many missions on so many worlds. Faces of Wanderers he had tracked and killed surfaced in his memory, unwanted, unbidden. For years he'd suppressed them, their faces only returning to him in dreams. Did that mean he was dreaming now?

"What is your current mission?"

The question had more bite in it. The voice asking him was getting angry. He was good at pissing people off. He'd been told it was a natural talent of his, but that was wrong. He worked at it. It took practice.

"What is your current mission?"

"Not gonna say," he said, but he thought of Kegsy, thrusting a photograph of Synjan towards him. It wasn't the only one that existed of her but it hadn't come from her Authority files. At some point, someone other than the Authorities had taken a photograph of Synjan without her knowing. Cameras were expensive on Trent—technology was being rolled out slowly to not overwhelm the populace. Photographs weren't unknown but were hard to get. Computers were unheard of, though he suspected that some criminals had them. Synjan worked for a criminal—for a man considered a minor drug lord by the Authorities, but they didn't know what Hawke knew. Ellis had enough influence on enough worlds that he could pull in orphaned Wanderer children. First Hawke, then Synjan and who knew how many in between who'd let the opportunity pass like he had?

"What is your current mission?" The voice asked, louder.

"Not deaf," Hawke mumbled, but he thought about Nakhari base, and Palua'a, and the Spies who'd tried their best to train him to lie not only with words but with posture and expression. Wasn't going to help him here. He couldn't tell them the process a Wanderer went through on Femme but he could certainly inform them of what a captured Authority could expect.

He heard tapping and looked up to see Yanjan Millana poking the tablet she held and then swirling her finger around like she was drawing a particularly abstract sketch. Her cheeks were round and pink, her eyes bright and focussed behind her specs. She reminded him of Cayden's wife Mary, who looked the part of a mother but who'd only ever treated him with resentment and suspicion. He'd invaded her house, her life and her family. As for Millana, he'd invaded her world.

She looked up and stared at him. Nothing was said between them, nothing came to Hawke's mind either, though he knew she was manipulating him somehow. Story of his fucking life.

"Do you think you're a puppet?" she asked.

"I have been one. Not anymore. I make my own decisions."

"Yet you answer to the Authorities," she said, putting the tablet down onto her lap. Hawke shook his head and noticed there was no table between them. Wait, had there been one at the start? He only remembered the couch. His hands rubbed the soft fabric of the cushions either side of him. But this was an interrogation room, wasn't it? The walls were still bland.

"Did the Authorities send you after her? This... Synjan?"

Hearing her name come out of Millana's mouth sent a spike of anxiety through him.

"Has she arrived in your world yet? Is she safe?" Hawke wanted to know.

"What do the Authorities want with her?"

"Nothing, nothing." He shook his head and thought about what the Authorities would do to her. Kill her, probably. What a waste. He had so many questions for her. So many.

"Do the Authorities know about her? Are you here because of her?"

"No... yes. Wait."

"How many missions are you on?"

Hawke didn't want to tell them, but he couldn't stop thinking 'two'. Millana must've read the number from his mind because she made a soft sound to herself.

"Both of them for the Authorities?" she clarified.

No, he thought.

"Is Synjan important to the Authorities?"

Not to them. Just to Ellis. Just to Kegsy.

"Then your mission is to find the Portal?"

His diplomat was supposed to deliver him to it but the mission hadn't been about that. It was about figuring out what sort of protocol the Wanderers went through while here. Woy refused to tell them and diplomacy required the Authorities not to ask. Femme had so many false Wanders—women showing up on Earth that would contact the Authorities as soon as they arrived—rendering the flare reports useless. Hunter research had shown that Wanderers that moved out of Trent were very slow moving through Femme. Painfully slow, to the point of Trent flares being ignored. Only Earth flares were relevant enough to draw the attention and pursuit of a Hunter.

Femme was the black spot, the wormhole where the trails died and nothing emerged predictably. While they were on Femme, the Authorities suspected Wanderers were being given a great deal of information about Wanderer powers and history. Hawke's mission had been to collect all that information and report back.

"What role did Ambassador Woy play in your mission?"

Hawke frowned, turning his head to the side in an effort to eject her from his mind but the image of her flying across the room surfaced. He'd replayed the incident many times, gaining no insight.

Millana paused, frowning at him. "Did you attack her?" Her tone was uncertain and part of him rejoiced that he'd managed to unbalance her.

"No."

"Then tell me what happened."

"Don't fucking know," he ground out. He didn't know what had happened, couldn't she understand that? He hadn't been responsible and he couldn't even remember what she'd been talking about when it happened. She'd been making predictions and then whoosh, off she'd flown.

There was some tapping and swiping on the tablet, and then, "Who is Kegsy?"

An Authority. A mentor. A friend.

"Who is Ellis?"

Hawke giggled, finding it very amusing that he'd be asked to define someone he'd never fully trusted or understood. Might as well ask about the stars and how they got there. Maybe Brita would know.

"Who is Brita?"

A flood of sadness invaded, casting him adrift. She was more than a convenience, he did love her, in his own way. Why couldn't he ever do right by her? Of course, if he loved her more, he wouldn't be here in this mess, on this ridiculous world, thinking about these bullshit questions. He'd never have left her to get into these stupid missions if she'd been enough.

"Did Ambassador Woy conspire to spread classified knowledge of our world to you?"

I will not betray you. Do not betray me. He blinked, able to see her very clearly as she leant over to warn him. It was the one thing he was determined to do. "No. She left me to find everything out for myself. Fucking bitch."

"How would you have returned to the Authorities? Travelled through Femme until you got to the Portal and then used it?" Millana asked, tapping and prodding her hand-held device as she talked, making notes on everything she gleaned out of his head.

It would've been so easy if he could've done it her way. It made more sense than sneaking back to Nakhari base.

Hawke watched her put the tablet down and they stared at one another again.

"Why break your cover by going back to Nakhari? Why not just Wander out of the world?"

Because he couldn't. Because he didn't have the blood. And now that he knew that the Wanderer Portal had a fucking bomb up its ass and could mess

116

with whoever was hostile to it, he wasn't going to get anywhere near the thing.

"Are you only a partial blood Shielder?"

Only? Fuck you.

Millana laughed, a guffaw that filled the entire room and made him jump. He glared at her, angry without knowing why—he knew she was laughing at him, even though he couldn't remember what it was he'd said, and that was enough. No, she was laughing at what he'd *thought*. Whatever that was. Had they been questioning him about Synjan? He remembered Yanjan Millana saying her name. What had he been telling them?

"Have you ever seen the Portal, Hawke?"

He envisioned the large metal cylinder that usually held eighteen chairs. He could almost feel himself sitting down in one; comfortable and at peace even though he knew that the machine ripped the fabric of the multiverse somehow, that it tore through into—

"The Wanderer Portal, Hawke. Have you ever seen the light?"

Snow. He thought of snow, blinding white and biting cold. He remembered whoops of joy and grinning faces peeking out of bundled scarves. He remembered being held while someone else reached out to touch... nothing.

Yanjan Millana grunted, the noise one of dissatisfaction. He didn't know what it was she didn't approve of—the Wanderers who'd stolen him out of his world or the fact he hadn't been able to see the Portal for himself. Maybe both?

"You chose your own life, after that," she spat.

Something else, then.

Hawke woke up on a polished concrete floor. It was hard and cold and his body was fatigued from resting on it. When he struggled onto all fours, a wave of nausea had him dry-heaving. His stomach ached, as though he'd already emptied it several times. Nothing came up except for spit, which he ejected from his mouth into a puddle on the floor. He contemplated it. He was desperately thirsty and it was water. He hadn't liked the slimy sensation of it before it was out of his mouth, so he didn't know why he thought it would be better going back in. He crawled backwards and hit a piece of furniture swiftly enough that its legs scraped against the floor. Hawke sat heavily on his backside and turned.

He used the chair to help him climb onto it and discovered a bottle of water in the middle of the table. He blinked, astonished that he'd been provided with anything. Hawke grabbed it and undid the cap, taking small swallows. The water was at room temperature but he didn't care—it was glorious. He made himself stop. There was half a bottle of water left. He spun it between his hands.

Memories of his questioning were unclear. He knew that he'd been unable to keep them out of his head. They'd led him into thinking about—

Synjan.

Oh fuck, he remembered saying her name. He'd been asked about his mission and he'd talked about *her.* What had he said? If she was on Femme already, they might tell her about him, or that the Authorities knew about her. She might never leave and his one ticket to come and get her had expired.

What had he been thinking, coming here and chasing after her? It would've been smarter to head to Earth and wait for her to make an appearance there. If too much time passed and it was obvious she was staying on Femme, he could've gone to Nakhari at *that* point. This was the biggest fucking mistake of his entire life. He'd failed in his mission for Kegsy— the one time his friend had asked for help and Hawke had launched straight into pursuit without planning.

He had never gone on a hunt without a plan. Everything was always laid out with direct ideas and contingency plans in case things didn't work out, or if the Wanderers were wilier than he expected. Why had he gone off without thinking things through this time? Nakhari Base had been on his mind because of Brita's dickhead friend mentioning it, but was that a legitimate reason to go straight there without taking a moment? Kegsy had shown up, asked for his help and then Hawke had portalled into Femme without a second thought.

What the fuck was that about?

It was too hard to figure out and he had half a bottle of water in front of him begging to be drunk. He finished it all and then regretted not rationing it. What if it was the last water he was given? It felt almost like a reward—that he'd been a good little informant and surrendered every secret on the Authorities that he knew. Not that he knew many.

But the Hunter Division. He knew a lot about that and it was obvious that Wanderers were helped on this world.

Also, if he managed to get out of here, he would be held at Nakhari Base for an indeterminate length of time while forced to relay every piece of information he knew, so the Authorities would know what Femme had on them. He didn't want to be kept there for any length of time. He didn't want to be considered a liability. He didn't want to be forced into retirement or dishonourably discharged. He didn't want to be considered a traitor and incarcerated or executed.

He thought he understood now, the perilous tightrope that Ambassador Jinwa Woy walked between her native world and the Authorities. It was one that he would have to walk now, too.

If he ever managed to get out of here.

CHAPTER NINE

In The Belly Of The Beast

DAESON SAT BESIDE Roman in a large open room, doing his best to ignore the roar of voices as hundreds of men had conversations around him. His ears felt like they were cringing into his head. His fidgeting attracted some advice from Roman.

"Focus on someone's conversation, it'll help."

Daeson looked over at the other man, surprised by the tactic offered. He did as suggested and focussed on the first conversation that was in Authoritan.

"...and she took me to the beach after that."

"Even after she threatened to make your life miserable?"

"Yes. She does not mean anything she says."

"It sounds like you get treated well."

"Only once she finishes tormenting me. When she feels guilty."

"A guilty mistress is the best mistress."

Laughter.

Daeson didn't want to listen to that conversation anymore but the others closest to him were in a different language. Another option was to talk to Roman. Daeson hadn't wanted to speak to him about the sensitive topic of Wandering after being warned not to do it in the open but there was little else he could think of that they had in common.

He opened his mouth but a loud tone over the speakers drowned him out. A message was given in two different native languages—he could tell there were two because the second one didn't have the clipped and gargled sounds of the first. Daeson struggled to hear the Authoritan translation over all the men fastening bags, talking with their friends and moving around. "Attention. You are now to board in groups of twenty. Make your way to processing."

His skin tightened at the word 'processing'. It had been the start of his problems in Gredann City, when the Authorities had wanted to process civilians to find and register Wanderers. He'd faced an uncertain future.

Roman looked impatient, standing at a lean in the direction he wanted to go, looking back over his shoulder at Daeson. He nodded to Roman, thinking it was nice of the other man to have waited — there was no obligation for him to. They'd barely spoken on the train and if the two diplomats hadn't been friends, they might not have met.

Synjan had taken a quick dislike to him, though.

"We're cattle," Roman said. He spoke so little that Daeson considered his words, discouraged that the other Wanderer had broken his silence only to point out something derogatory. Daeson glanced around at the men shuffling through the doorway—not pushing but not being kind to one another either. Perhaps he was jumping to conclusions and Roman wasn't badmouthing them.

"Do you come from a farming background?" Daeson asked. It would be something else they had in common. Roman gave him a wry look but didn't respond, not even with a nod or shake of his head. He was a curious one.

They joined a queue while women in silver dresses patrolled along it. One of them stopped to stare at him. Daeson stared back in a manner he hoped wasn't confronting. He didn't want trouble.

"You, come with me."

Daeson's heart plummeted. He looked at Roman who stared straight ahead. No help there.

"I'm travelling with Diplomat Nama, she—"

"I understand. You can go front of the line," she commanded.

"I'm with him," Roman said. The lie gurgled in Daeson's belly even though he was glad that Roman hadn't abandoned him after all. What trouble would be waiting for them at the front of the line?

The woman in silver spoke to another who was dressed the same. They both stared at Daeson for a long moment, then broke into broad smiles. He couldn't see their eyes behind their silvered specs, but the smiles looked genuine enough to make him relax. More conversation followed, and within the chatter they said something Daeson recognised.

Sorcha.

Somehow they knew. Their specs had told them. Would every woman know what had happened? He tensed and then the silver-dressed women waved him and Roman through, to join with another handful of men who'd already been processed. Processing seemed to entail being looked at and nothing more.

They walked up a gangplank and into a large, open space. A wall of glass separated them from impossibly large golden coils and Daeson would've found the sight fascinating except he felt sick over the idea that everyone on this world would know what had happened to him. How would other women react with the knowledge he'd lain with their High Priestess?

"That must be what makes the ship fly, yeah?" Roman said.

"What?" Daeson asked, pulled starkly out of his thoughts and struggling to catch up. "*This* is the thing that flies?" It seemed too huge, too lumbering to fly. He'd thought this was the station.

"It's an airship," Roman said, pointing to the golden coils. "Those things... when they power up they give it lift, something to do with magnets and gravity fields. The captain then pilots the airship with rudders and air-currents and we dock after four days."

It was the longest conversation he'd had with Roman. Daeson was grateful for it as he could focus on something other than his loss of anonymity.

"How do you know all this?"

"There weren't any Diplomats when I arrived so I got dumped at a hotel while I waited for one. A woman was assigned to me so I wouldn't run off. She called herself a Duty Officer and I figured she might not know what she could and couldn't tell me. I pumped her for information and she said I'd probably be catching this airship. It's called *Katori Nian,* which translates to Golden Rain." Roman laughed like he'd told an extremely funny joke. "I'd hate to be under the flight path!"

It took Daeson a moment to understand what Roman meant, for he'd heard the words 'Golden Reign'. It made more sense in a world filled with golden-haired women in charge.

He didn't point out the possibility of an incorrect translation to Roman. It didn't matter and travelling would be easier if they were friends.

They smiled at one another and moved with their group farther into the belly of the ship, where a staircase led upwards. On the next level they were assigned quarters—narrow spaces that fit two single beds. Behind a black glass screen was a tiny bathroom. Even though it was compact, Daeson thought it charming. Roman placed his bag on the left-hand bed, claiming it. Daeson sat on the right and put his backpack on the floor.

Roman closed the door and leant against it, staring at Daeson and then at his pack.

"You're carrying too much. You're advertising yourself as a Wanderer to anybody who bothers to look at you."

Daeson looked from his huge pack to Roman's bag.

"So what do you have in there?"

Roman stepped forward and showed him by emptying everything out and sorting it on his bed.

There were two little rolls of clothing that Roman said held two outfits. Another bulkier roll of clothing was his winter necessities in case of a world with snow. There was a small box that he called a 'first aid kit' and pointed out that Daeson wouldn't need one so could travel even lighter. There was a peculiar look on his face as he said this, like he was holding back more comments. Then he touched each item and named them. A strong lamp connected to an elastic band was called a 'head torch'. A tiny plastic packet was said to be a 'raincoat'. Three square plastic bags were 'zip locks'. Inside one of the bags were strips of coloured plastic that he called 'zip ties'.

An odd little grey box was a 'water purifier'. The biggest item was a large green roll identified as a sleeping bag. Roman declared it to be worth the space due to cold climates. Tucked inside it was a small canister of bug spray. The last thing he showed Daeson was a tool that had a knife, scissors, can opener, spoon and other things that could open out and fold away.

"You have no money," Daeson said.

"Money's useless."

"But if you need something from a shop?"

Roman shrugged. "I don't go into shops. Cities that have shops will have shelters."

Daeson was quiet for a moment.

"That's why you don't have a tent?"

"Tents are bulky and difficult."

"I have a pop-up one. It's easy to put up."

Roman put all of his things away while Daeson watched. There was an almost mechanical method to it. Roman packed his things like they were part of a puzzle game and he knew where all the pieces went.

Once he was done, he turned to Daeson and stared at his chest for a moment before reaching over and toying with the collar of Daeson's tunic. Perhaps his neckline wasn't straight—the material was too soft and wispy for him to be able to tell, but he didn't like Roman pawing at him. He smacked the Navigator's hand away and Roman drew back, his expression pensive. The silence grew between them until Roman filled it.

"What you're doing is dangerous. I've been Wandering for years and a Hunter has only noticed me once. I lost him in a matter of days."

"How do you know a Hunter noticed you?" Daeson asked.

"Because I used to travel with my father and he was killed by one."

The revelation was so shocking, so blunt, that Daeson reeled and hit the backs of his knees on the cot behind him, forcing him to sit heavily on it. Roman didn't comment, choosing to buckle and lock his bag instead. He turned a sly look towards Daeson, who couldn't figure out what Roman was thinking. It had all been true but the expression on his face was so similar to Omerri's that they could've been related.

Goosebumps broke out on Daeson's skin. Was Roman using the truth to manipulate him? Using shock as a tactic?

"They don't ask questions," Roman continued. "They don't try to arrest you or make you join their side. They just shoot you from a distance. Wandering is dangerous but Hunters are lethal. And that bag of yours is a target on your head."

Daeson felt like he'd been punched. His head was spinning with realisations and emotions—irritation at Roman for delivering the news so callously, gratitude that he would share the information at all. Fear at having taken unknown risks, self-deprecation for being so careless and stupid. Synjan had been ignorant as well, even while trying to help. She'd loaded them up with things that would make their adventures more comfortable while ignoring the biggest danger—the Authorities.

"Why would you tell me like that? After revealing your father is dead?"

Roman's face showed apparent confusion. "How else would I tell you? It's the best way to drive the point home."

Had he intended to smack Daeson down with the upper hand?

"Most people would soften the news."

"How softly would you like me to present you with the fact of my father's murder?"

Daeson blinked again and saw Roman's expression shift. "I'm not... I don't say it to..." he pulled a face, obviously struggling with his words. Daeson felt bad for him, realising that Roman's caustic nature was more due to leading a solitary life than his desire to shock.

"My father died too. With sickness. I watched him wither away. I knew death was coming for him but it didn't make it better."

Roman stared at him for a long moment and Daeson held his gaze, wondering if sharing that information had made things worse between them.

"Did you Wander together?" Roman asked.

"No."

"You Wandered out of your homeworld after he died," Roman guessed. Daeson nodded and Roman copied the movement. "Makes sense. By yourself or with your girlfriend?"

Roman must have meant Synjan.

"She's not my girlfriend and she's not from my homeworld. I met her in the next one."

Roman nodded slowly, thoughtfully. "How long have you been Wandering together?"

"Uh, not long." The days on J'Bdyamn had blended together. There was a calculating look on Roman's face that Daeson was wary of. Synjan had taken an instant dislike to the other Navigator but Daeson wasn't so quick to judge. He thought he knew why she didn't like him. Roman didn't share his thoughts with others—and chances were that his opinions weren't great. Synjan shared everything that was on her mind and had earned Daeson's trust. Her words were without guile and she always spoke the truth. Roman was more reserved and suspicious but Daeson could forgive him for that. He'd been on his own for a long time and it sounded like he'd gone through many worlds that had been difficult for him. Much like Omerri had made Daeson more suspicious of others, Roman's survivor past had done the same. He couldn't think ill of a person who was a result of his circumstances.

"You helped us on the previous world," Daeson said, wanting to make friends.

"How so?" Roman asked.

"You sent the portal to us when you touched it. It was a long way off."

"I didn't like the world before this one," he said.

Daeson nodded. "It was hard, but at least the natives were helpful."

"I didn't see any natives. There was nobody near me and I travelled for months."

"Months!" Daeson replied, horrified that Roman had gone through the trials of J'Bdyamn on his own.

Roman shrugged one shoulder like it wasn't important. "How many different worlds have you seen?" he asked.

"Including this one, five, but one of them was using a mechanical portal. I think it's a world not far up ahead. Mwavey, it's called."

Daeson watched as surprise overtook Roman's face. He thought he would be asked a multitude of questions about the mechanical portal. Quietly, Roman proved him wrong. "So, you've Wanderered four—no, three times. And you've been with Synjan for two?"

"Yes."

There was a pause, then, "Something bad

happened between you."

Daeson shook his head.

"But she decided to join you when you went to the toilet," Roman pointed out. "Not normal behaviour for someone who's not a girlfriend."

"She had to escort me. I couldn't go alone."

Roman gave another half-shrug.

"Do girlfriends normally join their partners on the toilet?" Daeson asked.

Roman laughed. "She wanted to talk to you without me overhearing, yeah?"

"Yes."

"What about?"

"Why do you want to know?"

Roman hadn't seemed the conversant type. He'd been tight-lipped until they'd arrived in this room and now suddenly he was full of questions.

"Because I'm curious about you and you look like you want to talk. I've been Wandering for sixteen years and in that time I've seen over two hundred worlds. I've seen so much that I don't think anything left will surprise me. Whatever you share, whether you just want me to listen or offer my thoughts, it will stay with me."

It was an appealing idea, to talk to another man about what he'd gone through. Synjan's reaction had been so dramatic that it had become much bigger than what it was. Roman would be able to tell him if it was normal to think of his experience with Sorcha as unusual and fun, but offensive on later reflection.

He told Roman everything, starting with Yun's seduction and how she'd joined him in bed, describing how Sorcha had interrupted them with her assistants in tow, that they'd watched as Yun moved off him and Sorcha had taken over, only to leave immediately once they were done. By the end of the telling, they were both lying on their cots, staring up at the ceiling.

"So they tricked you into donating Healer sperm, the natural way," Roman said, turning his head on the pillow to make eye contact.

"They knew I wasn't staying."

"It's a bit weird they didn't get you to put it in a cup."

"I wouldn't have."

"So why have the sex?"

Daeson blinked a few times, unable to answer the question in a way that didn't make him sound foolish or immature.

"Yeah, don't bother answering that," Roman laughed before he sobered and tilted his head at Daeson. "You know you're lucky they let you go."

Daeson frowned at him. "They were very polite. They said they wouldn't make me a prisoner."

"This is a slave world. I bet they *would* have if you had some other power they wanted. You're only okay because Healers are holy."

Daeson considered Roman's words. If he hadn't heard the truth behind all the promises made to him, he might've been scared about becoming enslaved. His fears had been put to rest very early, though they'd still managed to trick him.

"I wasn't holy enough to be told directly what they wanted."

"Nothing's direct on this world. It's smoke and mirrors. I was told Diplomat Nama was on her way to collect me. She was supposed to take me to the Portal. Then, change of plan, suddenly she's unavailable and some woman named Diplomat Ashiq is now on her way, but it'll take an extra day."

Daeson sat up, leaning back on his elbows, staring at Roman.

"Synjan and I took your diplomat! Why would they do that?"

"How quickly did you tell people you were a Healer? Maybe she switched to you. Healers are important on this world, yeah? They're important on every world, really... but Healers are also spiritual leaders here."

"How do you know so much about this place if you were only here an extra day?"

"I already told you, I had a Duty Officer," Roman snapped before taking a breath and forcing a chuckle. He continued after a small shake of the head. "She was stuck at the hotel with me and I wasn't allowed to leave so she told me a bunch of stuff. I did a bit of sightseeing anyway, my power's good for that," he grinned.

"Sightseeing?" Daeson asked, confused. "Isn't it just the lay of the land? A grid pattern?" By what Synjan had explained to him about her mapping, he'd imagined it as a bunch of lines with coloured blobs on it that represented people.

"Only if I look at half-strength," Roman said, scoffing. Daeson figured out from his words that Roman must be able to see the world like he was flying over it. What a magnificent talent... that Synjan was missing out on. When he went quiet, Roman returned the conversation to his experience with the High Priestess.

"So did they ask you to live at the palace?"

"Um, I was supposed to live in a resort with other male Healers until I was called up for 'duty'," Daeson said.

Roman's eyebrows shot up before he cackled,

holding his belly. At first Daeson was affronted but then he laughed too—it was hard not to when Roman's laughter was so infectious. But he wasn't seeing much of a funny side.

"That's priceless," Roman gasped. "Slavery, premium edition!"

"Yeah." Daeson lay back down and Roman's laughter abated.

"So how are you doing now?"

Daeson hadn't expected Roman to ask how he felt. The surprise of it pulled a more revealing answer out of him. "I'm okay with it, but isn't it strange for me to be okay with it? I mean, aren't I supposed to be upset?"

Roman stared at him until Daeson felt self-conscious. He was about to retract the question when the other Wanderer finally answered.

"I think however you feel is the way you're supposed to. Who knows better about your feelings than you? After going through the amount of worlds I have, you start seeing a pattern in every society. This is normal, that is not. If someone you love dies then you have to grieve for this long, but not *too* long because then you're not mentally healthy. Rules are made and when someone dares to break those rules—by not feeling guilty or sad or happy at the right times—then everybody says they need help, just because they feel something different. I don't understand those kinds of rules—I don't ever want to understand them, or conform to them. It's why I'll never fit in. The World of Worlds is all I have left."

Daeson was astounded by Roman's insight. He supposed that with all that time to himself, Roman had the opportunity to think about a lot of different things. He felt freed by Roman's words—his emotions *didn't* have to make sense. Someone had said that to him before, and recently. Or had it been a dream? "Is it real?" he asked.

"I hope so. Because if the worlds connect in a circle and I end up at the place I started, it'll be a cruel fucking joke."

Daeson had to backtrack to realise Roman was talking about the World of Worlds. "How are you planning on getting there?" he asked.

Roman told him.

CHAPTER TEN

Out Of Control

QUIET FEET WHISPERING across grass matting catapulted Ellis from his slumber. For a few heartbeats he was disoriented, confused about where or when or why. As light seeped into the hut with the rising sun, understanding followed and he sat up, swinging his legs over the side of the bed.

"Paki?" he queried, his voice thick with slumber.

"Yes. Ellis," came the warbling response. The effort put into speaking the two words was audible in the hesitant pronunciation and he wasn't surprised; she was intent on making a good impression. She also seemed to be kneeling on the floor between the beds.

"What do you want?" he asked, speaking slowly to assist her comprehension.

"I breakfast," she replied.

He squinted but could only make out a shadow on the floor before her. He deduced that she'd brought them breakfast.

"It's very early," he chastised.

"Eat bed?" she enquired as a hand travelled

suggestively along his bare thigh. He admired her in that moment because he'd been right about her.

"No," he argued and removed her hand decisively.

Paki huffed her disappointment but she wasn't willing to abandon the chase at the first hurdle. He expected nothing less. "Synjan," she entreated, shuffling closer so that she was beside his feet.

Fyfe chose that moment to sit up and yawn obnoxiously. It was only when the Navigator's mouth closed that Ellis realised the sun had risen enough for him to make out details in the room. He looked back at Paki.

"I know you knew Synjan. Tell me about her."

Paki merely looked at him, her eyes glittering.

Deciding he'd like to test the bounds, Ellis clamped her chin with his hand, his fingertips digging cruelly into her flesh. "Tell me about Synjan," he ground out.

"Ellis!" Fyfe cried in alarm.

He lifted a finger in the boy's direction, warning him to shut his mouth and not interfere with the staring contest he was having with the woman. He could tell from the way she was looking at him that she knew exactly what was at stake, yet she was unwilling to yield unless she got something in return.

"Paki. Wandruh."

"There it is," he whispered, releasing her face and shaking his head at her. "No. Paki will not Wander with us," he said.

A kaleidoscope of emotions crossed her face, the dominant being frustration. With an animalistic growl, she snapped her teeth at him and surged to her feet. She stormed out of the hut with all the noise she'd avoided when she'd snuck in, leaving Ellis looking austerely at Fyfe.

It wasn't that Ellis was unable to relate to Bannan's self-styled totalitarian regime—he'd done much the same thing when he was young and Wandering with Omerri and Kegan—it was simply that he was impatient to be gone. Halfway through the morning he was shifting restlessly in his seat, bored with the scenery and unable to stop thinking about Synjan.

She would have looked imposing amongst these women with her long, golden hair and arrogant gait. Forced into Paki's position, Synjan would have known to surrender sooner, to take attention off herself long enough that she might gut the posturing megalomaniac where he stood. She would never have tolerated the savage's nonsense, although his talent was an uncounted factor. What was he? Would Bannan have bested Synjan—his heart—if she'd met him? Ellis doubted it. Perhaps his demise wouldn't have been immediate, but it would certainly have preceded her exit from the world.

"Ellis?"

Startled from his reverie, he looked at Fyfe, who'd spoken his name. The bearded redhead was also peering around Fyfe at him. What had been said? He'd fallen into his thoughts when they'd started discussing where the Portal was—again—and nothing significant had triggered a need to attend in the last few minutes.

"Hmm?"

"I said you're stronger than you look. Bannan thinks we're not going to be able to row to the Portal," Fyfe repeated, looking annoyed. "Where'd you go?"

"Nowhere," he briskly dismissed the reference to his preoccupation and focussed his gaze on the grinning king. "Why do you think it will be a problem?"

"Because you are puny men and the seas of my world are monstrous!" he announced with a brazen laugh. "You will need a great deal of muscle."

"We need a boat more than we need muscle," Ellis muttered.

"I will bequeath you my loveliest boat—when the time is right. The morning after you arrive is *not* the time, especially with this afternoon's imminent festivities!"

"This afternoon?" Fyfe enquired.

"Yes, little brown Navigator, we will have a hunt before the sun finishes this day and you will enjoy the spoils with my people," Bannan extolled. He leant down and cupped Paki's face, turning it so she was glaring up at him. Bruises and fresh swelling made her hate-filled expression more beautiful and Ellis could understand Bannan's desire to admire his handiwork. "You will taste the end of your people for yourself, my sweet," he crooned.

Paki narrowed her eyes and opened her mouth but appeared to change her mind. "No," she said deliberately.

Bannan's face lit up and he surged to his feet, hauling Paki with him. "At last!" he exclaimed to no-one in particular and embraced her passionately. Swept off her feet—literally—she had no choice but to accompany him to his hut. The sounds of enthusiastic sex and screaming were easily heard from Ellis' position on the royal lounging throne not long afterward.

"Fucking animal," Fyfe muttered

Ellis sighed. "Forget it. It's not your fight."

Fyfe bristled, getting to his feet so he could stand over Ellis. "No? Then whose fight is it, huh? She's not strong enough to fight for herself!"

A calculated narrowing of his eyes had Fyfe retreating from Ellis. He balled his hands into fists instead.

"You underestimate her," Ellis drawled.

"She's a punching bag."

Ellis' lips pursed. He didn't reply until he was certain their host hadn't heard Fyfe's impassioned words. "Like all women, she is so much more than you give her credit for. Every being is only as strong as the fires that forge them but women have a particular talent for being tempered by flames that melt men—men widely considered invincible. Men that think themselves strong have been ended by circumstances that don't even make women blink. No," he shook his head, slouching lower on his furred cushion. "You're insulting Paki. I have concerns about your intelligence if you think she's unaware of what's going on. Wake up."

Fyfe looked like he was ready to explode. His fists worked, his cheeks puffed and his eyes shone with fury. Instead of unleashing his rage on Ellis, he stalked off through the village, disappearing quickly. Ellis was surprised by his wisdom. He wasn't interested in arguing with the child or listening to his whining for extended periods. The sooner they got away from the Techatachenti, the better.

When Bannan returned half an hour or so later, he was alone. Ellis observed this as the giant redhead fell onto the lounge beside him, sweating and reeking of sex.

"Where's Fyfe?" the canny king asked.

"He and I had a difference of opinion. He has gone to stew in his own juices, I suppose. Where is Paki?"

"Gone to clean off *my* juices," he guffawed. "What is the nature of your different opinions?"

Ellis gave the wily redhead a sidelong glance, understanding that they were too alike and too well versed in life for there to be much subterfuge between them. He respected the man's intelligence, even as it dismayed him. "Paki. He objects to the way you treat her."

Bannan's eyebrows lifted and he grunted. Ellis thought he might have surprised the old fox with his honesty.

"The boy thinks he knows better, eh?"

"He's twenty-one," Ellis shrugged. "He's convinced he swims in the font of all knowledge like all young men too stupid to realise they're merely paddling in life's swill bucket. Everyone he meets, he wants to play some sort of sport against, fornicate with or impress with tales of his prowess. Generally, all three at once. He has no idea."

Bannan laughed heartily and slapped Ellis on the shoulder. "You are funny!" he declared. "But if that boy touches my woman, I will send him into the forest and tear him limb from limb." There was no smile to soften the threat and, as Ellis watched, something brutal rippled across the redhead's face, intensifying his expression alarmingly. It took every atom of self-control Ellis had to keep his own expression neutral, to hide the fact that he knew exactly what talent the self-declared king of the Techatachenti had—and was awed by it.

"I would appreciate it if you wouldn't," Ellis requested mildly. "I need him to get to the next world."

Bannan tilted his head and looked at Ellis thoughtfully. "You know what it is to rule people," he stated.

With little else to say, Ellis nodded.

"And to lose people," Bannan continued. "The boy. He doesn't understand what it is to be betrayed. He doesn't know how you will have to punish your woman once he helps you catch her." A grin spread behind the bushy beard and dark satisfaction twinkled in golden eyes. "He won't like it."

"His opinion won't matter. By the time he figures it out, I won't need him anymore," Ellis dismissed, deciding to change the subject and share one of his perceptions with his host. "There are a lot of pregnant women in this village," he observed airily.

Bannan chuckled appreciatively. "Yes. There are. None of them are mine."

"You are sure?"

"I *make* sure," the redhead boasted, "but I use the pregnant ones freely because my seed is fierce and powerful!"

Ellis nodded, his suspicion confirmed. There was no room for succession in the Techatachenti. Bannan was leader and he wasn't interested in having his authority challenged. Fyfe would be appalled to know that any offspring suspected to belong to Bannan would be killed at birth—a common practice in most despot-ruled societies.

"Do the men of the village respect your right to fornicate with their women?"

"I am their *god*," he reminded Ellis. "They challenge me at their peril, as you will soon see for yourself!"

Ellis had no idea what to expect from the

afternoon's promised 'festivities' but the amount of relish with which Bannan spoke was enough to unnerve him. The fact that Paki and Fyfe were both absent at the same time—probably beyond anyone's supervision—also dismayed him but he wasn't going to bring it up. It was necessary, in fact, as long as Fyfe got intelligence about Synjan.

If it was Paki in control, however, they were doomed.

They didn't return for close to an hour but, thankfully, Paki came back first. When Fyfe reappeared, he came from a different direction and was keeping company with a small group of youths younger than he was. They looked like they'd been playing some sort of game or swimming, as their bare brown limbs were glistening with moisture and their camaraderie was palpable, even from Ellis' position on the royal couch.

Lunchtime arrived but the meal delivered to them was meagre. Bannan laughed it off, telling them they needed to save their appetites for the evening's feast. Ellis was dubious in his hunger.

Paki was back at Bannan's feet, looking generally defeated whenever the king was paying attention but shooting Fyfe little smiles when she could. Ellis could only grit his teeth until the light began to lengthen and wane towards dusk. At that point, Bannan shooed them off the lounge and headed towards the nearby stage. Ellis took his chance and grabbed Fyfe by the upper arm, physically steering him away from

Paki and anyone else that might overhear.

"What do you think you're doing?" he growled in the Navigator's ear.

"Nothin'," came Fyfe's sullen reply as he yanked his arm free.

"I certainly hope so," Ellis finished before they were collected by the wave of villagers heading towards the stage.

Various Techatachenti workers had been crafting the scene for hours, re-packing lamps and setting them alight, sweeping the wooden platform and stringing flowers around it. The busy work had contributed to the buzz of anticipation among the villagers and it increased with every step forward. When a naked Bannan bounded before them and spread his arms wide, his people cheered, waving their arms and banging their shields and weapons together. Drawn by the clamour, Ellis gazed around and saw that many were armed and sporting fresh camouflage paint.

"Friends, visitors, enemies, listen well!" the barrel-chested redhead boomed, his voice and stature dominating the area.

Ellis edged quietly to the side of the crowd, deciding that if the large clump of warriors were preparing to hunt, they'd all turn to run off at some point and he didn't want to be caught in the stampede. Fyfe begrudgingly followed him with folded arms and pouting lips.

After Bannan was sure he had everyone's attention, his voice lowered to an intimacy that had his audience leaning closer. It was clear to Ellis that he had a great deal of experience as a showman and that the villagers were his rapt fans.

"Just a few full moons ago, the gods spoke to me

and whispered that they were willing to share their bounty, that the Techatachenti were deserving of this island and its spoils, for we were plentiful in number and diligent in our worship!" The villagers cheered on cue. Bannan stalked from one side of the stage to the other, flinging his arms for emphasis and banging his chest when his message became particularly impassioned. He towered over those clustered closest to the stage, pointing, grinning and winking at them, to great effect. The crowd's devotion reflected in their upturned gazes.

"'Move to our island!' they told me. 'Allow your people to flourish as they deserve!' And so we began our long, heartbreaking move to our new home. The gods were, indeed, happy for us to come here, for have they not provided us with the perfect site upon which to build?" The crowd nodded obediently, turning to consult their nearest neighbours before they stared up at Bannan again. He seemed disgruntled by their lacklustre response, so his next question was more rousing. "Have we not found food in *abundance* and clean, clear waters to *nourish* us?"

"Yes!" the villagers responded, realising their duty to respond with enthusiasm.

"And have the winds not favoured us with *glorious* fishing hauls, *pristine* beaches and *stunning* views?!"

"YES!" the crowd roared, stamping their feet and clapping their weapons again.

Ellis marvelled at Bannan's skill, thinking back to a time some fifty years before when, in his childhood with the Corona of Chi, he would watch the leaders stand at the pulpit and preach to the congregation, espousing the wise and awe-inspiring gods watching over them. Bannan was more than a king, he was a supreme pontiff worshipping in and ruling over the

Church of Bannan as well.

"But then there were the *Mukake*." Bannan dropped his voice to a menacing whisper for the last two words. It had his audience hissing appreciatively. "They sought to rise above their place. They chose to argue with the will of the gods and fight us for this, our *gift*!" The booing and noises of dissent rose, along with the rattle of weapons. "We had no choice but to prove them wrong, to *defeat* them in combat and cow them in the *sand*, in the *forest*, in the *sea*!"

Bannan was a brazier of light and noise and movement, punching the air on the words he emphasised and crowing the Techatachenti's victory to the purple sky above. The village was a roiling mass of adoration and fervour, ecstatic and zealous, frothing to unleash their rising ardour upon something. Their leader spun to face them, feet braced and arms once more flung wide in the middle of the stage as he roared his climactic message.

"AND STILL WE DOMINATE THEM!"

This appeared to be a cue, for a man was pushed onto the stage from the side. He stumbled from the force propelling him forward and caught himself not far from Bannan, attempting to pull himself up to his full, dignified height but flinching due to the injuries he'd sustained. Ellis recognised his as one of the beaten men from the cage.

No sooner had the man arrived than Bannan began to change. His entire body rippled as he hunched over and became stockier, his shoulders rounding and his stomach flattening. Thick, springy orange fur sprouted over him. With a sickening crunch like snapping bones, his human face elongated and became that of a wolf. His arms and legs shortened and turned into the clawed paws of a bear to match his powerful body. He tilted his head back and emitted a terrifying roar at the dusky sky, his elongated teeth glinting murderously in the firelight.

The terrified Mukake warrior scrambled off the stage and ran for his life. The hooting villagers parted before him, allowing him the chance to run. Bannan roared again and his people screamed their ecstasy as he leapt into their midst. They danced and chanted around the beast that was their leader until he decided it was time to pursue his quarry. The sun was almost gone and the shadows would make the hunt more of a challenge. Ellis doubted it would last long, regardless.

In the wake of the throng ebbing away, Fyfe turned to stare at Ellis with wide eyes. "Werewolf? Bear-beast?" he asked hoarsely.

Ellis sniggered, thinking that Fyfe had never looked so pale. "Transmuter," he clarified.

"That's a Wanderer talent?" the twenty-one-year-old choked out. "I've never even heard of it!"

"Not everyone has. Particularly the Authorities. They're very rare," Ellis mused, finding he was more than a little disarmed by Bannan's talent himself. He'd deduced it earlier but that had not prepared him for the sight he'd just witnessed. He hadn't known a Transmuter could invent their own creature. Fyfe had to be reeling. "He has to be a full blood to do *that*."

"He's a psychopath and a genuine fucking *monster*, dude!" Fyfe shuffled close to hiss his words at Ellis. His lack of volume did nothing to hide the note of hysteria. "Why the fuck are we dangling here and not running?"

Truthfully, it did shed a new light on things. Ellis

didn't disagree with Fyfe's desire to abscond immediately but they were handicapped by their inability to traverse the world. "We need a boat," he reminded his companion.

"Let's just steal one!"

Ellis raised his eyebrows at Fyfe, waiting for him to see the stupidity in his statement but his fear was definitely governing all cognitive functions. "A man that can grow fur, claws and sharp teeth can just as easily grow gills and fins and sharper teeth and swim right after us," he answered patiently.

Fyfe hunched over and hurried away to vomit beside the stage. When he straightened, he used a trembling hand to wipe his mouth and returned to Ellis. "What the fuck are we going to do?" he asked thickly.

"Play nice. Pay our dues. Behave ourselves and collect our reward when his majesty deems us deserving." A triumphant howl sounded from the depths of the forest not too far away. "You know, he's really not very far from a god, after all," Ellis observed thoughtfully.

Fyfe stumbled towards the royal lounge, lowering himself awkwardly onto it. Paki had made herself scarce in the hubbub and Ellis didn't blame her. He sat beside Fyfe and waited for the show's inevitable conclusion.

It didn't happen quite the way he expected. A large fire had been stoked in the centre of the village but when the crowd returned, the prey was still alive. Carried over Bannan's head, he screamed and writhed, clutching at the spear perforating his lower intestine. The Transmuted leader took the stage once more, completing a few victory passes with his prize before he lowered him. With a final growl, he ripped out the man's throat with his powerful jaws.

Before the last pulse of arterial flow faded, he spat out the remains and transformed back to his human form, dropping the corpse on the stage. "Now we *feast!*" he bellowed, rubbing fresh blood across his bare chest. As his people came to collect the body for cooking, Bannan looked around, yelling for Paki when he couldn't see her immediately. Four men dragged her towards him, each of them doing their best to hang onto one of her heaving limbs. Bannan directed them to his hut and followed after them, leaving Ellis wondering what vegetarian options were available on tonight's menu... and just what sort of meat they'd eaten the night before.

CHAPTER ELEVEN

An Unexpected Reality

HAWKE LAY ON the cot in his cell, thinking up strategies of escape that became more fantastical with every pass. In his experience, the simplest plans were the ones that worked—most times, blunt was best.

Footsteps alerted him to someone's approach. He recognised their rhythm as belonging to Funny-Bitch, also sometimes referred to as Stomping Bitch. The other guard—Platinum—was light on her feet.

Hawke got up off the cot, expecting a bathroom break and toying with the idea of overpowering Funny-Bitch and nabbing her gun. It would be hard when his senses were still muted by whatever chemicals they were adding to his water. He couldn't even summon up anger about it anymore—only tendrils of offence. He was too grateful for being given water at all.

Funny-Bitch glanced up at the retinal scan that released the shield-wall and Hawke approached her, stopping only when she levelled her bubble-gun at him. This was new. She normally didn't aim it at him when they walked to the bathroom together.

"What?" he asked.

Instead of replying, she shot him.

The goop flew out and hit him in the chest. He was horrified to go through this ordeal again but relieved that she hadn't shot him in the face like the last Enforcer. They weren't big on talking when they aimed their bubble-guns—it was just lift and shoot.

His arms were pinned to his body as the goop connected at the back, encasing him in a hard shell.

He was surprised by how little either of them was saying—usually he and Funny-Bitch exchanged many unpleasantries. This time there was only the noise of their footsteps, the strange wet sound of the goop as it had moved and then hardened, the clicks and swishes of Funny-Bitch holstering her weapon and then pulling out what looked like welder's goggles.

She moved into his cell—the first time she'd ever done so—and attempted to put the goggles over his head but Hawke flinched away.

"Nope."

"You are being removed," she said with a huff.

Removed? What a strange word to use. Funny-Bitch didn't look like she was enjoying the task of 'removing' him, either. He suspected that he was being relocated somewhere more secure. This place could be a temporary holding cell.

It made a horrible kind of sense—he hadn't had his own bathroom and he hadn't seen many guards. It was possible he wasn't meant to stay here longer than a day. Why had they kept him here for so long, then? And how long *had* he been here? It felt like maybe three weeks. Had there been negotiations in that time? Was that why they'd questioned him without torture, so that he could be neat and presentable when returned to the Authorities? Or had the negotiations fallen through and now he would be sent to a worse hole-in-the-ground than this?

Funny-Bitch was coming at him with those damned goggles again. Fuck her if she thought he was going to make it easy.

"Where am I going?" he asked, feigning left and then stepping right when she fell for it. She looked exasperated before glaring at him. He laughed—this felt comical to him, though there was a touch of hysteria in his laughter that he didn't like. Was it the drugs or his mental state finally being challenged for holding in his anger too damn long?

"I will shoot you in the face." She put the goggles on the table and unholstered her weapon. It sobered Hawke immediately.

"No, you can put the goggles on." She looked at him uncomprehendingly, her weapon half-raised. "Those things. Whatever you call them. Put them on me."

She re-holstered her bubble-gun and took the goggles from the table, stretching the band as she advanced. He wasn't told what they were properly called because Funny-Bitch wasn't much of a sharer. After they were on his face, he was surprised to be greeted not by darkness but by an image of a beach.

And then it started moving, like a television had sat on pause and now knew to play for its wearer. He not only saw but heard the waves as they surged forward and retreated with a hiss. The cry of gulls had him looking up and they wheeled above his head. He could *smell* it, too—the salt of the water and the heavy wet odour of seaweed and marsh plants that perched at the edge of the sand. It had been a long time since he'd visited a beach and the experience the goggles gave him was so vivid, so *real* that all he could do was look around himself and gape.

He got a push from behind and he started walking, looking over at an outline of a woman. There was a peculiar rune in the centre of her head, and as he looked at it, it opened out into a selection of five different women. Three of them were blonde but there was a redhead and a brunette. His gaze was drawn to the latter and after a lingering moment, the woman beside him filled in with the image of the brunette. He was reminded of Brita even though they looked nothing alike. His stomach hollowed as though his insides had been scooped out and he felt short of breath.

The brunette that looked nothing like Brita scowled at him as they walked up the beach. She held something out to him—it looked like a wand—and touched his chest with it. He felt the hard casing turn back into jelly and it slimed itself away, leaving no trace. How did that work?

"Door," his escort said, and pointed.

Hawke looked ahead and there was a smooth metal wall in front of him, with an open doorway that he could step through. He could see more of the beach beyond, and he marvelled that it hadn't been here before when he'd looked around. He wouldn't have missed a wall this large. The goggles must be giving him a representation of the real world and decided to plop down a metal wall for reference.

He stepped through the door. There was another metal wall and doorway up ahead but the beach was otherwise open. To test out how clever the Virtual Reality was, he moved suddenly to the right, wondering if he would mash against a wall.

The programming was incredibly smart. One of the gulls overhead swooped at his face and he flinched away. Then Not-Brita (Funny-Bitch?) grabbed him and firmly escorted him towards the doorway up ahead. The VR was far better than anything the Authorities had access to.

They stood just on the other side of the door and Not-Brita made some peculiar gestures in the air with her finger. They left a trail and he raised his hands to wiggle his fingers to see if they left a trail too.

That was when the VR programming revealed its flaw. He was looking at a woman's hands. Long and elegant fingers, thin wrists and lightly tanned. There was a moment as his mind wrestled with the peculiarity of inhabiting a woman's body and then he disassociated with it. The golden skin was flawless, the nails perfectly manicured and without the oddities that unpainted nails showed. He looked further down to see what kind of breasts the goggles had given him but he was apparently disembodied— all he could see was sand.

He was catapulted straight up into the air and his head swam with the suddenness of it. If not for the firm grip that Not-Brita had on his arm, he would've stumbled.

The beach fell away and he broke through the surface of a landscaped park, with paved walkways and clusters of flowers.

He must've been in a lift. The VR had represented the rise and then loaded another program when it couldn't deal with his flight. Had Not-Brita known? She was more considerate because Funny-Bitch would've let him flounder so she could laugh at him.

No, wait. He was confused.

"Walk," Not-Brita said, tugging on his arm. He walked.

They followed the path and walked through a pair of large, ornamental wrought iron gates where a carriage awaited.

"This is romantic," he announced. Not-Brita gave him a look of such complete surprise that he laughed. He was shoved inside the carriage—which admittedly was less romantic—and then Not-Brita pushed her way in and slammed the carriage door shut. "Do we kiss now?" he joked.

Her fist came up quickly, intending to smash him in the nose but the VR was capable enough to portray it as it happened and he blocked her. His reactions were shit, his mind was dull and he blocked her anyway. A thrill travelled up his spine at the idea of not being helpless.

And then the bitch made a second attempt that he wasn't ready for and his nose flared with pain. The goggles flickered their picture when they were jolted, showing him the reality of where he was—in the back of an egg-shaped car—and then the carriage returned.

Hawke nursed his nose and tipped his head back, allowing himself to be lulled by the clip-clopping of hooves. He'd always found it fascinating that every world had gone through, or was going through the process of rearing horses and using them to pull wagons and carriages. Some worlds used larger animals—like elephants—and others had smaller— like dogs—but horses were everywhere and were used everywhere.

Being taken somewhere with his VR 'blindfold' on and no longer restricted by a hard shell of goop, Hawke was optimistic. There was no point blindfolding a dead man or one who would be locked away forever, unable to share the sights he'd seen. He looked out the window to see a rolling digital landscape of lush green meadows and hills. They repeated often. The programmer hadn't bothered detailing the scenery, which was odd since a carriage ride was supposed to be scenic. The repetition made him sleepy and he dozed.

"We have arrived."

Her voice cut through into his awareness and he turned to see Not-Brita reaching for the goggles. His mind protested the strange shift in light and scenery. He was sitting in an egg-car, very similar to Woy's, and it was parked in front of the Nakhari Base gate, on the footpath—because there were no roads up to it.

He'd been right. He'd been bargained for and returned to Authority care.

"Get out."

Hawke didn't need to be told twice. He didn't even give Funny-Bitch a parting comment as he scrambled out of the car. It drove away and he found himself staring at two surprised Authority soldiers in full assault garb. He saw one of them twitch with her gun—a subconscious desire to lift it perhaps?—but the other one snapped to attention and saluted. The twitchy one followed suit.

"Hunter Hawke Donovan, sir! Welcome back to Nakhari Base, sir!"

Hawke didn't normally salute soldiers back, contemptuous of the obligation to offer a sycophantic gesture to those above rank. He saluted this time and was aware of a heavy pressing sensation inside his chest that was making it difficult to breathe. Was it relief? It felt too big for that.

"Uh, sir?"

He looked at the soldier, the one who'd recognised him. Her rifle was held in one hand now, pointing it at the ground. Her other hand had unclipped her helmet strap, presumably so she could talk more comfortably. She looked vaguely familiar but he didn't know why.

"Yeah?"

"Would you like me to show you back to your room? You can change before debriefing."

It wasn't the typical manner of conversation for a soldier of Nakhari Base, where everybody shouted their orders or spoke like the regulation handbook. She was treating him like his ordeal had weakened him, as though he couldn't just slip back into his role.

Maybe it was true—his outrage had disappeared.

"Sounds good. Yeah."

He wondered if Synjan's time on Femme was any better.

CHAPTER TWELVE

Pretences And Propositions

RUSTLING SHEETS AND cautious movements propelled Synjan out of slumber. It took a moment for her consciousness to catch up but then she realised what had alerted her; Anwar was leaving the bed. Inhaling loudly, she sat up and squinted through the darkness.

"What time is it?" she asked, her voice husky.

"Just before sunrise," he whispered. "Please, go back to sleep." A muted thump and a muffled exclamation signalled his difficulty negotiating the dark.

"Nah, s'okay," Synjan mumbled, turning on her bedside lamp. The windowless room sprang into stark relief, causing both of them to flinch. "Shit, that's bright," she said apologetically.

Anwar chuckled as he pulled on his second sandal and hunted for his clothes. Synjan admired his muscular physique while it was still on display. She found his gold and silver hair as enchanting as when they'd met in the bar the night before—well, about five or so hours before. Their unexpected encounter had stamped her second night aboard the airship as her favourite experience in the world so far—not that the measure was particularly high in that regard.

Missing Daeson and resenting the fact that he was content to spend all his time with Roman, she'd decided drinking might provide the distraction she needed. She'd declined several propositions—delivered with varying degrees of severity and desire from her fellow 'sisters'—by the time Anwar had approached, capturing her attention with his twinkling blue eyes and suggestive quips. He was much older than her—in his late forties, she thought—but his body was strong from hard work and gentle where he touched her and she'd quickly considered him in her bed. He'd said his mistress was an early sleeper and never minded where he spent his time as long as he was by her side when she needed him. They hadn't stayed in the bar long.

"Do you have to get back to your mistress?" she enquired around a yawn.

Anwar watched her as he belted his tunic, a smile flirting with the corner of his mouth. "Are you ordering me to stay?"

"I… no. Do you want me to?"

"It is not my place to clarify your thoughts, Synjan."

She thought it was a positive thing that he was using her name rather than calling her 'mistress' but she was confused by the conversation. Given that she'd only had about an hour's sleep, that wasn't surprising.

"What do you want me to say?" she tried again.

"I want nothing more than the taste of you on my tongue, your flavour marking my body and the swell of your breasts haunting my palms. Speak and you may take that away from me," he warned as he came to her side of the bed.

"Huh?" she asked, tipping her face up to be kissed.

"What words have you settled on?" he whispered against her mouth.

"Does this mean you're going?"

"As you wish," he said obediently and straightened.

With a bow, he was gone and Synjan still wasn't sure what had happened. She turned off the light and snuggled back under the covers, deciding she definitely needed more sleep before she faced the day properly.

It was mid-morning when Synjan awoke again. She stretched and mapped Daeson, unsurprised to find him with Roman. Apart from little trysts the male Navigator had experienced with two other slaves, he and Daeson were always together. They shared a room and had spent their first night aboard ship talking for many hours. During the day, they joined other slaves in what must be some sort of common area for them, never far from one another.

The slave quarters were in the bowels of the airship and they seemed like they'd be overcrowded and stuffy. Diplomats Nama and Ashiq hadn't ventured down there to bring the two Wanderers to the upper decks (where all slaves had to be accompanied by mistresses) so Synjan decided she would. They must be starved for different scenery by now. She was certainly hungry for Daeson's company. She didn't dare hope that he felt the same, not after the way they'd parted in Anjiang, but she had to try.

She was more nervous than she'd anticipated by the time she showered and left her room. She'd spent too long fussing with her hair, trying to twist it into some of the odd styles she'd seen on the other women, only to go back to the braid she normally wore. She selected a simple burgundy dress from the choices in her wardrobe and used some of the makeup provided at the dressing table, pleased with the way it highlighted her features. The appreciative smiles she received on the way to the elevator boosted her ego and made her feel more positive than she had in days. The hours of sex hadn't hurt her mood, either.

When she stepped out of the glass lift and onto Daeson's floor, she got an inkling that her actions were unusual. As she passed, the looks she received from slaves ranged from guilty to suspicious to outright hostile, cementing the feeling that she was invading a private area. None of them said anything but all of them stared at her as she negotiated her way along corridors.

The ripple of awareness preceded her as she walked across the games room towards Daeson and Roman. They were sprawled on some couches, watching a pair of slaves hit a small white ball back and forth across a table. The ball was snatched out of the air and the game suspended as the players watched her stand in front of Daeson.

"Hi," she said quietly, unable to resist following Daeson's gaze as he glanced around and realised they were the centre of attention. "I was wondering if you wanted to, uh, come up for some air?" Synjan asked brightly. She looked at Roman so that the invitation included him, but he was busy staring at Daeson's thunderous expression. Her heart sank.

"Is the air much different up there?" Daeson challenged.

Shocked whispers rippled around the room. Synjan kept her eyes fixed on Daeson.

"No, it's just an expression, I..." she had to stop to swallow the spit that was flooding her mouth at being met with resistance she hadn't foreseen. She felt like a fool and she'd only armed herself with the truth. "I wanted to spend some time with you."

Daeson's gaze was unreadable as he considered her words.

"Are you sure you don't want some *other* slave to take care of you?" Roman interjected.

Daeson frowned at him and Synjan was aware of subtext but unable to decipher it amongst the torrent of her own heightened emotions. Still, her verbal response to the other Navigator was swift and certain.

"Daeson's not a slave."

Absolute silence resounded, the absence of noise pressing on her eardrums more noticeably than the whispered comments had. Stupidly, she looked up to be sure everyone was still there.

"He meant the guy you were with last night," Daeson clarified.

Understanding tingled down her spine, swiftly followed by offence. It was bad enough that her encounter with Anwar had been noted by Roman but his satisfaction at sharing the information with Daeson was galling. "You—"

Her remonstration was cut short by Roman's gloating demand. "Don't like being spied on?"

Synjan pressed her lips together, unwilling to add fuel to an already-smouldering situation. She watched Daeson—who finally had the grace to look guilty—and thought of their last conversation. He'd obviously shared his opinion with Roman that Synjan had spied on him! She couldn't decide which part disappointed her more.

"Can we talk?" she asked Daeson.

"You mean can you make more excuses," Roman sneered.

"Sure," Daeson agreed, then looked at his male friend. "I'll catch up with you later."

"Sure," Roman echoed, glaring at Synjan as Daeson got up to join her.

She felt his gaze boring into her back until they were out of the games room, and he remained an invisible presence between them all the way up in the lift. It was only as they exited onto the topmost deck of the airship that Synjan began to shake off the shroud of Roman's disapproval. She led Daeson past lush gardens, glittering bars, bubbling fountains and swimming pools glinting invitingly beneath the broad blue sky. Comfortable loungers, tables with chairs and enormous plush cushions held pride of place all across the open-to-the-air deck and most of them were filled with women lazing about chatting while a few had their men standing silently by, waiting to be needed.

The scenery was beautiful—backgrounded by the views floating beneath them, visible through the glass walls that towered into a sheltering curve—but it didn't match Synjan's emotions. The turmoil provoked by her distant relationship with Daeson was an ugly stain on her insides, marring everything around her. She found them a remote place to sit, at an ordinary table and chairs near the dessert bar. Apparently desserts weren't very popular with guests eternally concerned by their looks because they were the only ones there.

"It's very pretty up here," Daeson said, his tone even.

Knowing his words were meant to appease didn't lessen Synjan's resentment. Roman was still a presence between them. "So he speaks for you now, does he?"

Daeson's lower lip protruded and his voice lost all sense of conciliation. "He's not saying anything I disagree with."

"So you think the same things as him?"

"I can't believe you took a man," he dropped his voice and glanced around before he continued, "into your bed."

She narrowed her eyes at him. "What about it is so difficult to believe?"

"I didn't think you were the type to take advantage of someone."

Synjan blinked, surprised by the accusation. "That's what Roman told you happened?" she scoffed.

"I don't need details. All men are slaves here, remember?"

For a moment, all she could do was stare at him. Maybe this wasn't Roman's doing. Maybe Daeson actually thought she was the type of person to order a helpless man into her bed so she could have her way with him. Did he honestly think she was no better than those women in the High Palace? She wasn't sure whether she wanted to laugh or cry so she settled for speaking through gritted teeth. "I think the details are pretty fucking important," she ground out, stabbing the table top with the point of a finger to reinforce her words. "It was mutual."

"You don't know how the men talk downstairs," he countered.

"Have you spoken to Anwar, then?"

"Who's Anwar?"

She merely looked at him, getting her answer and waiting for him to put it together.

"Synjan, this is a slave world. He's a slave and you're a Mistress," Daeson argued, apparently resigned to his view no matter what she said.

"I wasn't a *Mistress*. I was lonely and he approached me."

Daeson's expression changed to something hopeful. "*He* approached *you*?"

Synjan huffed, contemplating Daeson. She was twenty kinds of grateful that his accusation about her taking advantage of an innocent slave wasn't because he thought it possible of her; it was all because that bastard Roman either hadn't seen or had chosen to leave out how her interlude with Anwar had begun. The world-wandering prick had deliberately riled Daeson into being angry with her—for what purpose? She'd have to tread carefully and do her best to keep watching Roman for the rest of their time together. For now, though, she was winning and she could afford to be gracious in victory.

"He approached me," she repeated.

"Details matter," Daeson admitted with an embarrassed smile.

"That's what I said," she pointed out, unable to resist a parting shot.

"Sorry."

Synjan was surprised. She hadn't heard him apologise before, probably because of his truth talent—he could only say the words if he was genuinely sorry, not just to appease someone. That fact made the word even more important. "You're forgiven. I'm worried about Roman's influence on you, though."

She realised the mistake she'd made as Daeson's expression shifted into a glare. "He was looking out for me."

"I think you're capable of looking out for yourself," Synjan argued, swallowing the anger that bubbled up in response.

"Do you? Because you don't act like I can."

Synjan's hand flopped on the table in appeal. "What do you want me to say? That I'm wrong for worrying about you? I'm over-protective? I'm suddenly the worst person in the worlds because I care about you? Should I just leave you with him?"

Daeson folded his arms and pouted. "No."

"Good, because I miss you terribly and losing you is the last thing I want. But I think Roman is trying to come between us and *that's* worth worrying about. He's telling you select things so that you doubt my integrity and I hate it."

"Roman's not trying to come between us. He's just not good with people."

Synjan did her best to limit her response to pulling a face, wanting to yell at Daeson for regurgitating Roman's bullshit. "What?" she demanded.

"He's been on his own a lot more than he's interacted with others. It's a survival thing, I think, when he pushes others away. He's seen a lot of bad things on different worlds so it makes sense that he doesn't want to be responsible for someone else. Don't you think so?"

"Maybe," Synjan mused, releasing her breath in a discomforted puff.

"I think it's because his father died while they were Wandering together."

She raised her eyebrows. "It sounds like you two have talked about a lot of meaningful things."

"Yeah. I told him about my father, too. And about some of my experiences when I entered your world."

"Did you tell him about Omerri?"

He didn't answer straight away and she wasn't sure what the pause was in aid of. It wasn't as if he could lie. "Some of it," he admitted at last.

"Which parts?"

"The cheating part."

"What did he have to say about that?"

Again, there was a pause before he spoke but she knew why his words were so measured this time. "He, uh, wasn't kind in his opinions. I had to distract him from badmouthing her by telling him about the holiday she took me on. He was pretty curious about the portal we used."

Synjan frowned, wondering what he meant. Clearly, he couldn't have used the Authority Portal with Omerri and he hadn't Wandered naturally, which left only one choice.

"You mean she took you through *Ellis'* portal?"

He looked disconcerted by her shock. "Uh, yes. Omerri brought me through it a few times."

"She what?!"

A male coming over to take their order paused as Synjan's screech echoed around them. She noticed his awkward posture and discreet glances, hoping that her tantrum would pass. In an attempt to diffuse the situation, she welcomed him loudly and made contrite enquiries about the menu the dessert bar offered. She ordered something unknown for herself and prompted Daeson to order for himself. The waiter was startled but he took it in stride and hurried away.

She turned back to Daeson and spoke as dispassionately as she was able. "Let me get this straight. You used the criminal portal more than once with Omerri while you lived in Trent?"

"Yes," he answered, watching her warily.

"I was never allowed to use it," she told him in disgust.

"That's just as well because they never put me to sleep properly."

Synjan tilted her head, frowning. "They must've. You'd be dead."

"That's why I just pretended to sleep. It was too much hassle to explain something I didn't understand anyway."

She spluttered the beginnings of numerous words in an attempt to find an explanation, her hands twitching like they might suddenly reveal something useful if she could just perform the correct choreography.

"And it has you stumped as well," Daeson laughed.

She sighed in concession. "But I know you should've died! Don't you dematerialise and get put back together?"

He considered this theory. "No, I went into this tunnel with streaming colours and ended up in a strange room with my mother."

Synjan raised an eyebrow. "Because she's dead, and *you* were... dead?" she posited

"I don't know. I never figured that out. She didn't talk to me again after the first time. She told me not to use any portal other than the natural one, though," Daeson said, sounding definite. As he spoke, he leant back so that the waiter could place their desserts onto the table, allowing Synjan some extra processing time as well. Daeson's dessert bowl was shallow enough that she could see a cube shape in it, which looked like purple sponge-cake. Her own dessert was similar to ice-cream, with a fruity note to it.

"Omerri went to sleep when she used the portal, right?" she asked.

"Every time."

"Do you think you Healed the medicine that was supposed to put you to sleep?"

"Maybe so. I always woke up before the portal sent me."

Synjan deduced that all Healers had to be able to go through mechanical portals awake and survive. It was the only logical explanation, as contradictory as it was to all her prior knowledge. Daeson's talent had stopped him falling asleep as he should have but also Healed any attack the process made on his body, ensuring his survival.

"Where did Omerri take you?"

"Every year, for her birthday, she would run away to a resort world called Mwavey. She took me each time."

It struck Synjan that Daeson was discussing Omerri and his relationship more candidly than he ever had. He seemed fully adjusted to life without her now. "How long were the holidays?"

"A couple of weeks."

Synjan thought back to her life in Gredann and was surprised to connect Omerri's weeks-long absences with extra attention she'd received from Nick. Now that she had a reference point, it *had* been the same time each year that Nick had been more interested in gracing her bed.

It was odd to think about her ex-lover. He'd been everything to her but she'd never been more than a distraction to him. Considering the cynical manner with which she regarded memories of him, she realised now that she'd been as guilty of convenience as he. She'd thought it was love but it had merely been proximity and lust.

"Oh, I've been wanting to tell you something Roman shared with me about Wandering. Have you heard of Folds?"

"Um, I don't think so?" Synjan pondered, putting her detached realisations aside to concentrate on Daeson's information.

"A Fold is when all the Wanderer powers get together and can create a Portal to get to the World of Worlds. But it's a cheat, it's..." He struggled to find the right words to clarify before shaking his head, implying the effort needed to hunt them down was too great to bother with. "Anyway, when he was a kid Wandering with his dad, they were going through this really unpopulated world and they left a forest and went into some tall grass, and Roman walked into his dad, who'd just stopped for no reason. But when he looked, he saw this circle of dead people, all wearing packs and travel gear, like Wanderers. There was no reason why they would be dead—no bullet holes or burns, and they were all different ages and stuff, so the memory stayed with him. He'd counted them and there were exactly twelve and he told me that it was a Fold and said to never join a Fold. He said he doesn't understand why this world's religion centres around something that would kill them."

He spooned purple cake into his mouth, clearly finished talking. Synjan blinked, digesting the torrent of information she'd just received. She thought of

Phoak, vomiting words of adoration and Wanderer purpose at her like any zealot reciting scripture. He hadn't mentioned anything along the lines of Roman's theory and had been nothing but encouraging and worshipful about Wanderers' roles in travelling the worlds. He'd spoken of Wanderers deserving their place in the World of Worlds, but she couldn't remember his exact words. Still, there was something about Phoak's devotion that convinced her Roman must not have the whole story. Phoak would have warned her about Folds if they were that dangerous, surely?

"That doesn't make sense," she began but Daeson was quick to argue.

"It does to me. Roman called it a shortcut, and it makes more sense that the World of Worlds would be reserved for those Wanderers who take the full route, who don't take the easy way out, but go to the very end, like Roman's doing."

She considered the nuance, again comparing it to Phoak's adamance. "I don't know Daeson, he's just one person and as you say, this whole world's religion is centred around the Fold. Surely they know more than he does?"

"You really don't like him."

Again, she blinked, offended that he thought her argument was merely a method of opposing Roman, rather than a reasoned decision, but she didn't have enough facts to discredit him outright. "Well... no," she admitted.

Daeson frowned at the remainder of his dessert before he pushed his bowl away. It spoke volumes of his loyalty to Roman and only alarmed her more.

"You haven't asked him to join us, have you?" she asked worriedly.

"Your invitation to come up here clearly didn't include him."

She didn't bother arguing. "Not for dessert," she sighed.

Daeson stared blankly at her, causing her to emit an impatient noise deep in her throat.

"Put it this way: he's Wandering through every world, while *we* are still looking for a place to settle down, right?"

"It doesn't sound like you want me to invite him."

She uttered a sound of complete exasperation, her fingers flaring in his direction. "Of *course* I don't!"

"Then why bring it up?"

"Because you're a nice person, it's likely that you will have run your mouth and asked him to join us."

"Run my mouth? I wasn't going to ask him, but now that you bring it up, maybe I should."

"You're going to spite me by asking him? He won't say yes anyway, he dislikes me as much as I dislike him," she dismissed the notion as soon as she brought it up, trying to squash the annoyance Daeson had riled in her. He hadn't thought of asking his newest, bestest friend to join with them? Was he kidding himself?

Daeson seemed horrified by her words and she couldn't figure out why until he spoke. "Maybe, I don't know. He hasn't said how he feels about you."

Synjan pressed her lips together, clamping her tongue between her teeth so she didn't shout about Daeson's ignorance. That wasn't the message she wanted to convey at all. "That's because he isn't a good enough friend to be honest with you," she managed, her words crisp. "*Ask* him what he thinks about me."

Daeson's expression became stony and he stood

abruptly. "I'm going downstairs," he declared and spun on his heel. Synjan observed the stiffness of his spine as he walked away from her, doubting he was going to do what she asked and believing he was merely running away from an argument wherein he'd be forced to make an admission he didn't want to. He couldn't lie and he didn't want to tell the truth, so there was only one solution. Run away. He'd done it before and it was her least favourite trait of his. Weary of fighting with him, she rocked back in her chair and contented herself with glaring at his retreating form instead.

No sooner had Daeson stepped into the outer limits of the swimming area than he was summoned by one of the women on the soft bag-type loungers. He heard her call and stopped, his hands fisting at his sides before he walked over to her, doing his best to act the part of the obedient slave.

As they conversed, Daeson's body language shifted to a greater level of discomfort. Synjan watched, in a bad enough mood about him running away from her that she rather enjoyed seeing him squirm. He helped the woman to her feet and Synjan saw that the woman was quite elderly. She leant heavily on Daeson once she wobbled to her feet, smiling gratefully up into his blue eyes and clinging weakly onto his muscled arm.

It was only when the old fish reached down to squeeze Daeson's backside that Synjan suspected there was more going on than her companion helping an elderly sister out of her lounger. Daeson shot her a worried glance before he turned away, still carefully supporting the woman as they headed for location unknown. Synjan ran after them.

"Daeson!" she cried, stepping in front of the pair.

"What are you doing? I instructed you to go and get my scarf!"

The elderly sister looked between the two of them. "Oh, you don't mind, do you, if I take advantage of him for a little while?" she told Synjan, as if her agreement was a foregone conclusion. "I've never had one from the South before!"

"The south?" Synjan asked, momentarily thrown by the woman's breezy attitude and confusing statement.

The elderly woman caressed Daeson's brown hair, cooing up at him through weathered lips. "Such lovely dark hair. Is it everywhere?" Her gaze lowered to Daeson's crotch.

"Hey!" Synjan interrupted before the woman's hand could follow. "Let him go right now, he's mine. Release him to do… my… bidding," she declared as authoritatively as she could, disconcerted by the words she'd chosen and certain they'd show her to be a fraud.

Fraudulent or not, her declaration had the desired effect and the older woman unwound herself from Daeson. "Grubby sympathiser!" she hissed loudly, causing a few sisters nearby to turn and stare at Synjan. The elderly woman walked off without looking decrepit or needing assistance.

"Thank you," Daeson said humbly.

"Let's go to my room," she instructed, keeping him close as they walked. He didn't argue and she wasn't in the mood to speak, though the bitter taste the encounter had left in her mouth. The fact that personal violations were social mores in this world was something she would never get used to.

She closed the door to her room with a profound sense of relief, watching as Daeson got a drink of water out of the bubbler fountain set into the wall. It had a cup placed conspicuously in the lee of the two water spouts but he ignored it in favour of sticking his head into the niche and slurping directly from one of the nozzles. A ghostly smile on her face, Synjan sat on the end of the bed, taking his hand in both of hers when he joined her.

"That was pretty awful. I'm sorry I didn't get there sooner," she told him.

Daeson shrugged one shoulder. "I tried to tell her the refusal phrase but it wasn't the truth so I couldn't speak it."

"What's a refusal phrase?" Synjan asked, startled.

"The diplomats taught it to me and Roman before they sent us downstairs. They told us to say, 'I am sorry but my mistress does not permit me to be shared'. But it's not true so I couldn't say it."

"This world is fucked," Synjan declared, hating the necessity of a refusal phrase and despising Daeson's truth talent for prohibiting him from using it.

"There are worse worlds I've been told about."

"What you've gone through in *this* world is what breaks my heart," Synjan ground out, tears pricking her eyes. Daeson looked at her and she was embarrassed by how emotional his trials in this world had made her. His vague smile was reassuring and also made her feel proud.

Daeson took a deep breath and expelled it. "You don't have to be broken hearted. I've made my peace with what happened. I wasn't even upset over the action so much as the deception before it. It was a strange situation but it was... pleasant." He shrugged and nodded.

Synjan wasn't sure she'd ever get over the guilt of exposing him to the predators in charge of Femme but she could take comfort in his resolve. There was no point picking at a healing sore to punish herself. "If you can be okay with it, then I can be okay with it," she told him.

"Roman helped me figure it out," he added, giving her a wary look.

She swallowed and paused to give her words the gravity they deserved. "Then I have something to thank him for."

Daeson visibly relaxed and Synjan mentally forgave him for running away from their discussion. He was caught in the middle of two Navigators. The fact that one was manipulating him needed to arouse her sympathy, rather than her anger. Roman was playing a game that Daeson couldn't see and Synjan couldn't win. Not if she followed *his* rules. She had to stop being predictable or speaking without thinking. It wasn't natural for her but until she had a better idea of what was going on, she had to try.

CHAPTER THIRTEEN

Withholding Trust

ENERAL IRIAN CAYDEN was waiting for Hawke in his assigned room. He stood the moment Hawke entered. Hawke noticed the stiff way his superior was standing, fists clenched. His ordeal wasn't over but this part was one he could face. A torrent of emotion washed over him and he found himself unable to speak. The soldier who'd escorted Hawke excused herself and left, closing the door. Hawke looked at the back of the door, still unable to remember why she looked familiar. He flinched when he turned back around because Cayden was close to him, bringing him in for a hug. Hawke's hands moved automatically around him but it felt awkward. It wasn't the kind of homecoming greeting he'd expected. It all felt like a pretence, like they were mimicking reality. Had that VR helmet done something to his brain? Was this Femme's final 'fuck you'?

Cayden pulled away and his hands held Hawke's face. The gesture was so foreign that Hawke was complacent, staring up at Cayden who'd become a giant. Hawke was a little kid again; helpless and vulnerable.

Then Cayden released him and took three strides away before whirling around. "What were you thinking?" he exclaimed, throwing his hands in the air as he paced the room. "You let them throw you to the wolves and now they're blaming *you* for this disaster. You're lucky your mind is even intact!"

"I was only gone eight days," Hawke said, even though he didn't believe it. It had felt much longer. It was embarrassing, how badly he'd lost track of time. The first time he'd heard how long he'd been missing, he'd challenged the soldier to repeat herself. Twice.

"Eight days where they could throw themselves against your Shield. Eight days to wear you down," Cayden said, jabbing an accusatory finger in Hawke's direction as he made his point. "Eight days where an Intuit can find out who you are and turn you into a vegetable."

Hawke frowned. "That's not how Intuit powers work, they can't—"

"Do you think they can't torture you?" Cayden snarled. Hawke couldn't stop his eyes from widening at how angry his superior was.

"They were too logical for that," Hawke replied. His words were calm as he tried to influence Cayden's temper.

"You were fucking *lucky* that they didn't know what you are!" Cayden yelled, spittle flying from his lips.

Hawke was struck by the statement. "What am I?"

Cayden gave him a look of bafflement. "A Hunter. To them, a murderer."

To *them*. "Right."

Cayden paused in his tirade—like someone had

flicked a switch. Hawke met his stare and wondered what was going to come out of Cayden's mouth next. What role was he going to play?

"What happened?" Cayden asked, sounding like he'd tapped out of his emotions finally.

"You'll find out during the debriefing. I don't want to talk about it twice."

Cayden's jaw tensed and he pressed his lips tight. Hawke expected to be blasted with an order but none came. Instead, Cayden rubbed his face with his hands, his shoulders drooping.

"Have it your way."

Hawke didn't know what the issue was, why it was a big deal. What did it matter if he heard the story along with everyone else? What would the advanced hour give him? Hawke didn't think the whole story would fit into an hour anyway. For someone who'd seen almost nothing, he could say a lot.

He had a choice, he realised, to spare Woy to the Authorities, or sink her. He knew that she was playing both sides—and he was fairly sure she'd played him. He was confused about her role and it sounded like the assholes in charge of Demkoi weren't sure about her either. So far he'd witnessed unwavering loyalty on the Authorities' side, but that couldn't be trusted.

The Authorities trusted no-one.

Not even their own.

When Hawke left the debriefing room four hours later, he was met by Cayden.

"Were you waiting long?" Hawke asked, surprised.

"I was messaged."

Hawke couldn't remember anyone making subversive moves but he wasn't surprised by that. After such a long interrogation, he wasn't at his sharpest. The debriefing room was supposed to be closed, though—no devices allowed. He'd faced the Division Overseer Palua'a and his superior, the steely-eyed Division General Loris. Dr Fellows had also been invited to a seat at the table but there was nobody else.

He and Cayden walked together, heading down corridors that were no longer a maze to Hawke, yet knowing them was like knowing something out of a dream. A sense of unreality pervaded everything.

"Why didn't you tell me you wouldn't be at the debriefing?" Hawke asked. He wondered if Cayden would make him repeat it all.

"Because it doesn't matter what you did for those assholes. I don't need to know, unless it's going to affect you. Is it going to affect you?" Cayden asked, staring at Hawke with an intensity that made him uncomfortable.

"No, it's not going to affect me." He wasn't sure if he'd ever told a bigger lie.

"How sure are you of that? What they did could've..." the General lingered on his sentence, seemingly unable to finish his thought. Hawke stepped in before it was done.

"I hated being helpless, but nothing bad happened."

Cayden was quiet for a moment and Hawke thought that was going to be the end of it.

"There's something I don't recognise in your voice. And on your face." So he knew it was a lie.

"I hope it wasn't that salad sandwich I ate."

"Maybe you are your usual self," Cayden said with a grunt. If he was going to let it pass, then it would be for the sake of convenience.

"Do you know what the Authorities negotiated to get me back?" Hawke asked.

"A base."

Hawke stopped walking and Cayden took two more steps before he paused and looked back.

"Did you say 'a base'?"

"It was the start of one in the Southern part of Femme. A tiny hole set up with a pioneer portal. Three people were stationed there."

"So... someone is going to be left behind?"

"To dismantle it, yes. Can't leave that tech for Femme."

"Fuck."

"You're more important, Hawke."

"I guess the Authorities haven't finished with me."

Cayden's face went a deep red. "*I'm* not finished with you! I *fought* for you! You think they wanted to give up that ridiculous base? Scientists can be found anywhere but there's only one of you!"

Facing Cayden's second wave of anger, Hawke was oddly touched. He hadn't had much acknowledgement from the people in his life and for some reason he was starting to crave it. But why now? Why was he wanting more now, when everything had been fine before? What had changed?

Synjan.

The woman who'd taken his job, following a parallel life meant for him. He'd kept tabs on her, curious about the life he hadn't chosen, so when she left it, he had to know why. He had to know where it was she thought she was going. Why would she risk everything, leaving her life behind when she knew the dangers? What did she know that he didn't?

A piercing, clanging noise echoed up the corridor, like it was a warning bell for dangerous thoughts.

Cayden looked at his watch. "A drill was organised for today—I didn't realise how late it was. Come, let's get to the portal before the foyer fills up."

They hurried through corridors and into the large space of the foyer. Hawke watched as soldiers trickled out of the deployment funnel, looking so much like an inverted anthill that he couldn't help but stare. As each soldier landed, they scurried to different parts of the room and stood to attention in tight units of six.

Hawke followed Cayden around the farthest wall and down the corridor of artful photographs towards the portal's waiting area. Instead of approaching the Transport Officer, Cayden took a seat and stared expectantly at him. He sat beside his superior and waited for the conversation to start again.

"You're not returning to Othello, are you?" Cayden said.

"No."

"This Femme bullshit wasn't the thing you were really doing, was it? You were looking for someone on this world."

Hawke licked his lips. "I made a mistake. I rushed into something without assessing it properly. I shouldn't have come here."

"What should you have done?"

"Gone to Earth and waited."

"You're in a big hurry to get this person."

"Yes. As a favour for a friend."

"Kegsy?" Cayden guessed.

Hawke was struck by how casually Cayden had

brought up Kegan Frederickson's name. He shouldn't have been so surprised that Cayden would accurately guess who Hawke's friend was... he didn't have many. Brita had already pointed that out. Only one friend was worth the trouble he was going to — Cayden knew Hawke had the utmost respect for the man who had mentored him in fighting. The man who'd trained him in a wide range of skills. The same man who'd trained Synjan.

It was so strange, the things he shared with her, but it was the differences he craved an explanation for. She had to have answers for him, because everything he'd just endured had assured him he had none. He'd always known he didn't fit in anywhere, not with the Authorities, not at the DOME, not with Brita, and not Hunting. Still, he'd played a part in all of those things, maintaining a role that had kept him grounded, if not camouflaged.

In chasing after her, he was surrendering all of it because he saw now that none of it mattered. That was why he didn't feel real anymore. It was one thing to understand that he didn't fit in, it was another entirely to realise he was lost. The only way he could find his way back was continuing forward, finding her and extracting her secrets.

"I'll take your silence as affirmation," Cayden said.

"Don't ask me for more details," Hawke said while shaking his head. He didn't want to betray Kegsy. He felt like he already had.

"Don't worry. I'll stay out of it."

"It would be easier if you could write me down as on mission," Hawke said. "So I can be done faster."

Cayden pursed his lips then nodded.

"Alright. I'll check in from England. Are you going back to Red Rock?" Hawke asked, saying normal things but not feeling normal at all. The banality of the conversation didn't help to ground him.

"Yes."

Red Rock, the small but high tech Authority base designed as the Hunters headquarters. Since Cayden was the Division General, he likely had a lot of work to catch up on.

He left Cayden with a handshake followed by a salute and Hawke checked in with the Transport Officer. While sitting in the portal, being hooked up and waiting for the coordinates for Earth's London Portal to be punched in, he couldn't shake the feeling that Cayden was up to something.

CHAPTER FOURTEEN

Arrival In Na'ala

DAESON SAT IN the collections hall beside Roman, waiting for Synjan and their diplomats to arrive. The bench was hard but the room was magnificent. The ceiling was a dome of green glass above a spectacular eight-tiered fountain. Grand images of benevolent Goddesses were sculpted on the walls. Arched windows of dizzying height revealed lush gardens beneath a starry sky. This was a rich world, a grand world that could have been perfect for him—except he would never accept slavery, regardless of its form. Whether he was the slave or Synjan, it wasn't the kind of society he wanted to live in. He puffed air harshly enough to attract Roman's gaze but the other Wanderer said nothing.

With a new perspective he looked at the men around him. Some were chatting but not all were smiling. Many had empty gazes. He didn't know if they were bored or if their spirits were broken. It was hard to know and too horrible to find out. He felt both lucky and guilty that he hadn't been born into this world and that he was able to escape it.

"Daeson and Roman."

He stood when Diplomat Nama called his name and joined the two women and Synjan, who stood behind them. The two diplomats were tall, regal and gorgeous, carrying themselves in a manner that exuded confidence and awareness. In contrast, Synjan looked apologetic and small, like she didn't want to be there. He loved her for that.

He surprised her with his hug but her hands readily embraced him with a sound of delight from her lips. He'd rejected her, neglected and argued with her during their time on the airship but she'd forgiven him without hesitation. He felt obliged to show her the same loyalty. He promised himself to defer to her more often.

"Come along," Nama said, her tone impatient yet excited. He wondered if she was looking forward to being rid of them. "The Portal is close."

Their backpacks and bags arrived on a trolley, rolled to them by a tired-looking teenage boy.

"You're driving," Ashiq told Nama as the boy removed a square token from his pocket and held it out to them. Nama plucked it out of his fingers as she spoke with her friend.

"Are you still banned?"

Ashiq replied in her language and the pair of them laughed. Daeson held his tongue, feeling restless and wanting to get moving. He couldn't sense the Portal the way Synjan could, as a pulling, but it agitated him in other ways. He remembered how he'd been on his homeworld, walking blindly through the forest. It had happened again on J'Bdyamn, he'd tapped into a renewed energy for rowing once he'd come into its sphere of influence. When he chose a world to stop at, he would have to live somewhere away from the Portal... or he would never feel settled.

They moved through the carpark, with Daeson pulling the trolley and Roman behind it. It wasn't difficult to deal with but he resented the chatty guides for walking at a quick pace and not once looking back. Synjan had tried walking alongside him but the wheels of the trolley were in constant danger of catching the hem of her gown—a pretty aquamarine one today. As lovely as she looked in it, he knew she wouldn't have chosen the dress for herself so he was gentle when he pointed out why she should walk ahead.

Their car was too small to fit the luggage. Their bags went into an even smaller vehicle which looked like a car but was referred to as a trailer. It was programmed to follow them at a certain distance. Nama gave a long explanation about how the car and trailer interacted but Daeson stopped paying attention about halfway through. Both Synjan and Roman seemed to understand how it worked, which annoyed him.

When they were ready to leave, Daeson was the first one in the car, inadvertently leaving Synjan to sit between him and Roman. Already he was breaking his promise to himself, acting without consideration. He'd just wanted the window seat, he hadn't thought about her potential discomfort sitting beside a man she didn't like. He realised his own selfishness but now that the car was moving, he couldn't do anything about it. He offered Synjan a smile as a poor consolation and received a warm smile back. It only made him feel worse. He looked out the window instead.

A red half-moon hung low over dome-like houses.

There weren't any tall buildings other than a few spindly towers too narrow to live in. He wondered what they were for because they all had violet burning flames at their tops.

The southern city—he couldn't remember the name of it—was filled with domes. It was as if the builders couldn't move away from what they knew best. The only points of difference were the accessories on the roofs. Some had flagpoles, statues, furniture or even gardens up there. Each turn in the road presented him with more of the same until he lost all sense of direction. He looked for signposts but none of them were translated into Authoritan. The dome houses gave way to a grassy clearing with shaped hills and sandpits before they appeared again.

He could hear a strange, distant roar over the gentle hum of the engine—he'd never heard anything like it before. Several minutes passed before somebody addressed it.

"It sounds like word's got ahead of your departure," Ashiq said, looking over her shoulder.

"Is that what that noise is? The crowd?" Roman asked.

The crowd? Daeson both understood the source of the noise and didn't. How could there be so many people gathered together that they sounded like a large animal roaring? Now that the noise had been identified, he could hear the pulsing volume of a chant.

"What are they saying?" Daeson asked. There was something familiar in the incantation but he couldn't properly make it out.

"Lots of things," Ashiq laughed.

"No, they're chanting something."

He could sense everyone listening, as they

collectively held their breaths. The car engine was silent enough not to block the words.

After a moment, Synjan spoke: "I only recognise 'Portos' in that. Are they chanting in your language?"

"Yes," Nama replied. "They're saying 'may the blessing of Portos guide you'."

Tingles travelled along Daeson's spine and in the tips of his fingers. Cleric Faelin on Kharltae had sent him on his way with the blessing of Portos. It had been of his own doing on Trent, when he'd instructed Jade to say the words. Nobody had been around to bless him when he'd Wandered out of J'Bdyamn but now he had an entire crowd of people to make up for it.

"Portos," Daeson whispered.

"A Wanderer God," Roman clarified. Daeson tilted forward in his seat to stare at him. Synjan faced the other Navigator as well. "Didn't you know?" Roman asked, as though they should've.

Daeson slumped back into his seat, overwhelmed by the knowledge. Synjan had passed on the information given her at the High Palace—that Wanderers were messengers of the Gods and were given the power to travel between the worlds to spread the word. He didn't feel like he was a part of that. It centred around the idea that all Wanderers desired to travel. He'd never wanted that, he'd never pined for adventure or desired to see the sights of multiple worlds. He was curious but not that curious. He would prefer to sit with a travelling Spinner and listen to the tales they spun. He wasn't comfortable taking a risk each time he touched the Portal, never knowing if the outcome would be good or bad. He just wanted a home, to find someone to love and be loved back. To make a family.

Out the car window, a couple of young men waved frantically at the car. Behind them was a woman wearing a flared silver dress and carrying what looked like a pipe with bulges in it. She stood beneath a mobile lamp-post with a light so bright that it hurt Daeson's eyes to look at directly. As soon as Nama drove beneath the light's influence, it turned into daytime. Scores of similar lamp-posts had been set up, keeping the night at bay.

Clear plastic barricades followed the kerb and curve of the road. They were tall enough to stop people from entering the road but short enough to climb over. The trickle of people standing behind them turned into a throng, two people deep, then three people deep, then they were countless bodies squashed behind the temporary blockade. The only people Daeson could see were the ones in front holding makeshift signs—many of the messages were written in Authoritan. 'Blessing of Portos' was written on a lot of the signs, but there were also plenty with 'Defy the Authorities' and 'The World of Worlds has chocolate!' which Daeson thought both peculiar and amusing.

The crowds grew exponentially and the cheering became so loud Daeson could hear nothing else. It was a wall of sound. He leant into Synjan as something sprinkled against the windows.

"What is that? Are they throwing something at the car?" he asked.

"Pebble glitter," Diplomat Nama explained through a broad smile. "It's a metaphor for showering you with gifts."

Many times they drove close enough to the crowd for men and women alike to lean over the barricades and pat the car. Fingers smeared the windows, and through them Daeson saw faces so elated with joy that they looked fanatical. It was terrifying.

The car pulled up to a small building—yet another dome—with many women in silver dresses surrounding it, keeping the crowd at bay.

"Alright, Wanderers. When I say go, you are to get out of the car and enter through that door there. Once inside you will be handed your packs. Take out travelling clothes best suited for a warm climate and wear those. Return to the car with your bags on your laps and I will take you the rest of the way to the Portal. It is not far."

"I can feel it," Roman declared, a hand on his chest. He looked overwhelmed. Daeson didn't know if it was the crowd or the sensation of the Portal tugging at him that made him that way. Probably both.

The car door opened. Daeson was swamped by the roar of the crowd. Faces blurred as he rushed past them. When he stepped inside the building, it was sparse. Everything was white. Two tables and four benches were assembled in the middle of a round room. Six cubicles without doors were set against a portion of the wall.

He turned, his shoulder bumping Synjan because she'd followed him so closely. He apologised and noticed a woman in a silver dress with a downturned mouth. She carried his and Synjan's pack in each of her hands. His pack was dumped at his feet while Synjan had hers handed to her. Another woman in silver handed Roman his bag with a smile.

After both women left, Daeson entered a cubicle with his bag and undressed, selecting shorts and a cotton shirt. He put on sneakers. Wherever they were going, regardless of the climate, they were going to be walking. Synjan and Roman were dressed in similar gear. Synjan must have packed her outfit and shoes because he could see his and Roman's Femme dresses dumped on the cubicle benches but not anything of hers.

They returned to the car without speaking and bundled inside with their packs.

The drive was short. Daeson could see the Portal out the window even as it thrummed within his body like an electric current. He felt energised. He felt *vibrant*.

Before they exited, Nama turned in her chair and reached out a staying arm. "Wait!" she cried, her eyes wide behind her translucent specs. She seemed to be focussed on whatever she was seeing on the glass rather than on the Wanderers. Her gaze changed focus. "Synjan. I've received an important notice that you have been offered asylum here."

"Asylum? What for?" Synjan asked, sounding as alarmed as Daeson felt.

"We've been informed that the Authorities are aware of your Wandering and have sent a Hunter after you. This message is days old—it must've been sent while we were on the airship, out of range."

"A Hunter?" Synjan turned wide eyes to Daeson. His stomach lurched, but not because of any spoken lies. This time it was fear. Roman frowned at them both.

"I understand if you want to stay here, but I can't," Daeson said, thinking Synjan might want his permission. He didn't want to make the decision for her.

She gave him a crooked smile before placing a hand on his arm. "I'm not staying, either."

"Alright," he said. "Let's go."

They climbed out of the car and stood at the foot

of a rolled out carpet, bright blue in colour. There were no barricades here but everyone respect the carpet and lined up at the edge. The carpet ended at the Portal. Someone had laid it out for him, Synjan and Roman to walk on. Somewhere along the way, people had learnt their names because they were screaming them out between chanting the blessing of Portos.

"Maybe that's how it happened," Daeson guessed. "Maybe at the start some Wanderers spread the word of their Gods and it became a belief."

He knew Synjan and Roman wouldn't hear him. His voice was drowned by the crowd. It made sense that some devout worshippers had passed on the stories of their religion. The idea that this was the Wanderer's *only* purpose didn't feel right. He didn't believe that he couldn't choose his own path.

Roman passed him on the carpet, then Synjan passed him. She looked back and reached out her hand. He linked fingers with her and together they followed Roman to the Portal.

Many citizens of Femme were crying—tears streaming down their faces as they proffered gifts for the taking. Daeson didn't want them to feel bad but there were too many gifts to take them all. Many were impractical. Not wanting everyone to feel bad, he took some of the smaller items—a small bejewelled horse and a rainbow-hued reclining woman. He sampled whatever food there was— shoving a small cake into his mouth and eating it quickly, drinking an odd coloured liquid through a straw that tasted sweet and refreshing, tasting a cookie from a plate full of them and then tugging Synjan back for her to take one as well. Cheers sounded when she bit into it and she pulled a exaggeratedly happy face, gesturing with the cookie. He could only read her lips, 'It's good, thank you, thanks, got to go, thank you'.

They moved farther down the line. When they were almost at the Portal, a young man leapt out from the crowd—causing a surge of booing and angry cries as he reached out and clung to Synjan's arm.

"Take me, Mistress! Take me with you! Please, I can't stay here!"

Daeson could see the horror in Synjan's face. She looked to Daeson and he shrugged, unsure of what to do. When faced with their indecision, the native threw himself at Roman, tugging on his clothes as he fell to his knees, almost bringing the Wanderer Navigator down with him. There was a slight lull in the crowd as they stared.

"Get off me," Roman yelled, punching the man in the face twice to make him let go. Daeson was appalled to see blood spraying from the native's nose. Roman shoved him back into the crowd. Hands reached out and dragged the man back in among them, closing the space around him, making him disappear.

Daeson froze. He worried for the man who might or might not survive the punishment doled out to him for trying to escape slavery. Guilt overwhelmed him for not helping straight away. The man was already gone and there was a good chance Daeson wouldn't be able to find or help him. Synjan threw him a pleading look and he knew she would be able to find him in the crowd but his fear drove his selfishness enough to shake his head and move forward.

They had to leave this world immediately. He

couldn't jeopardise his escape from it. At the moment they were happy to let him go. If he and Synjan decided to interfere and went after this slave, who knew what would happen?

Daeson found the strength to continue—to walk with Synjan and Roman to the Portal. They linked hands and Daeson turned to Roman, perhaps to berate him, he didn't really know what he was going to say, but Roman got in first.

"You and me. I'll show you."

Before Daeson could think what that meant, Roman's free hand reached out and plunged into the light of the Portal and they were gone.

CHAPTER FIFTEEN

The London Portal

HAWKE ACCEPTED THE headache tablets and water bottle provided him upon entry to England. He pocketed the tablets, still wrapped in their company-branded blister foil and downed the water, discarding the bottle on his way to collect his bag before remembering he didn't have a bag anymore. He felt naked and vulnerable without it, angry that he would have to purchase a replacement. At least the city of London would offer options.

An Authority officer walked him to the elevator and they were both propelled upward at great speed. Hawke looked down at the metal floor and then at the soldier who was eyeing him.

"Wouldn't it just be easier on everyone to slow this thing down?" Hawke suggested, figuring the plebs on shit detail would be the ones cleaning up after all the nauseous visitors who boarded the elevator too early.

"Sure, but it wouldn't be as funny." The officer grinned and Hawke chuckled. Earth-Worlder humour was often a blend of sarcasm and darkness. Being an officer meant this man wouldn't ever have to clean up puke from unseasoned portal travellers so he could afford to be amused.

"Is Major Collins still designated Team Leader for the Hunter Division?"

"It's Colonel Collins now. He's still TL though. Likes it, I guess."

Hawke remembered Collins; weak of chin but not of mind. The man was a sharp observer and quick to act. His thinning hair and plain looks didn't add to his charisma but he had it anyway—because he knew he did a good job. He took pride in it. Hawke was certain that with Collins' help, he would catch up to Synjan in little time.

The elevator slowed to a stop—Hawke could tell by the way his body lurched upwards then sank back into his boots. The Earther adopted his ready stance just before the doors slid open.

Hawke entered a large room. Rows of open cubicles were occupied by suited civilians. All of them were tapping touch-screens and speaking into earpieces, creating a low rumble of activity. Very few people looked his way, intently focused on their own tasks of shuffling papers, writing notes or passing files to their colleagues. Hawke was led past the bustle, bypassing the main hub through the inner walkway rather than past the large windows. The Authorities owned this building that towered high into the clouds—a testament to the resources they mined from other worlds to create their own, shaping them to their own values and standards.

Out of all the Authority-created worlds, Hawke liked Earth the best. They were overdue learning about other worlds and attaching to the known

World Link but their efforts in space exploration had yielded results too good to ignore. The Authorities knew that their focus would change once Earth was aware of other worlds. Earth was the closest to colonising other planets—and that allowed the Authorities to test for the theory of accessing multiverses via a different planet. After living and breathing the Authority mindset for thirty years, it was obvious to Hawke why Earth was being left to boil. They were massively over-populated, they were currently in the middle of yet another spiral of social decline—this time facing a genuine threat of world-wide self-annihilation—but it didn't matter. If Earthers blew themselves up, the greatest loss to the Authorities would be the forced restart of a space exploration program elsewhere—using a people that might not ever match the intense desire of Earthers. Hawke respected Earth's interest in the stars.

"And we're here," the officer declared. 'Here' happened to be the west wall with a glass door. Through it, Hawke could see a cluster of desks where uniformed soldiers sat, facing multiple terminals that all fed into a large screen.

Before Hawke's attendant left, the man gave him a salute that ended with a wave-through. As he jogged back to wherever he had to be, Hawke supposed escorting a stray Hunter wasn't on his list of priorities.

As soon as Hawke stepped through the door, Colonel Collins headed purposefully towards him. The Team Leader looked nonplussed. His expression was atypical and a reason for Hawke to be concerned. He hadn't portalled a message ahead saying he was on his way but Hunters often arrived at the same time as their notice. They were always on the move.

Collins was too efficient to be flummoxed by something so simple. Something else was up.

"Hunter Donovan," Collins greeted formally, extending his hand. Hawke shook it. The clipped tone of his British accent was a familiar and welcome sound, for it was closest to the Varrell-Worlder way of speaking. Hawke had learnt Authoritan there and absorbed the accent. It had changed through the years in his travels but Varrell had become a home of sorts, since the Hunter headquarters was there. "Has General Cayden sent you to oversee the new parameters?"

"New parameters?" Hawke repeated, feeling his stomach roll as though in a belated response to the elevator. It had nothing to do with the short jaunt upwards and everything to do with what he anticipated out of Collins' mouth. "I'm on mission."

The look on the Colonel's face offered Hawke an instant realisation of his fuck-up before Collins even got a word out.

"I'm afraid the last flare we had... three days ago, was in Australia."

"Where's that?" Hawke asked.

"Other side of the planet, I'm afraid. Southern hemisphere. You would've been better off arriving at the New Zealand portal."

"Fuck!" Hawke balled his fists, looking around for something that he could punch or throw, but there was nothing. This room was functional and sterile. He stood tense and awkward as Collins made his excuses.

"We did enter it into the system immediately. If there was a miscommunication, it wasn't at our end."

Hawke glared at Collins as he went through the motions of saving his ass. There was another justification that he didn't properly hear because his mind was already turning over his options.

"I'll have to portal to the New Zealand base then," he said, wanting Collins to speed up his access. Inter-world portalling wasn't possible, which meant that he would have to portal out of Earth and then back into it.

"But you've only just arrived," Collins replied with a frown.

"In the wrong place," Hawke said, turning to go.

"I can't clear you," the Colonel said.

Hawke turned back to face him. Collins had a look of determination about him, the kind that went with no apology. Hawke's temper flared but it was countered by a knot of anxiety in his stomach that came from knowing why.

"You know of my reputation. You know I don't suffer the effects of portal travel like the others. I have to—"

"Not three times in one day," Collins insisted, stepping forward to close the distance between them so they could have a quieter conversation. He didn't want a scene and Hawke toyed with the idea of making one. "No, what you're asking me is even worse than that. You want three portals in as many hours. You've only just arrived, you intend on leaving now and returning as soon as you wake up. I will not help you suicide."

"I won't die," Hawke scoffed. "I've done same-day portals before."

"Not from here, you haven't," Collins bit back, "and you're not starting now. I won't clear you. You have to wait the minimum twenty-four hours."

"You're delaying the most important mission that I've—"

"Don't care," Collins interrupted.

"Fuck!" Hawke exploded. The expletive didn't make Collins blink even though it was delivered in his face. A few soldiers turned from their tasks to stare, not used to seeing their superior attract abuse from a Hunter. Considering their jobs, they probably knew who Hawke was and likely had opinions based on that, but none of them dared to speak or act on it.

"You can take a private jet, if you like. It'll take about twenty-one hours."

"So I'm stuck here for twenty-*four* hours before I can portal out or I could ride for twenty-*one* hours on a fucking plane?"

Collins waited him out. In hindsight the question was rhetorical—Collins had offered Hawke's only option.

Suddenly Hawke wasn't loving the fuck out of Earth anymore.

London was one of the most curious cities Hawke had visited. He'd portalled into it many times, catching up with Wanderers easily in a world that was security-conscious even beyond the usual Authority quota. The city always left an impression. The word that usually came to mind was 'conservative', though London was greatly nuanced and worthy of more descriptors.

Generally, the sky was unobtrusively grey. He'd heard rumours of blue skies but he'd never managed to catch any. The clouds huddled together and overlooked the city with an aspect that felt oppressive. The temperature ranged from cool to freezing, rouging cheeks and chapping lips.

In the city itself, the buildings were solid and stately, domineering the landscape with their monotonous uniformity. Crammed together and built from ancient stone or aged bricks, they watched sombrely over the residents and tourists like sentinels ensuring city-wide decorum. There wasn't much greenery—except for Hyde Park—and the river was tidal, regularly pulling away from its bricked banks. The dismal, filthy offerings that coated the Thames' walls seemed embarrassed by their exposure until the brown waters slunk sheepishly back to cover them up.

Everything was serious; outfitted in conservative tones that befitted the proud, staunch kind of city that London was. It was intimidating in a way that very few cities he'd experienced were. Traditional. Yet there were the odd tucked-away markets or places to buy tickets that lent it a furtive air as well.

Since he had some time to kill, Hawke braved the crisp streets to clear his head and go shopping.

The fact that his belongings hadn't been returned to him on Femme still irked him. He'd been very attached to his messenger bag. He headed for Harrod's, hoping he'd be able to find a bag similar to his old one. Harrod's was the only store that would allow him to use his Authority credit, so he couldn't take advantage of any other shops. He *could* return to the base to get some local currency, of course, but he didn't want to admit he'd been unprepared.

Three days. The time differential bothered him. After his warped experience in Femme's custody, time itself felt like his enemy. Knowing he'd probably missed Synjan's departure made him question himself. As much as he enjoyed the exultant sense of being freed, he knew what was waiting on the other side of that giddy flight.

A painful crash and crushing reality.

His expectations that a complete stranger held the answers to his most fundamental questions was ludicrous. She probably didn't have answers to anything. Just more questions. It seemed like every asshole was seeking enlightenment in one form or another. Why did he think she'd have what he was looking for? He'd become like his insipid sister.

The thought brought him up short and he stopped so abruptly that a couple walking towards him had to swerve to avoid running into him. He stared sightlessly at a mother taking photos of her children beside a huge lion statue, thinking about Giselle.

She'd been unable to make a decision about who to marry and was content to be told what her will was, because she had none. Of course she'd settled for status over sincerity. He'd been appalled by his family's ignorance when he'd visited Boronia all those years ago but he'd come to regard them with a sort of condescending affection in the time since. Oh, those simple people with their convoluted, petty lives, worrying about trivialities like land and prestige. He was out in the fierce worlds, ploughing through as many of them as he could to seek revenge for the wrong done to him, killing his abductors in as many forms as he was able.

His despair had less to do with Femme than he'd thought. This had all begun with Lyssa. *I don't belong anywhere. You cheated me out of belonging,* he'd told her. The truth was, he'd been falling for a long time, he just hadn't been willing to face it. The trail Kegsy had put him on was just a runnel within a much greater path he'd been traversing for a while. He'd heard philosophers going on about the journey being more important than the destination, but fuck that. Fuck them. They were all wrong. He was lost, he didn't belong anywhere and he wanted to get to the end to find somewhere that was *right* for him. It probably wouldn't be with Synjan but she might have some insight to impart about how she'd got to where she was. At least she was making decisions for herself rather than letting everyone else decide for her.

Hawke needed to do that for himself. Starting with getting ready to meet her. He began walking again, musing about his realisations as he went to buy a new bag.

CHAPTER SIXTEEN

Uncontrolled Lust

ELLIS HAD NEVER been known as a patient man. Nor was he stupid. Thus, his fourth day serving at the pleasure of the King of the Techatachenti was conflicted. The days had merged into one another with such ineffectual banality that he now saw the appeal of having a fight with a nearby clan. And of prolonging the disposal of their warriors; it was something to break up the monotony.

Of course, there were always things going on in a backwards cesspool such as the village but they were hardly alluring to men who'd come from civilisation. Looms and grass weaving and basket-making might be necessary for the function of a large group of people but they weren't even topics of conversation Ellis wanted to have, let alone tasks he wanted to participate in. It became clear why Bannan's humour was just shy of psychopathic and his interest in sex so prevalent.

Ellis spent his days doing his best to impress their host, listening to Bannan's opinions on everything from the Authorities to the benefits of buttons.

On the first day after the cannibalistic hunt and feast, Bannan had regaled him with his origin story. He'd begun Wandering as a young man, as part of a quartet. They'd travelled three worlds before their arrangement had fallen apart because he'd lusted after his Navigator's woman. The problem was, he'd been caught assuming his friend's form to sleep with her and, in the ensuing argument, he'd been forced to kill the Navigator. He and the two women had continued Wandering but he'd killed the object of his desire in Kharltae when she'd tried to slit his throat one night. Not long after, he'd finished off his own lover in Gredann when she betrayed him by trying to run away (Ellis could relate). Bannan had Wandered alone after that and finally found his home with the Techatachenti.

In relaying this eventful story to Fyfe in the seclusion of their hut that night, Ellis was reminded of just how inexperienced his companion was. Fyfe had come from Stonehearth in Kharltae so his knowledge of Wandering with a group was non-existent. Fyfe was appalled by Bannan's tale, which had surprised Ellis. It gave him something to ponder while lounging the next day.

Ellis also shared his own story—apart from the secret of his blood— but made sure he never said too much at once, lest he lose his intrigue. He needed to make a resounding impression—Bannan had to feel rewarded if he was going to willingly give up a boat. Ellis described his business ventures in Gredann, Synjan's role in his empire and what world travel using his illegal machine was like.

Bannan asked a mountain of questions. He wanted to know everything about the portal prototype, the worlds Ellis visited regularly and Synjan. The king was most enchanted with tales of Synjan. He listened to Ellis extoll her features and flaws at length, often closing his eyes to relish the vivid descriptions of her endeavours and encouraging Ellis to repeat his favourite parts.

It was understandable that Ellis felt the need to relieve his pent-up energy after his extensive stories about his Number One. Bannan made use of Paki while Ellis accepted whomever Bannan ordered to grace his bed. Of course, neither flesh nor tongues could fill the void Synjan's absence had gouged within him, but it helped to pass the time pleasurably.

The next day had been filled with village business for Bannan, leaving nothing but exaggerated tedium for Ellis. He'd tried a walk, some conversation with villagers and a swim in the ocean in spite of his hatred of salt water—but the day dragged. He welcomed the advent of mealtimes with an enthusiasm that likely communicated he was starving. The cause behind Bannan's flabby stomach became clear.

Fyfe spent as little time with Bannan and Ellis as he was able. He preferred to be away fishing, boating or swimming. He'd created a ball from a pig's bladder and was in the process of teaching the rules to some football game or other to those interested. He was not accepted by all residents. As far as Ellis could glean, Fyfe's adamant resistance to hunting was his primary drawback and showing too much of an interest in Paki was the other.

Bannan had heard of the youth's continued 'accidental' conversations with his woman but had accepted Ellis' explanation that he'd ordered the boy to gather all the information she had about Synjan.

To prove his loyalty to the redheaded leader, Ellis had also told him how Paki had tried to sway his interest on their first morning, bartering her knowledge as a reward for them taking her along. It earned the woman a deserved beating and was close enough to the truth that it suspended Bannan's suspicion of Fyfe.

The fourth day dawned with the world's habitual ambiguity. It was always hot and rained frequently but it was never enough to cool things off properly. Ellis was not a young man anymore and he had trouble sleeping through the night at the best of times. Add muggy weather, stinging insects and noisy neighbours into the mix and sound sleep was not something he felt he'd be acquainted with again.

"Still not sleeping?" Fyfe asked from his bed across the room. The annoying child had slept serenely every night thus far and never needed to get up through the night to wrestle with a bladder that released its bounty in spurts.

"No. But the charade persists," Ellis sighed. "Everything must appear well in Bannan's kingdom. You know, you and Paki—"

"Give it a rest, man," Fyfe groaned, sitting up and rubbing his face wearily. "It's barely daylight."

"That hardly matters."

"It's too early for your shit about her!"

"No time is a bad time for discussing tactics that will ensure our survival."

"Our survival?" Fyfe scoffed, flinging a hand in the direction of the leader's domicile. "What about Paki's? You got her beaten yesterday. On purpose. Is that part of your survival strategy, is it?"

Ellis also sat up and stared levelly at his Wandering partner. "*I* got her beaten?" he asked quietly.

"If you hadn't opened your big mouth, it wouldn't have happened." Fyfe stood and yanked his shorts on.

"Her actions were punished, not my recount of them."

Fyfe was across the room in two swift strides, leaning down and pressing his face close to Ellis'. "She's fucking desperate!" he hissed contemptuously. "She needs our help. Can you say you wouldn't do everything you could to escape, if you were in her position?"

Ellis considered his companion through narrowed eyes, drawing back to improve his focus. "She has you enamoured. You need to ensure—"

Fyfe growled and gesticulated at Ellis. It had the desired effect because Ellis fell silent and blinked as Fyfe pulled at his hair in frustration then strutted righteously out of the hut to find something to kick or spear, still snarling.

Pressing his lips together, Ellis considered the merits of the argument before he pulled on his own short pants and made his way to Bannan's lounge. It wasn't fully light but there was no chance he'd fall asleep again and, sitting in plain view, someone would eventually bring him a meal. He watched the sky change colours and pondered Fyfe's circumstance. Ellis had many misgivings about Fyfe's regard for Paki but he had no evidence the boy was doing anything stupid... yet.

The morning crawled along with yet another string of uninteresting visitors coming to the lounge to proudly show off their ordinary talents, as well as a lively debate about which animal had the tastiest eggs. Given this world didn't have chickens, Ellis' opinion wasn't even worth voicing. After lunch,

Bannan approached the couch with something behind his back. He came from the centre of the village, an unusual place for him to be at this hour, and there was no Paki being dragged along behind him.

Ellis squinted at him, taking in the broad grin behind his scruffy beard. "You look suspiciously pleased with yourself."

"I am! I have a gift for you!"

Ellis raised his eyebrows. "It looks too small to be a boat."

Bannan roared laughter. "You are funny!" the redhead declared and presented Ellis with a length of folded material.

"Oh, uh, thank you," Ellis murmured as he took the multi-hued fabric carefully. He opened it out and saw that it was a swathe of material that the men of the village generally wore as a sarong-style skirt. He wasn't sure what to say.

"Put it on," Bannan enthused, flopping onto his usual position on the lounge.

"Now?"

"You won't regret it."

"I think I will."

"Are you a babe? All I hear is fussing and whining!" Bannan declared, cocking his head and cupping his ear for effect.

"Name calling is beneath you."

"My kilt is beneath me, allowing my balls to swing freely and it is wonderful! You need to try it." Bannan shoved Ellis upward.

With a sigh, Ellis stood and walked towards his hut, looking at the material and thinking about underwear.

"Fuck, thank the Gods you're here!"

Fyfe had been pacing the floor of the front room, gnawing on a fingernail and sweating profusely. He stopped to grab Ellis by the upper arms at the doorway.

"What—"

Ellis was dragged into the room, surprised into silence as he was pressed down onto his bed.

"We have a problem," Fyfe said with all the seriousness of a doctor delivering news of a terminal illness. He was still gripping Ellis' upper arms, so Ellis slapped him away.

"What have you done?" he bit out.

"I, uh... " Fyfe began pacing again, this time wringing his hands. The sidelong glances he was throwing made it very difficult for Ellis not to panic and pressure him into speaking but he waited the boy out. "I didn't mean to. It just happened."

"What. Just. Happened."

"I... had sex with her."

"Gods," Ellis exhaled, slumping at the news. "When? Where?"

"Uh, in the forest. A little while ago."

"You're an idiot!"

"It's okay, though, she told me she wouldn't let Bannan find out," Fyfe protested.

His attempt at defusing the situation only stoked Ellis' fury. "You're as stupid as you are pretty, aren't you? The first thing that little bitch is going to do is make *sure* Bannan finds out, to tip our hand!"

Fyfe blustered momentarily, trying to find a legitimate argument for that point. "Well... I don't think she will, but even if she does, maybe that's not such a bad thing. She knows how to use their boats, she's strong and she's told me the three of us in one canoe will be able to get anywhere, no problem."

Ellis could feel his lip curling in disdain with every feeble word. The less he managed to say, however, the more Fyfe filled in the silence.

"Look, it's not as if I'm saying I'm in love with her or anything but she's a definite asset in this world and, frankly, as a fellow human being I can't stand by and watch her get treated like scum and not think about saving her. She needs to come with us."

"Curb your decency, gobdaw, because she's not. She's death and we want nothing to do with her."

"We have to!"

"We *don't*," Ellis growled. "We don't need her and we're not taking her."

Again, Fyfe puffed unintelligently, trying to think of a decent argument. "We are, or I don't go."

Ellis raised his eyebrows, looking pointedly at the child's swollen chest and clenched fists. "I'll make you."

"You can't Control me *and* Navigate!"

He was as impressed as he was disgusted by Fyfe's ability to have deduced the crucial limitation of his talent, but the child was forgetting that, as soon as they were far from here and in the middle of the ocean, Ellis could stop Controlling and Fyfe would be compelled to get himself out of trouble enough to concede.

As he opened his mouth to tell the young Navigator he was wrong, an infuriated roar travelled across the compound.

"WHOSE SEED DO I SMELL, WHORE? I WILL FIND HIM AND EAT HIS FUCKING HEART!" The telltale pops and clicks of Bannan changing into his beastly counterpart swiftly followed, leaving little doubt that he meant exactly what he'd said. Everyone knew where the first place he would look would be.

"Time to go," Fyfe gulped.

Ellis was already throwing things into his bag, ignoring him and the hoots coming from the villagers. They likely didn't know what was going on but seeing their leader change form was enough for them to get excited. "Sometimes choice is yours, most times it's not," he muttered to himself. "Accept, atone or attack." He straightened, pulling the strap of his bag over his head and looking straight at Fyfe. "Today, we atone and *run*."

CHAPTER SEVENTEEN

Roman's Plea

DAESON WAS SHAKEN awake.

"We've got to get going," Roman said. "Get your pack and come with me. We'll dump whatever you don't need in the next world."

"What?" Daeson asked, sitting up and rubbing his eyes. With his hands over them, blocking his vision, he was open to a warmth pulsing through his body and soft voices whispering in the air. The Portal was close enough to call to him.

He opened his eyes—almost expecting to find the pillar of light in front of him—but instead he saw Roman crouching by him. Behind the other Wanderer was a bleak and colourless backdrop, like someone had placed a dark grey shroud over the stars. There was a hint of purple in it, promised by a rising sun he couldn't yet see.

"Synjan's got a Hunter after her. We have to leave her behind."

"What?" Daeson asked again, though the question this time was not one of confusion, but of disbelief. Of course he understood—it was a practical, sensible decision. Roman would always make the best call towards his survival, even if it came with sacrifice. He'd impressed Daeson with his knowledge and experience, sharing examples of ruthlessness to survive—but now he was facing the reality of Roman's callousness.

"You need someone with experience to keep you alive. I'm the better choice for that. All Synjan's doing is putting you at risk."

And there it was; the truth at its harshest. Roman's knowledge and experience had always felt like offshoot rewards of bravery but now all Daeson could see was cowardice. Had his perspective changed simply because Synjan was the next offering for Roman's salvation?

Roman rose up and Daeson got to his feet, not wanting to speak from the ground.

"You can help us," Daeson pleaded in an attempt to convince him to stay. In his heart he sensed that the other Navigator was already committed to leaving Synjan behind, but he still had to try.

Roman shook his head and placed a hand on Daeson's shoulder, connecting them. "I can help *you*."

"You can help both of us," Daeson replied. Now that he was awake and standing, he could feel the pull of the Portal more clearly—it was very close—but he didn't dare break eye contact with the other Navigator to look.

Roman scoffed and dropped his hand off Daeson's shoulder to gesture at Synjan on the ground.

"I can't help someone who's been noticed by the Authorities. Who the hell is she, that they already know she's on the run?"

Daeson thought of Nick, who Synjan had been working with, and the unknown Ellis, who she'd been working for. Either of them could've informed the Authorities and sent a Hunter after her, but he had a different idea. Omerri was the most likely, for she was the most petty. She had Authority connections and her jealousy was toxic. Omerri had sent Synjan to bring him back and she'd left the world with him instead. He couldn't see Omerri letting that go, she would likely imagine that he and Synjan were romantically involved, exploring worlds together like characters in a storybook. She wouldn't let him have a fairytale ending at her expense.

"It might not be her fault, it might be mine. Please, Roman, help us. You know lots of ways to disappear."

"It's *her* name they have, and Hunters never stop. When a Hunter catches up with her, they'll find whoever she's travelling with."

He was right and Daeson hated that he was right. Synjan had attracted a dangerous foe and now Roman wanted to abandon her.

"Why did you wake me up, then? Why do you want me to come with you? I thought travelling alone was your preference."

Throughout their time on the airship, Daeson had felt like Roman was grooming him as a travelling partner. He'd asked leading questions, offered advice, listened avidly whenever Daeson had shared a memory and outlined many hypothetical outcomes that illustrated Daeson's chosen path had been the best. Everything towards him had been positive. But Synjan... Roman had never spoken about her. He'd carefully extracted himself from offering any opinions. Only carefully selected facts.

"Because we complement each other well and I like you." Roman folded his arms across his chest and looked uncomfortable. His words hadn't been a lie but it was unusual for him to speak from an emotional perspective. Daeson countered with the practical one.

"Between the two of us, I'm not the better choice. She's the capable one, she's the one who can defend herself."

Roman laughed. "But she's not the Healer. Your ability is better than anything she can do. We match perfectly—my Navigator ability and experience, and your Healer ability and personality. Plus, she hated me the minute she laid eyes on me. Admit it."

Daeson huffed but was unable to argue. Both Synjan and Roman had taken an instant dislike to one another and he didn't know how or why it had happened. He thought of the magnetism that attracted a Wanderer to a Navigator. Did it somehow work to repel Navigators away from each other? Was there never the option for Navigators to work together? No, that wasn't it. Synjan had spoken about her close relationship with her father and he'd been a Navigator.

"If she wakes up and finds me gone, she'd be devastated. I can't just abandon her," Daeson said.

"You're not abandoning her—you never agreed to anything with her. She just invited herself along, yeah?"

Daeson wished he hadn't shared the story of how Synjan had surprised him on J'Bdyamn. He'd forgiven it and now it was being used against her. He glanced at Synjan, guilty for betraying her trust.

"You're not stopping her from Wandering on her own," Roman said. "She's not helpless. You've just said how capable she is. She can look after herself, yeah?"

It was true. Daeson thought Synjan saw him as a

liability; someone to protect whenever there was trouble. It was evident in the way she put herself between him and the threat. She'd done it twice now. Could he travel with someone who felt obligated to protect him? At least Roman was offering equality. He'd explained outright that Daeson was a useful travelling partner. As horrible as this situation was, it was nice to be wanted as an equal member of a team.

Except Daeson already had a team.

"There's no point leaving her behind, she'd just catch up to us. Might as well travel together," Daeson countered. He looked over at Synjan, noticing that she was still asleep. "Why isn't she waking up?"

"Because you're not weathered. The more you Wander, the faster you wake up. She's going to be out of it for another ten minutes probably. It could be less, so we have to hurry." Roman pushed Daeson's pack towards him. "Come on, the Portal is right there."

Daeson looked where Roman had gestured. The pillar of light stood imposingly at the edge of the field where they lay. It was beautiful, intimidating, mesmerising...

"Daeson."

The purple-grey sky softened and mingled with blues. There was an artificial looking tree line nearby, beside a cluster of identical green buildings—they looked to be made out of metal and had no windows. Turning his head farther he saw distant houses, squat and square.

"Daeson."

He spun gradually around and saw fast-travelling cars on a road in the near distance—perhaps the same distance away as the Portal, only in the opposite direction. An impossibly long vehicle—it looked like a truck in segments with a hinge in the middle—zoomed down the road at the same speed as the cars. Daeson stared at it until Roman grabbed his shoulder and turned him back around.

"Stop daydreaming! I know the Portal gives you the gaga-feel-goods, but we have to get moving!"

Roman shouting in Daeson's face had the desired effect. He blinked, frowned and shook his head.

"I can't leave her."

"You can."

"She deserves better."

"Nobody deserves anything except what they take for themselves."

Instead of impressing Daeson, Roman's insight revolted him. Roman thought he was speaking the truth... and perhaps it even was the truth, on all the worlds, but it wasn't something Daeson wanted to align himself with.

"Come on, Daeson. I'm the better Navigator."

"But you're not the better person."

"She carries guns around with her. How good a person can she be, yeah?"

Again, Roman used information that Daeson had offered in conversation to vilify Synjan. But had he offered it in conversation or had Roman asked leading question after leading question in preparation for this moment?

"I trust her more than you."

Roman's lip curled. He lifted his chin and settled his bag more firmly on his shoulder.

"Have it your way. I'm not travelling with a dead man."

Daeson couldn't reply because Roman turned and sprinted towards the Portal. At first Daeson gaped at him, stunned that Roman's friendship had soured so quickly—but why was Roman running so fast? An instant later he recalled that when a Wanderer touched the Portal, it would move. Roman might have sent the Portal closer to them on J'Bdyamn, but he was intending on sending it away from them here.

Wherever here was.

"Synjan!" Daeson cried, crouching to violently shake her by the shoulders. "Synjan, wake up! He's running!"

Synjan's eyes fluttered open and, unbelievably, she smiled at him. "Who's running?" she asked.

Daeson shoved his hands into Synjan's armpits and hauled her to her feet. Her expression of alarm would've made him laugh if they weren't in the middle of being betrayed.

"Synjan, we have to get going right now!"

To her credit, she didn't ask him why, but reached into her shirt for her gun while trying to look everywhere at once.

"No, don't shoot him, it's Roman. The Portal is right there and he's going for it. Without us!"

He watched as realisation flooded her face.

"That fucker!"

CHAPTER EIGHTEEN

Losses And Gains

INSTINCT TOOK OVER. Synjan grabbed her bag and raced after Roman. The wind in her face cleared away the last tendrils of Portal slumber. She ran beneath an awakening sky, across shadowed grass and towards a sun that peeked out from behind the Portal. They were in a paddock? Trees, sky, grass, fences, none of it compared to the Portal's song rampaging in her veins, tightening her skin and provoking her soul. It was about a hundred metres ahead of her, swirling and enticing with its promise of rapture. So close.

No matter the world, the scent of dawn was unmistakable and the fresh, crisp air filled her lungs. The bloom of natural light above her hadn't fully reached the world below, so she could only hope that she wouldn't step in a hole—she leapt over the darkest shadows in case they could trip her.

Roman was a form in the distance, jogging at a sedate pace. He seemed confident that he wasn't being pursued and Synjan knew she was gaining on him. Her years of being a Runner for Ellis had formed muscles that recalled instantly what the flex of her legs and rush of adrenaline required of them. Despite carrying her heavy bag on her back, she flew across the dew-soaked ground, feet thumping in time with her hammering heart, her target in sight.

A noise from behind her drew her attention and she hesitated, her pace slowing. She was leaving Daeson behind. He had longer legs but he was a slower runner. Indecision caused her to falter and she came to a stop, her chest heaving as she studied the grey landscape behind her. Colour was leeching into the world in her wake and she could clearly see Daeson's expression. He was coming as fast as he could but it wasn't fast enough. She saw his gaze shift as he looked beyond her.

Daeson's eyes widened and he held out a palm to stop.

Synjan's head whipped around.

Roman had glanced behind him. He'd seen them coming. He sprinted towards the Portal, his lead unrecoverable.

Synjan took after him anyway, realising that she should've just kept going and tackled him. Even if she hadn't reached him in time, she could've shot him and let Daeson Heal him. Too late the idea came... too late for her to do anything but watch.

Roman ran headfirst into the column of coloured light that stood between them and the sun. He was silhouetted against it for an instant, the image burnt into her memory before the whole thing gathered into itself. Synjan stopped, staring, as Roman Wandered without waiting for them.

Instantly, the Portal glistened less. It was as if the column held its breath, shivered and then snapped at the base like an elastic rope severed by a blade. It retracted rapidly upward into the clouds, Roman's limp body arched in unconsciousness just above the bottom of the beam. The light and the traitorous Navigator hurtled to an unknown distance above them and then... they were gone.

Completely.

The lack of the Portal registered in Synjan's core, yet she closed her eyes to be sure, pushing herself harder and faster than she had in a long time. She couldn't find it anywhere on the world. Had it moved somewhere beyond her limits of perception, she knew she would still feel *something* in its direction but there was nothing this time.

The Portal was *gone*.

It felt as if she searched until the ache inside would consume her but she gave up after a few breaths and opened her eyes just as Daeson skidded to a stop beside her.

"What is it?" he gasped, concern warring with his need to catch his breath.

"The Portal's gone," Synjan mourned.

"I know... Roman... he took it, he—"

"No, I mean it's *gone*! From the world completely! I can't sense it anywh—" Her rapid conversation came to a stop when she was proved wrong. "It's back," she breathed.

Daeson looked confused but she ignored him in favour of closing her eyes and testing what she already knew to be true. She spoke while she searched, her words sounding dreamy even to her own ears. "That must be how it works. The Portal sucks Wanderers up out of the world they're on, takes them to the next world and then it returns, dropping back down in a new place." She gripped Daeson's hand as she opened her eyes and smiled up at him. "It was frightening but amazing. I had no idea it did that!"

"I doubt many Wanderers would know such a thing. How far away is it now?"

"It's a few hundred kilometres to the north, not *too* far away," she hazarded, "but we'll need to find some transport." She looked around and saw a vehicle moving along what had to be a road in the distance. "Over there. C'mon," she said and, keeping hold of his hand, began to walk in the right direction. She was pleased when he didn't pull away.

As they walked and discussed the Portal's behaviour, Synjan was very surprised to find that she was content with the outcome. Sure, she was annoyed that they'd had the Portal stolen from them but she was more than pleased with herself. Two worlds ago, she wouldn't have thought twice about shooting Roman to stop him from taking what she wanted but it had only been a belated consideration today. Daeson might have lost the battle with Roman but he was definitely winning the war with her. She was changing, becoming a better person, one that Daeson deserved as a partner.

A yellow sign on the side of the road depicted the silhouette of a very unusual animal. It looked like a mouse walking upright on two long, bendy legs, with a thick, curved tail for balance. Synjan assumed the sign meant the animals were in the area but they didn't see any. She and Daeson hiked parallel with the busy road but there wasn't much room on the shoulder. They jumped whenever a passing vehicle tooted at them, presumably warning them they were too close.

Reaching a blue sign that said 'South Grafton Industrial Area' was a two-fold relief. It confirmed that Authoritan was spoken here and also preceded a more established part of the city. The pathways were grassy and easier to walk on and the sun finally crested the horizon.

"It's pretty here," Daeson commented, openly admiring the colours rioting across the sky. "And there are farms."

"You miss being a farmer, don't you?" she asked, squeezing his hand.

He considered. "I miss the lifestyle, the simple way of things. I don't miss being a farmer. I was no good at it."

She chuckled at his clarification. "What do you see yourself doing, then? When we find the right world?"

"I liked working in the kitchen at the Queen. The head chef said I had talent. I'd like to open a bakery or something."

Synjan hadn't expected the answer she got. She stared at Daeson for a long moment. "Like bread and cakes?"

"Or stews," he said with a smile.

"So you want a restaurant?" Synjan hazarded.

"I just want to cook," he replied. "I think I'd be good at it."

"I think it's great that you have a goal."

Daeson looked pleased. "Do you have a goal?" he asked.

"I don't know what I'd be good at." She couldn't imagine how her skill set would translate to regular employment.

"Not singing," he said, chuckling until she punched his arm. "Ow, okay. Do you think this world could be what we want?"

"Maybe," she answered non-committally. Part of her would be terribly disappointed if they'd found a world worthy of settling in; it was too soon. She wasn't ready to stop Wandering yet and it had nothing to do with the Hunter on their trail.

It wasn't long before they came to a roadside diner with numerous huge vehicles parked on the dusty land around it. One pulled away as they approached, its engine growling deeply and its undercarriage hissing as it lumbered out onto the roadway.

Heading inside the sprawling building, Synjan and Daeson paused just beyond the threshold and looked around, getting their bearings. The air was a scent-cocktail of baking bread, old plastic and warm grease. To one side was a dining area with tables and chairs that were occupied by a few people. Straight ahead, past some shelves with a variety of colourful products on them, was a counter with a cash register. A young woman slouched behind it. Beside the open counter was another one, supporting a glowing glass box filled with food. Synjan's stomach growled, reminding her that she hadn't eaten for many hours. She walked between the shelves, intending to speak to the girl but receiving a queer look before she even opened her mouth.

"You haven't got the rig at pump five have you, sweetie?" the native woman asked.

Synjan had no clue what she meant. "Uh, no? We were wondering if you could advise us about getting transport northward?"

As she spoke, the brunette relaxed. She nodded and curled a hand around one slim hip, looking satisfied. Synjan was pleased she'd somehow said the right thing.

"Didn't think so. How far up you going?"

"Up?"

"How far north you going?" the woman clarified.

Synjan was happy to be able to answer this question—the grid she saw using her Navigator talent was accurate for calculating distances. "About three hundred kilometres."

The woman gave her another odd look. "So... Brisbane, then?"

"Sure."

The woman gave a snorting laugh and lifted her chin towards the dining room. "See that fella over there? The one in the hideous floral shirt and blue shorts? That's Kev. Go see him about a lift." Her voice had been raised to get the attention of the man in question and he looked suitably affronted by the girl's description of him.

"Oi!" he bellowed back. "You leave my shirt alone, Jess. I have better taste in clothes than you do men."

"Ah, piss off," Jess jeered, then lowered her voice as she leant closer to Synjan. "He's a good bloke. You can trust him," she assured before turning away.

Synjan glanced awkwardly at Daeson, seeing him shrug then nod before she headed towards the man named Kev. Approaching him made her feel uncomfortable, as though she knew something incredibly intimate about this stranger that she shouldn't. "Hello... Kev, is it?" she enquired as she stopped hesitantly by his table.

"Yeah, g'day," he confirmed, wiping his hands on the seat of his shorts as he stood and then extended it towards her. He was an older man, shorter than Daeson, with silver hair and a matching beard. His tattooed skin was leathery, his body strong and thin except for an oddly-large and rounded belly. He wore short sleeves and minimalistic shorts despite the coolness of the morning, but his heavy boots with thick socks spilling out of them looked warm—as did his twinkling eyes.

"I'm Synjan. This is Daeson," she said as she shook his hand, wondering how she had become the official communicator.

"Siddown," Kev said cheerfully, pointing at the other chairs at his table. He sat and resumed eating, watching them carefully. "So you two wanna' get to Brissy?"

"Um, well, we want to travel north about three hundred kilometres but we're not familiar with city names."

Kev nodded and Synjan was quietly relieved that her answer was acceptable. "Either way, that's where I'm headed. I'd be glad to give you a lift if you want it. There's room enough for both of you," he glanced appraisingly at Daeson, "as long as we stow your gear on my bed, I guess."

Synjan nodded hesitantly, uncertain about how the driver's bed would be travelling with them but unwilling to rebel until she knew for certain she'd be separated from her gear. She was learning to expect it.

Kev shoved some more food in his mouth and chewed, eyeing his passengers and grinning as he swallowed. "It'll be at least a four-hour drive plus roadworks. Do you two wanna' get some tucker before you go? Y'look hungry. I s'pose you don't have much money though, being backpackers. Listen, go tell Jess what you want from the hotbox and have her put it on my account. It'll be my treat," he grinned, apparently convinced just by looking at them that they were in a state of destitution.

Synjan glanced down at herself, dismayed by the threadbare appearance of her clothing. "Oh, no, we couldn't, we have—"

"Thanks!" Daeson enthused, cutting her off. His chair scraped loudly and he hurried over to choose some food from the glass box.

Synjan looked back at Kev and sighed, her cheeks turning pink. "Thank you. We really appreciate your generosity. Will you let us pay you back?"

"Yeah, nah. It's my pleasure, love. Don't mention it." Kev waved her onward.

She frowned, opened her mouth and then closed it decisively. It wouldn't do to question every word said to them. She got up to select something for their journey.

CHAPTER NINETEEN

Controlled Descent

AS UNDIGNIFIED AS climbing out a rear window was, Ellis thought it the best choice for escaping the monster hunting them. No sooner had Fyfe cleared the sill after him than they heard thrashing sounds at the front of the hut, signalling Bannan's entry. Ducking down, they hastened away, hearts pounding and sweat slicking their skins.

Ellis allowed Fyfe to take the lead. Apart from the fact he was a Navigator, he'd spent time traversing the village and its surrounds. He'd have a better idea of an escape route.

Once they'd managed to get behind some screening bushes, they straightened and moved faster. They found a thin trail of loose sand and overhanging creeper plants. It seemed promising, despite the poor footing. At least it led away from the village.

"This way!" Fyfe urged needlessly, his sneakers plunging into the sand with such force that every step elicited a high-pitched squeak. For a few moments, it was all they could hear; panting and squeaking and blood rushing in ears. Then the roar of something else happening in the village erupted behind them and they paused, looking back and then at one another.

"I think he's probably—" Ellis began but cut off when he heard people approaching from the forest depths. They were no doubt villagers running towards the noise at the heart of their encampment. The Wanderers leapt off the path so as not to be seen. Friend or foe, any Techatachenti they happened upon would likely attempt to drag them towards the action.

Ellis wasn't sure they weren't seen as they launched themselves into the spiky shrubbery but the footsteps didn't hesitate and moved steadily away.

"We need a plan," Ellis wheezed.

"We need Paki," Fyfe countered.

"You are insufferable!" Ellis condemned, getting to his feet with difficulty.

"The boats are this way."

"A boat is no guarantee!"

"I know, but if we get him alone—even if he's a shark—isn't that better for you to Control him?"

It sparked an idea and Ellis knew what he could do to get them out of this mess. It was ridiculous and irrational but he knew he had the skill to pull it off. Convincing his travelling partner wouldn't be as easy, so he decided to be vague. "I have a plan. Come on!" he urged confidently, heading the way they'd come.

"That's the way back to the village!" Fyfe screeched, obviously thinking Ellis had accidentally chosen the wrong direction.

"I know, we have to hurry. We have a show to put

on!"

Fyfe muttered behind him as he circumnavigated the village. It was the only way he might take the king by surprise. They approached the back of the crowd, where everyone was watching Bannan making a show of dragging Paki around by the hair and roaring, heightening the excitement of his brethren as he usually did before a hunt.

Ellis' sonorous voice cut through a momentary lull with maximum force. "BANNAN!"

A silence fell over the crowd, so pure that he fancied he could hear the hairs raise on everyone's arms. Bodies swivelled and a natural parting opened up between Ellis and the object of his attention, allowing them direct eye contact.

Bannan released his wailing lover and snarled as he padded towards Ellis, his huge feet-paws landing on the ground with muted thuds, his hand-paws flexing menacingly.

Ellis took one last breath and exhaled. Timing was everything. He watched the speed of Bannan's progress towards him for a few steps, calculated the distance and charged.

"I will not let you hurt Fyfe!" he bellowed as he went.

Bannan roared a response and starting thumping towards him too, his great, hairy arms lifting outward in preparation of the bone-crunching bear hug he was about to deliver.

Ellis ran headlong into the huge beast, throwing his mind forward and overtaking his opponent. One moment he was hurling himself towards certain death, the next he was overtaking a ravenous maelstrom of thoughts and catching his own limp form in huge, muscular arms. To mask the lack of violence, he tilted his head back and roared, greatly relieved by the Techatachenti peoples' responding cheer.

He realised he hadn't thought the next part through very well but he couldn't afford to hesitate or the locals would know something was amiss with their 'god'. He strode towards Fyfe and attempted to tell him to head for the boats but it soon became clear that the arrangement of his beast mouth wasn't conducive to human speech. All he did was growl. Fyfe wailed and shied away from him, shielding his face and looking as if he expected to have his head ripped from his body any second. Ellis was sorry now that he hadn't told his travelling companion anything about how his power worked.

Instead, he hefted his body into the crook of one arm and swatted at Fyfe with the other, encouraging him to get to his feet. He shoved him towards Paki, gesturing for him to get her and follow after him. It took more arm-waving than he would've liked but Fyfe finally proved he wasn't a complete moron and appeared to realise what was happening. Together, the three of them strode out of the village towards the boats, Bannan leading the way. When the warriors began to hoot and dance after them, Ellis turned and roared at them in his most dissuasive manner until they got the message that he didn't want them following. Confused, they trickled away.

Once they were alone, Fyfe risked a question.

"That *is* you, isn't it, Ellis?"

Ellis nodded his wolfish head.

Fyfe heaved a sigh of relief and grabbed Paki by the hands, pausing to face her. "It's okay. We're safe," he assured her, emphasising his final word before he pointed at the towering beast standing idly beside them, carrying Ellis' body. "That's Ellis," Fyfe instructed, pointing to Bannan's muzzle.

Paki did him the courtesy of looking from Bannan's beast face to Ellis' limp body in his arms and pointed to the human form instead. "Ellis?" she enquired, mostly keeping the singing from her voice.

"No. Ellis," Fyfe reasserted, pointing at Bannan again and then tapping the side of his own skull. "In his mind," he clarified, reaching up to tap Bannan's furry temple as best he could. "Ellis is in here."

Her expression might have been comical if someone watching her reaction hadn't known her history. She might be uncomprehending about the mechanics of the situation but it was clear that she accepted it when she grabbed a hunk of wiry orange fur in a fist and looked at Fyfe. "Kill Bannan," she said sincerely, her eyes glittering with hatred.

Ellis considered the variables. He'd been planning to Control Bannan until they were safely away in a boat but he acknowledged now that the idea had left a flighty feeling in his chest. Relinquishing his Control of such a powerful Wanderer on the open ocean was a risk and he wasn't sure they had enough weapons to satisfactorily end him out there. Delaying Bannan's death would also take time and they'd left in such a hurry, he didn't have a decent supply of fresh water to keep his talent active for long. It might become a disaster that would see all four of them dead in the boat, an endless ocean the only witness to their demise.

Paki's homicidal eagerness nudged him away from his hasty plan and towards a more efficient one. Ellis spun around and ran towards a more familiar path.

"Where are you going *now*?" Fyfe called. The sounds of their footsteps thumping along behind him was easy to hear when his own paws made so little noise.

Because they headed partway back to the village to find their desired course, they came into contact with a few more villagers. Ellis hefted his limp body triumphantly and growled convincingly, except the natives were puzzled by Paki and Fyfe. He knew it wouldn't be long before that disquiet became bold curiosity and they came after them. It spurred him anew.

Unfortunately, Paki became struck by the opposite impetus when they reached the cage at the outer limits of the village. The lone Mukake survivor huddled within, his eyes wide with terror as he caught sight of Bannan's beast form. Paki attacked the bamboo bars with unexpected zeal, tears rolling down her face as she sang rapidly at her tribe-mate. Initially, he seemed interested in the fact that she was freeing him and he stirred, but he couldn't trust the wolf-bear watching so he didn't move much after that.

Ellis didn't wait around to see how it was resolved. He didn't care if either of the enemy group survived, he only needed Fyfe and to be sure that *they* could get away. He strode determinedly onward, aware that Fyfe was torn but pleased when his companion hustled after him.

"I think she's trying to get him to run, man. Thanks for not hanging around to scare him."

Even if he could have responded, Ellis wouldn't have. Fyfe was an inconvenience and an imbecile at times but his approval was necessary for his goodwill. He didn't need to know the truth behind Ellis' departure.

A strong, clean breeze augured their arrival at the

top of the cliff. It struck him in the face as they rounded the last bend and shifted the hairs around Bannan's muzzle in a delightful, ticklish way. The sky was mostly blue after a morning shower but the clouds were thickening on the horizon and blowing in much darker than what was above them. Ellis had expected to be leaving the village with full fanfare and Bannan's best wishes, but this was a rather lonely and anticlimactic ending.

Ellis placed his body carefully on the ground and prowled to one side of the rope bridge, glancing at the monstrosity creaking gently and swinging in the ever-present breeze. He considered walking Bannan out to the middle of the bridge and off it but there was no guarantee he'd die, even from that height. A Transmuter as skilled as the redhead would probably have the wherewithal to change form into a bird on the long drop and fly away, if not become a fish and swim deeper at the bottom. No, Ellis needed something sharp and solid to smash the Transmuter's body into and he needed to Control him the whole way down to be sure.

After an inspection of both sides of the bridge, Ellis identified the best location to jump from and positioned Bannan on the precarious edge. Paki arrived just as he did and Ellis paused to look back. She was alone. When she saw him she ran at him, screaming a warrior's bloodcurdling cry of rage, victory and despair. With her push, he toppled backwards into open space.

As Bannan's body fell, Ellis tried to force it to turn so he could see the rocks and judge the moment of his mental exit but the wind and the velocity at which he was travelling had other ideas. Maybe his Control was also slipping in his concern because, as he was forced to stare up at an extremely sheer view of cliff face and expansive sky, he got a final impression of Bannan, a sense of redness and whiteness and absolute fury. Waving his furred limbs and writhing against the gale, he twisted silently, not allowing the ruthless dictator any last sounds but helpless to finish this on his own terms, either, because he couldn't see what was happening.

The explosion of pain was therefore unexpected and swallowed him whole, though it ended almost as it began. One moment Ellis was in a body suffused with torment as it was smashed apart on unforgiving rock and the next he'd snapped back into his own pain-free body. He gasped as he sat up, scrunching his eyes shut as he expected the insanity of murderous pain to continue but there was just... nothing. He opened his eyes, blinking because the view was different to what he'd been seeing through wolf eyes and because it was difficult to believe he was able to see anything at all. In between the agony and the freedom, there'd been a moment of blackness that his mind had registered and it had absorbed him.

"I died," he whispered, processing it all belatedly.

"Ellis!" Fyfe cried, stumbling off the bridge and rushing towards his companion. He fell to his knees beside him and engulfed him in a tight hug, yabbering in relief. "You did it! You killed him! He's nothing but a blood pancake on those rocks, it's fucking disgusting, oh by the Gods, I can't believe you just did that, that was insane!"

Ellis pushed him away and surged to his feet, imbued with an understanding only divinity could comprehend. "I have died and yet I live!" he roared. "Who is the god now?"

Fyfe blinked up at him, frozen in an awkward lean

back on one arm. "Did you swap minds with him or something?" he asked warily.

Ellis laughed heartily, grinning down at the ignorant Navigator like the fool that he was. Why had he ever been concerned about staying in the mind of the dead? He'd predicted he might also fall victim to that terminal end or, at the least, become trapped in a limbo, permanently separated from his own body and lost in a void. Now he knew. His mind was too strong to be captured by that quietus; he was tethered firmly to life. He could live through a thousand deaths, glimpse the truth of unknowable eternity, and come back to tell of it. He could taste immortality.

Nothing would stop him now.

CHAPTER TWENTY

Portal Bound

VOICES FLOATED OUT of the truck's dashboard radio, replacing the cheerful music and electrifying the cabin with an urgent tone. Synjan realised immediately that she was hearing a news update but the details were beyond her until partway through the segment, when a specific word caught her attention:

'... *Authorities have categorically condemned the bombing and are committed to responding with full force if peace negotiations fail. Hundreds of thousands will be killed should their arsenals be released, a political advisor has warned—* '

Their driver reached over and pressed a button. The woman's voice was immediately replaced by a singing man but the news reader's words reverberated in Synjan's mind.

"The Authorities will bomb them back?" she queried, her voice strained. What sort of place was Earth? She knew very little about it beyond the fact that it was on the Authority registry.

"Ah, the whole world's going down the shitter!"

Kev exclaimed in disgust, shaking his head.

Synjan looked to her left, to find Daeson staring tensely at her. "Was that close by?" she enquired, turning to her right again. "I didn't hear where it happened." She hoped Daeson would forgive her for lying because she *had* heard, she just didn't know where it was and needed to get an idea from their guide. Were they heading into a war zone?

Kev glanced at her and smiled, taking his eyes off the road to throw her a reassuring look.

"Nah, overseas, nowhere near Australia," he assured her, watching the road again. He had to be wary that 'road-hogging car mongrels' didn't 'cut him off' and Synjan was glad he was vigilant. More vehicles were swarming the roads than ants near a nest. She was dazzled and fearful about negotiating all the obstacles—bordered circular land masses and curious, changing lights on steel poles. She was impressed with Kev's ability as a driver.

"That's good," she said, though it didn't feel good.

Losing the Portal because of Roman hadn't been the setback they'd initially thought. It was the sort of good fortune they needed with a Hunter on their trail. Maybe all those faithful Docksiders that used to spout on about being helped by the Gods in their time of need hadn't been so far from the truth.

"So where are you two from?" Kev enquired.

Synjan widened her eyes at him, trying to look as innocent as possible. "Nowhere near here," she replied non-committally.

Kev chuckled. "I knew that the second you opened your mouth."

She regarded him thoughtfully, aware that the way they all spoke was very different. She admired Daeson's gentle accent as it was nothing like her own rounded manner of speech. Kev's broad, drawling pronunciation was difficult to understand. She couldn't be sure where one word ended before it rolled into another. He'd assumed they were from this world.

"Where do you think we come from?" she queried, hoping he'd tell her something useful. This was the first Authority world they'd Wandered into. They had to be smarter and more guarded about the information they gave out.

Kev seemed energised by her challenge and thought out loud to see if he could lure her into confirming his suspicions. "You, well, you I'd say come from northern England. Somewhere around Liverpool, maybe?"

Synjan smiled, hoping it looked mysterious rather than nonplussed.

"Thought so—I used to work with a Scouse bloke. And Daeson there, hrmm. Well, he's pretty quiet. I thought Dutch right off the bat, but the next thing he said sounded American, so I really can't pick him," Kev shook his head, glancing hopefully at Synjan. "I'm going with Dutch, though?"

"Wow, you're very good at this, you're right!" she exclaimed. "Daeson's well travelled. He's picked up a lot of accents, he's amazing with languages."

"S'that right?" Kev asked, his upward vocal inflection communicating his piqued interest.

"She seems to think so," Daeson answered dryly.

Synjan beamed at him, hoping she hadn't made him feel as uncomfortable as he looked. He was pushed up against the door of the truck to allow her to sit close to him and not interfere with Kev's driving.

"How are you coping with Aussie slang?"

"It's close enough to Authoritan that I can make it out," Daeson answered.

Kev gave him a bemused look, then laughed politely. Synjan could tell there was something in her partner's phrasing that had triggered that reaction but she couldn't define it.

"Good'o. Y'might've guessed that I make it a habit to give backpackers like y'selves rides when I can. It gives me some company on the run and opens me up to some cultures I wouldn't normally have contact with. Every single time I have someone new in the cab, they always tell me what a hard time they're having with Aussie English. I've been known to sling some wobblies every now and then so just ask if I've got you stumped and I'll explain it," he offered.

"Thanks," Daeson said and Synjan echoed the sentiment. She'd vaguely understood Kev's offer to clarify his language but even his help was difficult to understand.

Glinting sunlight drew Synjan's attention out the window past Daeson. They were travelling alongside water and she admired the way it reflected the blue of the sky overhead. Tall, leafy trees, tangled bushes and tufts of green grass separated the road from the river bank, while the wispy clouds overhead barely featured in the square of the window. The broad windscreen ahead made everything feel large and open, the pale blue dome above seeming infinite.

"The weather here is lovely," Synjan murmured, comparing the clear morning to the foggy clouds that usually supervised Gredann. "Everything's green so it must rain but the sky doesn't look like it ever would."

"Oh, we get our fair share, don't you worry. It's just not the season for it. They get more rain down here than we do up home."

"This isn't where you live?" Synjan asked, surprised.

"Nah, I'm based in Brisbane but I'm not there much. One or two nights every fortnight."

"Do you have a family?" Daeson asked.

"Divorced my missus about ten years ago now and the kids are all grown. They've spread out along the coast so I get to visit the grandkids while I work. It's a good life. In fact, last night the youngest tacker said the funniest—shit, hang on," Kev interrupted himself and his driving.

Synjan's heart leapt as he braked heavily and she and Daeson were thrust forward. The truck growled and churned as gears and brakes worked hard, forcing the huge vehicle to slow down.

"What is it?"

"Those authorities we were speaking of earlier," Kev muttered, glaring at a nondescript van parked on the side of the road.

Synjan's heart did a flip in her chest. "Where?" she cried, looking at all the vehicles around them as well as into the side mirrors.

"On the side of the road back there. Speed trap," Kev explained, frowning at her reaction. "You're not in trouble with the law, are you?"

Synjan's mind raced as she thought about how best to answer their host. She didn't want to say anything to jeopardise their ride but if the Authorities were inclined to set traps for motorists in this world, there was no telling how far they would go to capture them. It was clear that the Hunter pursuing them would find no resistance on this world. Kev might be in danger and she didn't want him to be ignorant of the situation. He deserved the right to decide.

"We're Wanderers," she admitted, holding her breath.

Kev took a few moments to digest this information and when he spoke, he cut to the heart of their dilemma. "Yeah, but have you broken any laws here?"

"Oh, no!" Synjan assured him, understanding that he was concerned about how much effort they'd exerted to avoid detection. He really must have given a lot of Wanderers a ride in his truck.

"Then you'll be sweet," Kev grinned.

Synjan relaxed back into her seat, exchanging a meaningful look with Daeson as she did. She felt guilty about not discussing the main danger following them but a Hunter would likely have been too much for Kev to stomach. She'd been numb to the news ever since it had been relayed to her on Femme but now that she had a moment to ponder it, it was noticeably scratching at her resolve.

She'd always known Wandering was likely to draw a Hunter but she hadn't been prepared for the swiftness of it. The Hunter would have to have picked up their trail the second they left Trent because there'd been no Authorities on J'Bdyamn and it had seemed that Femme was dedicated to covering Wanderers' tracks. They'd never been allowed unsupervised among the general populace and the Authorities were blocked from travelling freely in the world as well. There was no way it had happened on Femme, so...

Her skin prickled and hardened as a shiver ran down her spine. It wasn't natural discovery that had put a Hunter on their trail. It had to be Ellis. She imagined that, upon finding out that she'd Wandered, he'd been furious with her. She'd abandoned him and her responsibilities, after all. Brazenly run away. She rubbed her forearm with her hand, finding it difficult to get warm. It hurt to even contemplate but she couldn't deny the logic of it; Ellis hated what she did so much that he'd gone to the Authorities and reported her Wandering just so a Hunter would come after her.

The man who'd sheltered, raised and employed her, wanted her dead. The knowledge sat like an acrid weight in her stomach.

Daeson touched her arm, drawing her attention. "Are you alright?" he asked as his gaze searched her face.

"Yeah, I just thought of something," she admitted, summoning a weak smile and covering his hand with her own. "I'll tell you about it later."

Once he'd reclaimed his driving rhythm, Kev's bright chatter started up again. He wanted to know how old they were, how long they'd been together and how long they'd been travelling. Synjan was confused by the repetition of the question.

"We just told you, about a month," she replied with a frown.

Kev laughed like he thought she'd said something funny. "You're not getting me. When I asked how long you'd been together, I meant as a couple."

His encouraging stare failed to convey the subtleties of his meaning and Synjan hesitated.

"He wants to know how long we've been having sex," Daeson announced. Kev's braying laughter filled the cabin with a delight only he was feeling.

Synjan swivelled to stare into his blue eyes so quickly that her braid whipped around to hit her in the neck. "What?" she blasted.

"I know. Roman asked me, too. We're not a couple like that," he told Kev casually over her head. "We just travel together."

Synjan turned back to stare at the buttons on the dashboard in front of her, feeling the heat in her cheeks and aware they must be the colour of ripe bloodberries. The two men continued to converse without her input and she knew she shouldn't have been reacting like she was but what her mind knew and her body did were not the same. It took a lot of sifting through congested thoughts and feelings before she properly understood what was going on.

Humiliation. That was the heart of it. She wanted Daeson, had even tried to lure him into a shower with her and had been rejected. He'd been with at least two women who were complete strangers to him, and managed to sort through any mixed feelings he might have had about it without her. She was superfluous in Daeson's life and had been ever since she'd forced herself upon him during his escape from Trent. Having an outsider look at them and assume them to be intimate only compounded the awful realisation that once again, she didn't have the man she wanted in the way she wanted. She should acknowledge the reality and move on, shifting her regard for Daeson from a potential lover to a friend.

"Have you had any trouble from drop bears?" Kev asked Daeson in a tone so intriguing it managed to pull Synjan's attention away from her internal struggle.

"What are they?" Daeson frowned.

"Oooh, you wanna' be careful of drop bears," Kev warned, hissing in breath between his lips in a most disturbing fashion. "They're native to Australia, related to koalas but a vicious breed that survives on drinking warm blood. They live in our big gum trees and they wait in the low branches for unsuspecting visitors to wander underneath. Then they'll throw themselves off and DROP down to bite you!" their driver yelled, reaching over and digging the tips of his fingers into Synjan's nape for greater effect.

He laughed with satisfaction as she clenched her shoulders and yanked away from him, removing his hand when he'd got the reaction he'd wanted.

"They sound terrible!" Synjan spat.

"Deadly," Kev agreed. "Rip your throat out in under ten seconds. Though they're not our deadliest animal, I suppose, given they're so rare."

"Really?" she asked sceptically, sneaking a look at Daeson. His expression was unfamiliar and when he noticed her looking at him, he shrugged. Did that mean he didn't know if Kev was telling the truth?

"You're not aware we're home to some of the deadliest animals in the world?" the driver asked, sounding genuinely surprised. When they shook their heads, he took great delight in enlightening them. "Most of the travellers I meet are shit scared of our wildlife, even though they're more scared of you than you are of them. As long as you play it smart, you'll be right."

"What are we 'playing it smart' towards?" Synjan enquired weakly, uncertain she wanted to hear more. She was greatly disturbed by this unforeseen danger but she couldn't be sure whether she was most upset by the deadly animals or because she hadn't been worried. Certainly, she'd been unaware she should be, but every world likely carried such hazards. Small crawlers whose bites or stings could be Healed by Daeson were fine but what were they up against? She recalled the yellow signs with animals on them. Had they been warnings? They were lucky not to have encountered any of those strange beasts!

"We have the inland taipan and eastern brown—the two most venomous snakes in the world. We've also got the funnel web spider and saltwater crocs on land. There's a heap of sharks and the box and irukandji jellyfish in our oceans, not to mention the sea snakes, stonefish and blue-ringed octopus. Are you planning to go swimming at one of our 'lovely' beaches?"

Synjan knew Kev was joking because of his teasing grin but the list of menaces he'd identified sent spikes of concern across her shoulders and eroding chunks of her confidence with every word. "Definitely not," she told him firmly. "After what you've said, I'm not even sure we'll ever get out of this truck."

Kev tipped his head back and roared laughter. "Ah, you'll be fine," he assured as he sobered, patting the air in her direction in a soothing gesture. "Just watch where you're walking, look before you sit and stay out of tropical waters. Brisbane's a fairly safe city. Are you staying long?"

"We haven't discussed it, but..." Synjan trailed off and turned to look at Daeson, the question in her eyes. The Hunter meant that they couldn't afford to linger, they had to travel as soon as possible, yet Daeson's expression was wary. Unsettled, she turned back to smile stiffly at Kev. "We'll see. We'll definitely stay as long as it takes to get some new gear."

"There's a huge shopping centre not far from my depot. You should find everything there that you want," Kev said. "I'll show you where to go when we get there."

Synjan did her best to smile and agree but she was conflicted. The tendrils of control she'd always held so tightly were slipping beyond her grasp. She couldn't be sure whether it was better to drop them and push blindly ahead or find a quiet place to wait and hold them tighter.

There are none so powerless as those who believe themselves in control.

Keep perspective in the moment and an eye upon the cause.

As her mentors—Ellis and Freddie—warred inside her head, Synjan was no closer to an answer. She supposed the best she'd be able to do was trust in her training and follow her instincts when the time came. They'd got her this far, after all.

CHAPTER TWENTY-ONE

Controlling Destiny

TO AVOID CONFRONTATION with any of the natives, the trio climbed down the cliff directly to the beach, navigating the steep tumble of boulders and tufted grasses as swiftly as they were able. On the sand, Paki took charge and Ellis allowed her to, needing confirmation that she was worth the inherent drama. She took a moment to survey her sailing options, Ellis and Fyfe either side of her.

Ellis was surprised by how tall Paki was. She hadn't seemed it when grovelling at Bannan's feet. He also admired her glorious hair for the first time. It was usually gathered into a knot at her nape but it had undone and fell like a dark curtain to her waist. As she strode to the closest boat and removed the oars from within, her hair whipped around her face.

She straightened from her ministrations and sang at the two of them, lifting the paddles in her hand meaningfully. Ellis grinned. "Clever," he murmured as he and Fyfe set about gathering as many oars as they could.

Unfortunately, they'd only looted half the boats when Fyfe cried out. "We have company coming!"

Two Techatachenti women walked from the cover of the trees onto the beach. At first, they were engrossed in their conversation but soon registered the sight of three village enemies stealing their oars. There was a moment of staring before comprehension dawned, then they sprinted back towards the village to report to a leader they no longer had.

"We have to leave *now*," Ellis announced, striding towards Paki. She directed him and Fyfe to drop their bounty into the middle of a large, two-hulled vessel and urged Fyfe to sit in front with Ellis behind. Ensuring they each got an oar in their hand, Paki pushed the canoe beyond the breakers before she leapt in and began paddling.

As they cleared the immediate vicinity of the Techatachenti's land, another particularly tall island came into view. When their pace slowed noticeably, Ellis turned to find Paki staring across the waves at it, paddle gripped across her knees. Her expression was so raw, watching her felt like an invasion of privacy. He turned back to find Fyfe frowning over his shoulder.

"What's she doing?" he asked.

"Saying goodbye," Ellis snapped, stabbing at the water with his oar. "Keep rowing."

It wasn't long before they fell into a silent rhythm, believing that the Techatachenti would start after them soon. Paki's forethought would give them extra time but it likely wouldn't be enough. Revenge was a powerful motivator and the villagers didn't need more of a reason to capture the three foreigners.

"They ran around for a bit but they've found him

now," Fyfe panted. The island behind them was a line on the horizon but it still seemed close because it was visible. Their head start had been short-lived but life-saving.

"They'll come soon," Ellis said around gritted teeth.

He was proven right when much of the remaining fleet was sighted in the distance before the sun went down, each craft manned by a full crew of warriors. When night fell, they didn't stop rowing even though their muscles were aching and their bodies were ready to give up with fatigue. Half the pursuers fell away when the moon rose, leaving only the most dedicated to carry on; three boats.

Ellis was forced to stop rowing after too many hours. With an anguished cry, he dropped his paddle onto the pile in front of him and leant back, his hands cramping into claws.

"I can't. I have to... rest a moment."

Fyfe turned to look at him. "Drink some water. It'll help with the cramps and you're probably still needing it after what you did to Bannan. You've earned a rest, don't worry."

"Plus, I'm very old," Ellis sniggered, unable to stop his eyelids drooping and his chin from lowering onto his chest.

"That, too," Fyfe chuckled and it was the last thing Ellis heard until the sound of bloodcurdling screams propelled him from his sleep an indefinable amount of time later.

"What is *that*?" he cried, disoriented until the vast expanse of water around him reminded him of his predicament.

"They're getting closer," Fyfe told him grimly. "Think you can start paddling again?"

Ellis spared a look behind him. Paki rowed with the same determined rhythm, her features chiselled into stone by the moon's highlight. Beyond her, the sea was choppy and their Techatachenti counterparts were alarmingly close. They were excited by it, too. The sounds of their anguished cries and calls for blood carried over the ocean towards them, trickling into their ears, brought by the wind.

If Ellis didn't join in the rowing, they'd be caught suckling at exhaustion's teat and they were as good as dead. He considered plans for Controlling a man on each boat to attack their companions but his fatigue made his Control unreliable and there were three boats. He chose to paddle, hoping he was using his remaining energy in the wisest manner.

Just before dawn, the storm that had been plucking at the water like a puppeteer tugging on strings, struck full force. They paddled through waves higher than their heads, soaked to the skin but thankful for the relief provided by the pelting rain. They tipped back their heads and stuck out their tongues to catch what they could, wiping it out of their eyes and listening to Fyfe's updates about their location.

When the sun came up, they could no longer see their pursuers and it was invigorating to the spirit. They took turns resting, finding it difficult to sleep beneath a raging sun and through persistent winds but so exhausted that they surrendered to whatever peace they could find.

As the second day drew to a close, their pursuers lagged well behind. Their own rowing had become mechanical, their bodies numbed by exertion, their skin burned and cracked by the unforgiving elements. When Fyfe broke the silence with the news they'd been waiting to hear, they were too tired to properly mirror the elation the declaration deserved: "They gave up. They're rowing the other way."

They dropped their paddles and sagged, processing that it was over.

"We need to find a place to camp," Ellis murmured after a while, hauling himself upright so he could look around them.

Fyfe and Paki stirred to life as well. Islands were never far away on this world, and Paki pointed her recommendation.

"Maybe that's her home," Fyfe said, proving that he was still lacking in intelligence, despite being reliable in an emergency.

"Don't be ridiculous. We left her home far behind us when we rowed away from the Island of the Gods."

"Oh," Fyfe frowned. "We didn't ask if she wanted to go home." He shuffled awkwardly in the prow of the boat so he could peer around Ellis to squint at the native woman. "Paki, did you want to go home?" he asked. He might as well have been asking her if she wanted milk with her coffee. Ellis was curious enough to turn as well, so he could observe her reaction.

Paki smiled, her demeanour vibrating with a new energy that blazed in her eyes as she answered. "Paki Wandruh," she asserted.

"Guess she's coming with us," Fyfe announced before he reclaimed his oar and started paddling. Slowly they headed towards the island that would allow them to recuperate enough to continue the journey through this world.

Ellis said nothing. They'd triumphed over their first taste of adversity and, after sixty years, he'd learnt another facet of his power. He could die and live a thousand times if it was necessary and none could stop him.

He had been appalled by Fyfe's inability to follow instructions at the village but the resolution of their dilemma also reassured Ellis. He would be able to get them out of any trouble the brash Navigator's attraction to mayhem got them into. He was also better versed in the breadth of his companion's idiocy now. The boy knew little of the three pillars Ellis lived by but he would be forced to adhere to them from now on: loyalty, perseverance and wisdom. His commitment hadn't been forced but Ellis predicted it would start the moment he told the child that they were leaving Paki behind. It would have to.

Fyfe wouldn't like it, but Paki was perfectly suited to the next world and she would flourish there. They would take her that far. He'd heard stories of how Femme was a Wanderer haven, that they harboured his kind there. Paki's lack of Wanderer blood might be a detriment but her exotic heritage and gender would counteract that and bequeath her the favour of protection. She would be welcomed to a new home and they wouldn't be burdened by her in their pursuit of Synjan.

He wouldn't reveal that decision until they stood on Femme's soil. They couldn't afford any more distractions and Fyfe was bound to do something stupid if he was told sooner. Ellis could no longer be lenient. This journey was his and Fyfe was merely a tool of his choosing. Just as spades should not dictate which dirt they might dig, neither should his Navigator do more than guide and comply. Synjan was slipping farther away from them every day. She also needed reminding of her commitment to him and their life together.

Loyalty. Perseverance. Wisdom. He was poised to set everything right and the lessons he'd been taught on this world were part of a greater picture, reassuring him that he was exactly where he was meant to be and that his task was ordained by the Gods themselves. Nothing could stop him now.

CHAPTER TWENTY-TWO

Conscious Bias

DAESON JUMPED DOWN from the truck's cab. The heat was an oppressive furnace at his back. A hot wind blew on him from the undercarriage of the idling truck and he stepped away to distance himself. Tufts of yellow grass and weedy bushes lined the footpath, interspersed by strange looking trees with peeling bark and not much greenery. Gum trees, Kev had called them. Daeson thought they looked sickly.

He took Synjan's pack when she handed it down and watched her climb out of the cab.

"Thank you," she cried before slamming the door shut. They received a blast from the horn before the vehicle amble away with a lot of hissing and groaning. It turned right into another street and disappeared.

"What did Kev say about the shops?" he asked, turning to look at Synjan. She met his gaze as she finished adjusting her bra under her shirt. "Did you take your gun out?"

"No, I just needed to untwist a few things," she

said with a grin.

"Ah," Daeson said, then chuckled. Their instructions were to walk down the road until they arrived at a large cluster of shops on their right. Kev had mentioned they were at the northern lakes, but Daeson couldn't see any bodies of water nearby.

They got walking. Cars zipped past, causing light puffs of wind and dirt to wash over them in their wake. Each time Daeson checked what was on their right, he could only see a high wall with the rooftops of houses peeking over. They weren't at the shops yet but lots of people lived here so they must be close.

"I had a thought while in the truck," Synjan said.

By her expression, he knew it was the thing she'd said she would talk about later—it seemed this was the time. It scared her, whatever it was, and because of this and how fearless she was, it scared him too.

"Tell me," he said, because he couldn't say that he wanted to know.

"I think Ellis sent the Hunter after us."

"You do?" Daeson asked, surprised. "I'd already considered it was Omerri."

Synjan did a double-take and gaped at him. "Why would you think that?"

"She's a jealous kind of woman. She'd sent you to take me back to her but you took me away instead. That would have angered her and she can be a bit petty."

Synjan puffed laughter. "Yeah, like the sun can be a 'bit bright'. Omerri doesn't have the connections."

Daeson frowned. "I know for a fact she does. She has all kinds of Authority connections because of the Queen. She entertains the higher-ups personally."

"But Ellis does business with them. She just toys with them. Ellis is a serious businessman."

Daeson felt anger stirring in his chest and burning up his neck enough that he had trouble speaking immediately. His words dammed in his throat, building in pressure until they burst out. "Is nobody else as important as you? Why is only *your* boss a big deal? Why are other people too insignificant to impact on your life? Must you be the one who suffers most?"

He saw his words had shocked her. He may as well have slapped her, he thought. He knew his attack was melodramatic, that he was exaggerating what she'd said but it also felt right because even his guilt wasn't good enough.

Synjan scoffed. "Don't be ridiculous. What do you mean?"

Her accusation that he was 'ridiculous' didn't quell his temper.

"You aren't the only one in trouble. The Hunter is after both of us. I'm in this with you. Maybe it was Ellis, maybe it was Omerri. Why do we have to assign blame or ownership?"

Synjan took a deep breath and deflated. "You're right. It doesn't matter how it happened, but the Hunter's primary target does. If Omerri sent them—"

"The Hunter will kill us both if we're together. It doesn't matter who the Hunter is after," he said haughtily.

"It *does* matter, because if they're after me, I could leave you to keep you safe!"

The flaring in his temples lessened as his stomach knotted and his chest hollowed out. The anger was still there so he grabbed onto it, not wanting to acknowledge the other emotions swirling within. "You don't have to protect me. I'm not your job, your assignment or mission or whatever you call it. I'm the man you've been travelling with, the one that chose you over Roman. I could've left you, but I didn't. We're in this together." In the moment of silence that followed, a thought filtered into him and he realised he was working under a certain assumption. "Unless you don't want to travel together?"

He'd been awful to her on Femme and she might decide this was his true nature. She'd tried to help many times, she just couldn't. She'd seen him as a victim and he hadn't wanted to think of himself that way. Instead of explaining it to her, he'd shunned her. But he hadn't known at the time! It was only on reflection that he'd figured out what made him so uncomfortable with her. The idea of her turning and walking away squeezed his insides and filled his mouth with spit. He was unfamiliar with the sensation and thought it absurd to have such strong feelings. They hadn't known each other long. They weren't romantically involved. Yet, he didn't want to travel without her. It was during these realisations that he was the most confused about what she was to him, and what he wanted from her.

"Daeson, no! It's just... you... ugh!" Synjan spluttered, then surprised him by grabbing his head and pulling his face closer. Daeson resisted until she planted her lips on his and wrapped her arms around his neck. The kiss was gentle, seeking and comforting. He embraced her when he felt her trembling, then straightened and lifted her off her feet. There were no thoughts, just warmth. The moment was one worth savouring until a passing car blasted them with a horn.

Daeson put Synjan back onto her feet and pulled away, mystified and embarrassed and warm and tingly. He could still feel and taste her on his lips. She gazed up at him with glistening eyes and something in his heart clenched.

"I don't want to leave you," she whispered.

"That's good," he said, not knowing how else to respond. The moment between them was incredibly romantic even though the setting around them wasn't. He didn't know what to do about it, or if the kiss was supposed to mean something intimate. It had calmed his anger and quelled his fears but he sensed that wasn't the only reason she'd kissed him. He remembered her telling him sex was casual for her and he wondered if maybe she wanted a convenient partner in him. She knew he was looking for something permanent. If they wanted to be together, one of them would have to change. They weren't well-matched.

After staring at one another for a moment longer, Synjan tucked invisible hair behind her ear and shied away, continuing down the footpath towards their destination. Daeson followed, feeling like something more should have been said but unable to get the conversation flowing again. She started them on another.

"What was that you said about Roman?"

Daeson had to think back. "Uh, I chose to travel with you instead of him."

"When was that an option?" she frowned.

"This morning, when he woke me up. He knew there was a Hunter on us so he told me to come with him." Hunters were Roman's worst fear so Daeson could understand why the other Navigator had left them behind the way he had. After a brief silence he glanced at Synjan to see her eyebrows were raised.

"He tried to convince you to leave me before I woke up?" she asked slowly.

Daeson regretted mentioning Roman's offer and shrugged.

"That fucker."

"There are the shops," Synjan said, pointing.

A huge glass structure rose out of the ground, visible over the tallest trees. As they got closer, they could see other large buildings of different shapes and colours attached to it. It looked like toy blocks left behind by a giant child. Signs were plastered over every wall and the base was surrounded by a concrete moat filled with an impossibly large number of parked cars, every colour of the rainbow, laid out in neat rows and columns.

"Are you sure those are shops and not a factory?"

"It's where Kev directed us," Synjan replied. "There are loads of people inside that look like they're shopping... and eating and drinking. There are... huge rooms filled with people sitting down and facing one direction, like in a theatre, but nobody's performing." She shook her head. "I don't know about that part but a shop this big will have clothes."

"Look, the tower," Daeson said, pointing at the checkered pillar that ended at a strange funnel. "At the top it says 'North Lakes'."

"So where are the lakes?" Synjan asked.

"Maybe they're inside."

They entered through a large doorway into a wide corridor with shops on either side. Daeson was reminded of the High Palace because of its high ceilings and gold features, but the resemblance ended there. This place lacked carpeting and the hushed tones of reverence. Instead, it sounded like the people inside were yelling. Every shout and shriek was amplified as the noise bounced off the walls, floor and ceiling. A teenage girl laughing on his left, a child crying on his right and conversations held by passing shoppers at the top of their voices.

He and Synjan emerged into a large foyer where shops lined the walls and a river of people flowed in the middle. Hanging from the ceiling was a giant rectangular screen that flashed colours, words and pictures. A smiling woman appeared on it and made eye contact with him before she welcomed him to the centre. Daeson reached out and grabbed Synjan's shoulder, unable to make sense of what he was seeing, and then the woman's face disappeared to make way for more streams of colours and words. When Daeson looked at Synjan, her stare was fixed on the screen.

"Do you think she could see us?" he asked.

"I don't know."

"She was looking right at me."

"She was looking at me, too."

He recalled a large portrait of Omerri in the lounge-room of her house. No matter where in the room he'd stood, she appeared to be looking at him. Had this woman been like that, only a moving and talking variation? It was too difficult to rationalise.

"Let's find the clothes shop and get out of here," he said.

Synjan agreed and they moved down the long tunnel, looking into shopfronts as they went. There were giant pictures plastered on every window of men or women, or failing that, there were large sale signs. He saw a lot of dress shops that wouldn't have the right kind of travelling clothes for Synjan.

"Hello, sir." A female voice captured his attention. He glanced over and made eye contact with an attractive woman with long dark brown hair. She smiled at him and he instinctively smiled back. Daeson hesitated, sensing Synjan slowing beside him. "May I interest you and your partner in a special sample?" she asked. The woman had a rectangle pinned to her shirt with the name Charlotte on it.

"What kind of special sample?" Daeson asked, curious. The people here were friendly enough that he was willing to accept their help. They didn't seem to want anything in return, much like Kev. Perhaps, by the way he and Synjan were dressed, this woman knew who and what they were and wanted them to have something that would assist their travels. Charlotte's smile broadened and her eyes sparkled. Her tone changed to one of excitement.

"It's a new beauty product that I have loads of to give away," she blurted, then half-turned towards a counter in the middle of the aisle. "Come have a look," she insisted.

Daeson followed her, thinking that he didn't really want or need a beauty product but it would be rude to say no when she so obviously wanted to get rid of them. Charlotte moved to a counter and handed him a tiny packet that fit easily into his palm, while naturally grasping his hand and then exclaiming over how soft his skin was.

"You have such soft hands." She turned to Synjan. "Doesn't he have such beautiful, soft hands?" Charlotte turned her wide-eyed stare back to Daeson. "What product do you use on them?"

"Soap," Daeson said.

"Like a beauty bar? Something with moisturiser?"

her excitement was contagious and Daeson found her appealing enough to continue the conversation even though he didn't know what a beauty bar was. Omerri had moisturisers but he'd never bothered with them.

"Just soap and water." He couldn't tell her that it was his Healer ability that took care of callouses and scars. He was a farmer but he'd never had farmer's hands.

"How lucky you are!" Charlotte finally released Daeson to inspect her own tanned hands. "I have to do so much work on my hands to keep them nice. How are your hands?" she asked, reaching out for Synjan. Daeson watched Synjan step back with a frown. Charlotte didn't react other than to give Daeson her attention again.

"You know, it can be a lovely, intimate gesture to rub this lotion into your partner's hands," she suggested, glancing over at Synjan pointedly.

"Oh, uh, we're friends," he said, but he thought of the kiss and his cheeks warmed. He frowned, not wanting to discuss the moment with a strange woman.

"Then you can rub it into *my* hands," Charlotte giggled. Daeson laughed along, relieved that the attention had shifted away from him and Synjan but when he looked at her, she wore an expression that he preferred to ignore. "I love your accent," Charlotte said.

"We're not locals," Daeson said.

"Backpacking around the world? I'd *love* to do that!" Charlotte squealed. "I'm just not brave enough."

"Why do you have to be brave?" Daeson asked, thinking he could get some extra clues about the world they were in.

"Well, you know. It's a bit tougher for a single woman."

Daeson found world travelling tougher than Synjan did, but didn't argue. He had an idea that perhaps Charlotte was as soft as he was, when it came to dealing with trouble.

"Maybe you need to travel with someone who can protect you."

Charlotte giggled again and he heard Synjan mutter under her breath. "Daeson, we should get going," she said.

"Daeson? Is that your name? I really like it!" Charlotte gushed.

He grinned at her, relishing her happiness and the sincerity of it.

"How long are you staying?" Charlotte asked.

Her question revived the whirlwind of thoughts he'd been entertaining all day. As strange as this world was, as big and confusing as it happened to be, there were a lot of friendly people in it willing to help them out. The fact Charlotte was soft—like him—meant that this world allowed for such softness to exist. They were being too hasty, rushing through like they were. Maybe it was time to keep their heads down for a bit.

"We were planning on leaving but I would like to find out more before we go. Everyone's so friendly here." He looked at Synjan because his answer was more for her than for Charlotte.

Synjan gaped at him. "What?"

"We can stay a little while longer," he said, hearing the plea in his own voice. They hadn't talked it over because he hadn't the chance to collect his thoughts and he'd promised himself to be more open to

Synjan's point of view. Except she was intent on travelling without considering the repercussions. Moving without thinking.

"But you heard what Kev told us," Synjan said.

Daeson remembered what the truck driver had said about his family—about how all of his kids were raising kids of their own. This world might be safer than they thought. The Hunter wouldn't expect them to stop.

"Everyone's so friendly and helpful."

Synjan stepped closer to him. "That might be, but... what about, you know what, coming our way?"

"Won't moving on just attract more attention?"

Charlotte interrupted with her usual cheer. "Since you're staying, did you want me to give you a free manicure? I have this awesome—"

"No, thank you," Synjan said firmly.

This time Charlotte reacted to Synjan's rejection with what looked like embarrassment. Daeson hadn't wanted to shut her down in such a way, but he and Synjan had to talk about this in private.

"I'm sorry. I have to go," he told Charlotte, who smiled at him.

He wanted to learn more about this world in spite of its strangeness. Everybody they'd met had been friendly to them, and they spoke the same language. They should take advantage of those things and find a place to stay temporarily, like the shelters Roman had mentioned. If they explored this world a little more, maybe the Hunter would keep going ahead and eventually give up.

He would talk to Synjan about staying longer once they were out of the noise. They would buy the clothes she needed and pick up the supplies he was after just in case they decided to continue—but they would discuss it first. She'd always given him a chance to sound things out so he would do the same with her. He and Synjan would talk about their situation in depth and they would come to a decision together. They wouldn't be rushing into anything. If they did decide to continue into the next world, it would be with forethought and decorum.

CHAPTER TWENTY-THREE

Self-Defeating Prophecy

UNTIL TODAY, SYNJAN had believed she was very good at making decisions. She'd been proactive and efficient, in control and focussed. That had been changing since the day she met Daeson but she'd believed the consequences were only good. Now she knew better, because she'd lost control of her own mind.

All she could think about was that kiss—the feeling of Daeson's mouth against hers and the impression of heat his large hands had left at the small of her back when he'd picked her up. She'd wanted to discuss the giddy sensation she felt when she looked at him but he hadn't responded in kind when she'd initiated that discussion. He'd told her only that it was 'good' when she'd confessed she didn't want to leave him. Good. Not 'wonderful' or 'fantastic'. Just 'good'.

It had dealt a blow to her ego that she didn't know how to overcome. They'd kept walking and she'd managed to continue a conversation but everything was different after that. She'd kissed him to prove she felt more than just travelling-partner-committed to him and he'd kissed her *back* but neither of them seemed capable of taking another step towards the other again.

Every time she looked at Daeson, a queer sensation flipped around inside her belly. The way that girl had touched his hands and babbled about how soft they were had made her want to punch her stupid, smiling face. Rationally, she knew it was jealousy, and it was disquieting. Men usually argued over *her*, until now, and she didn't know how to stop the prickly sensation of possessiveness from ravaging her common sense.

"There!" Synjan cried, relief swamping her as they rounded a corner and she saw a booth labelled, 'Information'.

"Where?" Daeson asked, looking in the wrong direction.

Synjan hooked Daeson's arm with hers and steered him, dodging a woman with wires sprouting from her ears and a metal ring through her nose. She released him when they reached the counter and smiled winningly at the crisply-dressed woman behind it. "Hello. I was wondering if you could help me find a clothing store that would sell, uh, strong clothing?"

The woman picked up a glossy brochure but faltered before she put it down in front of Synjan. "*Strong* clothing?" she queried.

"Well, clothes that are made to withstand lots of different environments and worlds," she clarified.

The woman looked at her like Synjan was joking with her. "I see," she said, an indulgent smile on her face. "Are you talking about camping gear, maybe? For outdoor adventuring?"

"That sounds about right," Synjan nodded, trying to dampen the nervous flutter attacking her resolve because it seemed she was saying the wrong thing. It was hard to feel confident when people reacted like this—speaking with an accent was one thing but making unusual requests made them stand out in peoples' minds. If they were memorable, they were easier to track. It was exactly the opposite of what they wanted, with a Hunter after them.

The woman opened up the glossy pamphlet and revealed a map. She used a pen to draw a path while giving Synjan simple instructions to find the type of store she'd requested. They were soon walking through the sprawling city of shops again.

"What's wrong?" Daeson asked quietly, glancing from her to an older woman ahead of them, using a wheeled contraption to help her walk.

"I'm nervous! I don't want to stand out by asking weird questions," she admitted.

Daeson nodded and placed a hand on her shoulder. "You did great."

Synjan blushed and concentrated on the weight of his hand more than where she was going. She ended up in front of a wheeled cage filled with ungainly items poking in all directions.

"Careful," the person driving the cage called out while they wrestled with the cumbersome vehicle and tried to steer it around her. The thing had desires of its own and refused to change direction despite the woman yanking on it.

Synjan dodged and Daeson removed his hand from her shoulder. "Sorry," she apologised to the woman while mourning the loss of the touch. She received an ingenuine smile for her trouble.

Some twenty steps later, they were passing a

fenced collection of tiny children teeming over and around large plastic shapes when a baby crawled directly into their path. Synjan sidestepped the speedy infant but, to her surprise, Daeson scooped it up. A shrieking woman was with them an instant later, her demeanour frazzled and her speech high-pitched.

"Thank you, thank you, oh my God! You've no idea how you've saved me! He's such a fast crawler, he got away from me in a split second. All I did was look at my phone to text my husband and boom, he was gone!" she lamented dramatically, smacking her hands together to describe her infant's lightning-fast escape from the baby pen.

Synjan was dubious, especially because the woman was gazing less at her baby than she was at Daeson's face. She looked even more enamoured when Daeson spoke.

"I'm glad I could help out," he chuckled, prodding the child's round belly, unperturbed by the long line of dribble unleashed on his hand. When the baby squealed and giggled, Synjan noticed Daeson's delight by the way his eyes lit up.

"Sorry about that," the mother gushed, having the grace to be embarrassed by the drool. Synjan was quietly appalled when the mother bustled closer and lifted her shirt to wipe Daeson's hand dry, continuing to yabber on as if what she was doing was the most normal thing in the world. "He's got two teeth coming through at the same time, it's an absolute nightmare. I've barely slept for the last two nights. I was hoping if I brought him out for a while, it'd cheer him up. He's just miserable at home."

Daeson took this as his cue to peer into the boy's mouth and rub the swollen gum inside. Immediately after, the child made excited trills and kicked his sock-covered feet rapidly, grunting and squirming.

"He's so wriggly," Daeson chuckled, adjusting his grip so as not to drop the baby or interfere with his tiny, flying fists.

"Mm-hmn and those grunts probably mean he's filled his nappy again. You'll smell it soon," the mother laughed.

Synjan could only stare at her, amazed that she'd say such a thing out loud. She imagined Daeson would dump the baby back with its mother but instead he grinned and joggled the baby around, using it to make loops and lines in the air. Synjan was horrified, waiting for brownish sludge to ooze from the legs of the baby's clothes... but nothing happened.

"You're so good with him!" the mother enthused, finally sparing a look at Synjan as she asked, "Do you have one of your own?"

Synjan felt her face redden and her eyes widen. She shook her head adamantly.

"Not yet. Maybe one day," Daeson answered and the tinge of sadness in his tone was enough to snap Synjan out of her shock.

"Daeson, I think you should give the baby back. We have to get going," she said gently, smiling when he looked at her. She didn't miss the reluctant way he handed the infant over or the deflated look of the mother as they took their leave. The mother watched Daeson's retreating back with a hunger Synjan was unnerved by.

As they continued on, she was acutely aware of the silence between them. Synjan didn't know what to say. Daeson had told her at the beginning of their journey that he was looking for a world to settle in, one where he could have a family and now she saw just how ready he was. Was *she*? She didn't think so; she was still working on fixing everything that was wrong with herself. Surely she needed to be different before she could contemplate bringing a child into the worlds? Still, she couldn't help daydreaming about whether they'd make a Healer or a Navigator and whether it would have blue eyes and a gorgeous smile like its father...

Quite a few people gave her partner second looks as they walked by him. She'd got used to his beauty while travelling with him but exposing him to masses of strangers was an effective method of making her aware of Daeson's striking good looks again. And riling her jealousy. A group of young girls whispered as they passed, a woman held her little metal box discreetly in his direction and two separate men puffed up their chests and walked taller, pulling their female companions instinctively closer with brawny arms.

When they found the store they'd been looking for, it didn't take long before a wide-eyed young man with a lilting manner of speaking approached them.

"Hello, I'm Timmy and it'd be a pleasure to help you today," he purred, looking Daeson over.

"Thanks, Timmy, that would be good. We're getting a lot of things today." Daeson smiled back, eliciting an excited giggle from the native boy.

Synjan rolled her eyes. Everyone believed her partner was encouraging them when he was just being nice. She should probably be taking notes.

"I'll just get a trolley and you can tell me exactly what you're looking for," Timmy beamed, heading off to collect one of the wheeled metal cages.

They began their shop by locating new bags that fitted Daeson's (Roman's) parameters of discretion, then moved onto clothes and boots. Daeson delighted in pointing out everything in the store as either something they needed or a luxury that would take up unnecessary space. His attitude was a welcome change from the last time they'd shopped. While Synjan gathered sensible shirts—in long and short sleeve—and then went through the same evaluative process with pants, Daeson's attention flagged.

Sensing an opportunity, Timmy lured him towards the utensil aisle because he'd mentioned wanting an all-in-one tool like Roman's. Synjan found a sturdy pair of hiking boots to wear and pressured Daeson to come back and consider a new pair for himself. He was determined his boots were fine but he relented and let her talk him into a set of casual loafers.

By this time, the general mood had dimmed because Daeson hadn't found the tool he wanted and he was oblivious to the lingering looks Timmy was throwing him. It picked up again when they got to the register and Daeson found what he'd wanted all along—though he mentioned twice that it didn't have as many attachments as Roman's. Synjan pushed all the clothes and shoes through first, insisting all packaging and tags be left behind so they wouldn't have to deal with it later, then began digging into Daeson's pack for the money while the rest was rung up and bagged. Timmy was making a final effort at a good impression by arranging their purchases into numerous bags at the end of the counter, despite being told by Eileen, the register lady, that he should 'bugger off'.

Everything was bagged and tallied for their collection and Synjan, straightening up, carefully laid a wad of their stolen Authoritan dollars on the counter. She'd made sure she'd got enough to cover their exorbitant charges but, looking down at the lovely array presented to her, Eileen just laughed.

"What's wrong?" Synjan asked, concern causing her heart to flutter.

"Sorry darl', your Euro money won't work here. Got a credit card?" Eileen replied.

"Pardon?"

"We don't take Euros," Eileen clarified, speaking more slowly to make her point clearer. "You'll need to exchange your cash for Australian dollars or use your credit card."

A cold shiver washed down Synjan's back as she understood that she'd made a huge mistake. A litany of reprisal kept going around in her head. She knew Earth was on the Authorities' worlds register, had believed they were a presence here and had it confirmed by Kev. Or so she'd thought. The enormity of the mistake was too much for her embarrassed mind to sort through and identify where she'd gone wrong. It didn't even matter. At some point, she'd believed this world to be Authority-run and now they'd gathered an exorbitant amount of supplies and had no acceptable currency to pay for it. She should've known better.

Everyone knows something you don't. Treat them accordingly.

Unsolicited, Ellis whispered in her mind and she winced, pushing him away and doing her best to deny the truth of his saying. Kev had known much more than she'd got from him. She'd been content to accept what he'd offered instead of pressing for more. That was why she'd failed.

No. With grim determination, she focussed her broken thoughts on what security this world *did* have. Particularly this shopping centre. On their way to this store, they'd seen one pair of local authorities—dressed in a blue not too different from Authority uniforms—roaming around eating large, long sandwiches. They'd had guns and many bulky attachments on their belts but had seemed more absorbed in their food than in their job. There'd also been some store security guards dressed in white and black but they hadn't even had guns.

None of it was a challenge but therein lay her dilemma. She was doing her best to change, to become a better person. Following her instincts would destroy all the progress she'd made. She *should* just apologise for wasting everyone's time, explain that she didn't have a credit card and bow out of the store with Daeson. She could also pretend she was going to change her money to the local currency and just not come back. But... she *could* grab everything she was able to carry, signal Daeson and run. The latter choice was by far the most awful but it was the one she preferred. She *really* needed better clothes to travel in.

And she needed to keep travelling.

Daeson was entertaining the thought that this world could be right for them but, in that moment, only one thought was clear; she wasn't ready to stop. She didn't think this world was ideal. She'd made her decision. She hoped he'd forgive her.

"Synjan?" Daeson said uncertainly. She looked at him squarely as she spoke.

"They won't take our money. We can't pay for this stuff," she said meaningfully, loading the cash back into his pack and closing it for him.

"Oh no, that's unfortunate," he told her, turning to Timmy and Eileen, presumably to include them in his apologetic statement. They made grumbling noises.

"Put your pack on," Synjan instructed, pulling her own out of the open metal cage. Once they were both wearing their gear again, Synjan looked at Daeson, her mind finally quiet.

"Are you ready to follow me?" she asked, her words slow and deliberate. She was trying to warn him with her eyes as well.

"Follow you?" he queried with a frown.

"Run, now!" she yelled. He flinched as she pivoted and snatched the bags containing her clothes and shoes. Expecting he'd grab the rest, she took off, trying to remember where the nearest exit was.

Timmy valiantly threw himself in her path but she shouldered him away and raced between the plastic gates at the front of the store. It took longer than she would've liked for Daeson to come after her but he caught up and yelled at her as they ran.

"What are we doing?"

"We need this stuff!"

"This is stealing!"

"This way!" She dodged around seats in the middle of the walkway and cut across to a perpendicular wing of shops.

"Where are we going?"

"Out. We need to find a vehicle to drive to the Portal."

"Are we stealing that, too?"

Her heart quailed at his tone but she didn't answer as they pounded along the shiny floor, ducking and weaving around the other shoppers who'd stopped to stare. Daeson clearly didn't approve of the decision she'd made. She'd explain later. She'd remind him how, not so long ago, he'd chosen to steal a canoe to get them to the Portal. He'd understand then.

"Up!" she instructed, running at a black staircase.

It looked to be moving on its own but she didn't question why or how. It appeared to lead up and out, because people were riding it towards the sky. She was certain it would take them out of the confines of the shopping city.

As she stormed roughly past a couple on the staircase, she chanced a look behind her. Daeson was a few steps behind and there was no commotion in their vicinity. When she mapped, she saw people running towards them from two different directions, not far away. They'd communicated with each other somehow, because both groups were heading for her and Daeson. What if one of them was the Hunter? Would they be shot at? What if they were teams of Hunters? Or the real Authorities? None of it bore thinking on but it sent a fresh spurt of terror into her veins to mix with the adrenaline.

The midday sun had them blinking as they emerged in the open. They were now in a parking area, which helped Synjan's rough plan. Rows upon rows of shiny vehicles glinted beneath an endless pale blue sky, offering no immediate solace. Whipping her head back and forth, Synjan spied a woman a short distance away, loading groceries into the back of her vehicle.

"There!" she yelled, pointing for Daeson's benefit as she ran in that direction. The woman closed the back of the red box-like vehicle and walked towards the driver's door, head down, inspecting her keys.

As she ran, Synjan made a quick succession of decisions. They came easily because they were instinctive. As much as she'd regretted allowing them to take over at the beginning of this calamity, it was getting easier with each new problem. She shoved a fist through the holes in the bags she was carrying so she could slide her hand under her shirt front and remove the small gun from her bra. Daeson made a noise that she deliberately ignored as she ran up and grabbed the woman by the upper arm and spun her around to look at them.

"Excuse me," Synjan said, pointing the gun at the woman's chest.

She was chubby, in her forties and instantly terrified. "Is that a *gun*?" she screeched.

"Shut up!" Synjan hissed before looking around, hoping they hadn't garnered too much attention. "Yes, it's a gun but I won't use it if you help us out. I need you to drive us in that direction!" Synjan said, smacking her shopping bags into the woman's side when she moved her arm too quickly to indicate where she needed to go.

"Drive you?" the woman warbled, her eyes wide and glossy as she looked around the carpark for help. "Just take my car. Take it." The keys jangled in her shaking hands as she held them out.

"No, you have to drive," Synjan said, not even looking at the keys.

"This is a bad idea," Daeson said.

"Do *you* know how to get us out of this fucking place?" Synjan demanded, rounding on him with such vehemence that he pulled back.

"No."

"Neither do I!" she snarled, knowing she was being unreasonably aggressive but needing to keep the Earth woman convinced of her danger. "If this lady drives, she'll get us to where we need to go faster and then we'll let her go."

"You'll let me go?" the woman piped in hopefully, managing to stop her hysterics long enough to speak.

Synjan nodded and dropped her voice. "We don't

want to hurt you," she said as sincerely as possible. "We just need your help."

"You... want me... to drive?" the woman clarified, her words punctuated by hitching breaths.

"Yes," Synjan answered, gesturing towards the driver's door with the gun. "Get in. We'll get in the back."

They all climbed in. It took a few attempts for the woman to get the vehicle started—she couldn't stop looking in the rear-view mirror. Synjan leant forward and pressed her gun into the back of the woman's flabby arm. The barrel was placed where the woman could knock it back if she got feisty but was unlikely to get it out of Synjan's hand because of the awkward angle. They were soon underway.

"Don't go too fast. I don't want you to draw attention to us," Synjan warned as they headed for a downward ramp, bouncing over multiple speed-bumps.

"M-my name is Persephone Brown. People call me Peri," the woman declared. She sounded calmer now, though her voice wavered.

Synjan frowned, wondering why her name mattered. "Okay," she said non-committally.

"I have a husband, Dave," Peri continued. "Kind of... we're not officially married but we've been together for nineteen years. Longer than loads of married people. We love each other deeply."

"Okay?" Synjan repeated, confused.

"We have a cat. We rescued her from the side of the road. Poor thing was only a kitten. She's a bit on the crazy side. We called her 'Biscuit'."

Daeson gave a polite laugh and then turned to Synjan. "Why do you think she's telling us all this?"

Peri answered for herself. "I read that you should

introduce yourself to attackers so they're less likely to hu... hurt you," Peri explained but the words only brought her tears back. "I don't want to die!" she wailed, almost driving into a parked vehicle.

"You will if you don't watch where you're going!" Synjan yelled and Peri snapped the wheel back.

"Screaming at her won't help," Daeson admonished.

"Neither will being nice to her."

"I don't like what's happening," he muttered.

"Neither do I but... I'm sorry," Synjan whispered before she turned back to watch Peri, a lump in her throat making it impossible to speak. She blinked, unsuccessfully trying to clear her vision and her mind, wanting to say so much more but sabotaged by her body.

Apologising wouldn't change things. The urge to say it repeatedly was undeniable, as was the desire to justify. What she'd wanted to say was, *'What choice did I have?'* but that was pointless. There had been a choice—there had been numerous choices—and she'd made the one that had suited her. Not the one Daeson would have wanted, not the good choice or the right choice... but the one her violent instincts had urged her to make. Despair threatened to overwhelm her and she swallowed a sob, trying her best to hold it in.

There was no point having second thoughts but they were all she had. She gazed out the window as they drove past rows of immobile vehicles, a sense of trepidation settling in her bones.

It felt like they couldn't turn back now. She'd committed them to this course of action, as crazy as it was. She sniffed and wiped an errant tear as they wound their way cautiously forward. Maybe it wasn't so bad. Daeson didn't like it but no harm was done, really. Yes, they'd stolen things and yes, they'd scared this poor woman but all was fair in Wandering, right? This was the dark side, the part that had likely caused the Authorities to hate Wanderers in the first place; the chaos and the trauma they left in their wake. This was how a reputation was born. But it would be okay. They'd get to the Portal and leave Peri Brown to her life with Dave and Biscuit. They'd decide what they were going to do. Daeson might be upset with her, but he'd forgive her. Wouldn't he?

Once they were out of the main parking area, they approached an intersection controlled by light poles. "You need to go left," Synjan advised on a shaky breath, doing her best to focus and allowing herself to open up to the Portal's call. It wasn't far away. If they weren't in a vehicle, they'd have been able to see the brilliant beam connecting the ground with the sky in the distance. She didn't need to map to know where it was.

In her heightened state, Peri wrenched the wheel to the left, causing the car beside them to slam on its brakes and blast its horn. "I need more warning!" Peri shrieked as she cut off another vehicle and swung left. "I'm a very good driver. I've never had an accident!" she added as she turned the corner and forced herself into flowing traffic to the toot of another horn.

"I'm sorry, I don't know where the roads go, only where the Portal is!" Synjan yelled back, genuinely fearing that her decision to unleash an unstable woman onto heavily populated roads would be her undoing.

"What portal?" Peri squawked.

"Never mind," Synjan dismissed, feeling slightly

calmer as a light they were driving towards turned red. She knew it meant they would have to stop.

She and Daeson lurched forward as Peri stomped on the brake and Synjan looked at her travelling partner. His expression was grim and accusing as he looked back at her. She cringed inside, cleared her throat and forced words out.

I'm sorry. "Where's your stuff?"

"What stuff?" he asked.

I'm so sorry. "From the shop. Didn't you grab the rest of the stuff?"

"I just ran when you did!"

"Fuck," she muttered, looking forward again as the light changed to green. So much for the new bags that would make them look less like Wanderers. So much for forgiveness. He wouldn't do it, she was pretty sure. Nothing she could say would make this stupid idea all right. She could never be what he expected. She might want it desperately—want *him* desperately, even—but wanting and being were two vastly separate states. The fact that her resolve melted at the first challenge and she reverted to the person she'd always been, solving her problems with violence and bullying, proved it. She wasn't worthy of Daeson and no amount of desire and chemistry between them could change that.

She'd let him down and she'd betrayed herself in the process. The condemnation in his eyes bruised her every time their gazes met. Could she make him understand that she hated being forever Ellis' child as much as he hated seeing it?

A strange click and then the sound of a ringing phone filled the air around them, suppressing her self-loathing. Synjan had no idea where it was coming from—it seemed like it was *everywhere.* A woman's voice floated into the vehicle from the same non-existent place: "You have dialled emergency triple zero. Your call is being connected."

"What is that? Make that stop!" Synjan ordered, prodding Peri's arm with the gun, drawing a shriek from the woman.

"I have! I've made it stop, don't shoot me with that gun!" she cried over the top of the next message.

"It hasn't stopped," Daeson pointed out.

"Please don't shoot me!"

"Was that a telephone call?" Synjan asked, unable to comprehend how such a thing was even possible.

"It was an accident. I won't do it again, I promise," Peri said, tears and snot running down her face. "Oh my God, oh my God. My license plate is P-E-R-I, seven, three."

"I don't give a shit about your husband or your cat or your fucking licence plate. Shut up and drive, the light's green! Just go!" Synjan said angrily. The driver in the vehicle behind them beeped impatience as well. The vehicle lurched forward and Peri drove one-handed while sobbing with a tissue pressed to her face.

"Can you hear that?" Daeson asked, cocking his head.

"Hear what?" Synjan could only hear Peri's obnoxious blubbering.

Daeson frowned and looked out the window.

Synjan regretted the silence and the doubts circling inside her head reared up to grab her attention once more. The roads that led to the Portal were congested but straightforward and not enough of a distraction. Perhaps she would've been able to use Peri's car to get them here, though she was astounded by the sheer number of vehicles jockeying for position. It was intimidating. There'd been about twenty vehicles on Gredann's roads at its busiest. Here, it felt like there were twenty just beside them.

The road turned and the rainbow pillar came into view through the windscreen at last. Synjan frowned and swore again when they stopped at another set of lights.

"What is it?" Peri asked, looking into the rearview mirror, her expression betraying that she expected more terrifying news. She took the opportunity to exchange tissues.

"Up ahead, about... two kilometres. Are you going to be able to stop?" Synjan queried.

"Can I change lanes?"

"No, stay in this one."

"I can't stop in the right lane of three lanes of traffic, other cars will hit us."

"Hmm," Synjan peered around, wondering what to do.

"What is it?" Daeson asked.

"The Portal's right in the middle of this stupidly wide road," she explained, gesturing at the three lanes of traffic to their right as well as to the two to their left. "We'll either have to pull over and run out to it or drive straight through it and hope."

"Pulling over is a good idea," Peri enthused as a loud siren erupted behind them. Synjan and Daeson swung around to stare at the white vehicle's array of flashing lights. The two inhabitants were local authorities, gesturing towards the left side of the road. They were ordering them to pull over.

"Don't pull over!" Synjan screamed as she swung back towards Peri. She prodded Peri's arm twice to convince her.

"I won't, I won't!" the older woman said, pressing

the accelerator obediently.

"Drive faster!" Synjan urged, cringing at the volume of the siren following them.

"I can't! This guy—never mind," Peri stopped mid-complaint as the driver in front decided the siren behind them was too much pressure and got out of the way.

"Go!" Synjan enthused.

"I'm driving away from the police!" Peri shrieked.

"Do it faster," Synjan said, seeing the lane ahead of them continuing to open up as they sped ahead of their involuntary escort. A similar set of flashing lights was coming towards them on the other side of the road but Synjan only had eyes for the Portal by then. The swirling, multi-hued column was hypnotic in its beauty, dominating everything around it. As she slid her gun back into her bra, Synjan marvelled at the amazing effect of vehicles driving ignorantly into and appearing magically out of it.

Ensuring she had her shopping in her lap and a grip on her backpack, she held out her free hand towards Daeson. "Ready?" she asked, emotion clogging her throat once more as she gazed at him. She understood what she was seeing in his eyes when he looked at her now and it was far worse than anger.

It was disappointment.

Daeson took her hand. As the sirens blared and the lights swirled, Peri drove her vehicle directly into the Portal and they were gone.

With an unconscious driver behind the wheel and two sleeping passengers in the back seat, the humble suburban utility vehicle burst into a strange and sandy world with its engine revving and its wheels churning. No-one was awake to apply the brakes. The vehicle launched off the top of a twenty-metre sand dune, landing and rolling from halfway down. Eventually, the vehicle slid to a stop on its crumpled roof, the sleeping inhabitants flung about like floppy dolls, crushed and broken, seeping as much liquid as their mechanical coffin was. Blood and petrol leaked into the thirsty desert as the two Wanderers and their accidental hostage slumbered.

Coming 2018

Wanderer of Worlds

BOOK FIVE

Femme LIGHT

A WANDERER NOVEL

Kaley Blackburn is sent to Femme in her final year of University. The world is a socialist utopia of low crime, great health and advancements in technology.

It is a place that attracts female tourism, as all men are slaves, obliged to cater to women. Kaley knew about the culture of slavery but didn't think she would have to participate—until she is assigned a slave for the duration of her stay.

Mecca is handsome, intelligent and obedient, but Kaley has growing concerns. Does Femme hide an ugly truth beneath the beautiful surface and can she trust her feelings for a man whose duty is to make her feel special?

www.wandererofworlds.com